Eggnog EXPERIMENT

MELODY TYDEN

*For all the women whose happily-ever-after
included a curveball or two.*

Chapter One

DESTINATION WEDDING

~Gemma~

Cole's voice in my ear still had the power to make me shiver, even after more than thirty years together. "That seatbelt is such a tease. I can't wait to get you properly restrained when we land."

His words conjured so many memories, all the way from that Christmas when he first wrapped his ties around me to much more recent adventures in our personal dungeon at home.

As much as I wanted him to tie me up that night too, we had to be realistic. "We have the welcome dinner tonight with Julien's family, and jet lag is bound to catch up with us. It might have to wait."

"I'll be thinking about it until it happens," he murmured before settling back in his seat and turning his attention back to the others in the plane with us. Grey strands streaked through his dark hair these days, but it only made him look more distinguished and possibly even more handsome than he had in his youth. I barely noticed the lines on his face, and he certainly never commented on mine. "Are you alright, Olivia?"

Our daughter-in-law sat across from us on the other side of the table on our private plane, next to our son, Noah. I hadn't noticed how her hand had gone to her mouth, but Cole picked up on it. He didn't usually miss much.

Olivia swallowed, tucking her blonde hair behind her ears as she lowered her hand. "My stomach is a little queasy but I'll be fine. I can't remember the last time I got motion sickness on a plane."

"You should eat something," Noah suggested, taking his wife's hand supportively. At times, he looked so much like his dad, it felt like being in a time machine when I looked at him. He wore his dark hair differently than Cole had, and his green eyes came from me, but otherwise, they had everything in common. "You hardly ate any dinner."

"I'm not hungry," she assured him, looking like she'd rather be talking about anything else. "It's probably just the long flight."

None of us could argue with that. It *had* been a long flight. Even with a shortened refuelling stop in Hawaii, we were coming up to 24 hours since we left New York, and no matter how nice the Stamer private plane might be, we were all anxious to arrive.

"I'll feel better when we're on the ground," Olivia insisted even as Cole and Jackson exchanged pointed glances across the aisle.

Our best friends, Jackson and Holly Hanmer, also happened to be Olivia's parents, and I knew exactly what Cole and Jackson were both thinking even though neither of them said a word. Unbeknownst to our children, their fathers had a secret wager between them about which of them would be a grandfather first.

They were both a little chagrined that it hadn't happened yet. Noah and Olivia had been married for almost three years and together for six years before that. Olivia's sister, Noelle, had been with Aaron for three years, though they only got married earlier that year. It had been at their wedding that Cole and Jackson made the bet in the first place, enjoying the evening with a drink or two, and the young couple sat across from Jackson and Holly on the plane, completing the group of us making the trip together.

Our daughter, Eve, met her fiancé, Julien, the previous Christmas, and we were all travelling to Australia that December to celebrate their wedding, the last one in our extended family group.

Holly and I tried to explain to our husbands that many young couples chose to wait to start a family.

"Just because you knocked Gemma up the week you met her doesn't mean everyone should do it that way!" Holly told Cole bluntly when we overheard the men talking about it one day. "They'll have children when they're good and ready to."

"It's all in fun," Jackson protested, shrugging his shoulders sheepishly even though Cole remained unmoved. "We'd never put any pressure on them. It's just a silly rivalry between us. And if Olivia and Noah are the first, we both win."

We left it there, but I could read in their eyes as we started our descent into Sydney that they were both wondering if Olivia's nausea had anything to do with a potential baby. I would love for Noah and Liv to start a family *if* they both wanted it, but they hadn't said a word to me about it, and if Olivia talked to Holly, Holly hadn't mentioned it.

In the end, unless they asked me to get involved, it wasn't really any of my business.

"Tessa's going to have a car waiting for us?" I asked Olivia to help change the subject.

She threw me a grateful smile. "That's right. Our baggage will all be brought separately, we can go on ahead as soon as we're finished with immigration. Everything's taken care of. We're getting the VIP treatment, even more than usual. Tessa pulled some strings for us."

"It's lucky that she knew the owner," Jackson piped up. "I took a look at the resort online and it looks beautiful."

"Yeah. It's a lucky break for all of us," Noah agreed, giving Olivia a smirk that I hoped Jackson didn't catch.

When Olivia enlisted her college friend, Tessa, to help plan Eve and Julien's wedding, I expected something classy but not too showy, keeping in line with the less extravagant lifestyle that my daughter and her fiancé led. Maybe a historic house outside of New York, or maybe even something close to where Julien grew up in Québec.

So, when we had a video call with them in October where Eve shared their plans with me, Cole, and Noah, their chosen location took me completely by surprise.

"Australia? In December? But... *why?*"

They might as well have said they wanted to get married on the moon for all the sense it made to me.

"Julien and I are really busy," Eve reminded me. After spending two months in Africa in the late summer, they'd moved on to Asia and the Pacific islands to meet with charities who might be interested in joining Eve's new international internship program. Her charity matched young, ambitious college graduates, the companies in the United States who were interested in hiring them, and charities around the world who could benefit from some extra help. The young people got some real-world experience and perspective, the companies benefited from that when their new employees joined the workforce, and the local charities got dedicated, hard-working, well-educated volunteers.

Although they'd just started, the program already had a waiting list of people wanting to apply, and so Eve and Julien had gone to recruit more charities and vet them in person, to make sure the experience would be a safe and successful one. Their travel plans had them booked well into the new year, but they had agreed to take a week off at Christmas to get married.

"With such a short time available, by the time we flew back to North America and got over the jet lag, we'd only have time to get married and turn right around again," Eve explained. "I know that you all have three weeks off over the holidays, so if you come to this side of the world, you can make a real vacation out of it and we'll all get to have Christmas together."

That part appealed to me, as she knew it would. Christmas had always been my favourite time of year, and I'd never had one apart from my children yet.

There was just one little problem. "It's summer there! How is it going to feel like Christmas in the summer?"

Everyone laughed as if I'd been joking. "It'll feel like Christmas because we're all together, Mom," Noah promised. "And I'm sure if you want it to snow, Dad'll pull it off somehow."

A glance at Cole made it clear he was already considering how he might do that, so I quickly nipped that in the bud. "I don't need snow. But how are you going to plan all this in two months in another country?"

"Tessa's one of the best wedding planners in the city," Noah piped up. "She'll pull something amazing together, I'm sure."

"I don't know if 'amazing' is necessary," Julien piped up warily. He sat next to Eve on our computer screen, the two of them wearing cool, loose clothing in the Vietnamese heat. "We were just planning to go to the local registry office, nothing fancy."

"She'll make sure everyone's happy," Noah promised, and as soon as we hung up with them, he turned to me and his dad, his eyes sparkling. "I know just the place. An acquaintance of ours opened a resort in Australia a couple of years ago. Their ethos is to literally provide whatever their customers want. It won't be cheap but it'll feel as low-key and casual as they want it to. As long as Eve doesn't see the bill, it'll be perfect."

"Will they have availability on such short notice?" I wondered.

"They will if the price is right," Cole remarked. "How do you know this 'acquaintance'?"

Noah didn't mince words, being as honest with us as usual. "I met him in the voyeur scene. There's a private club attached to the hotel too, for any kind of kink you can imagine, but it's extremely discreet. Unless you're specifically looking for the place, you'd never know it's there."

I had to ask the obvious question. "You're not suggesting we have your sister's wedding there just because you want to try this sex club, are you?"

Noah laughed, taking that as another joke. "Of course not. I really think this place would be perfect. The club is a bonus, and not just for us. I'm sure they've got BDSM rooms too."

Although I loved that our children felt comfortable talking to us about anything, every now and then I had to imagine what my own father's reaction would have been if he could hear half of the things that were said around our dinner table.

Cole seemed to be onboard, at least to consider it. "Let's see a proposal and we can go from there. But if we decide to go with it, whatever you do, make sure nobody tells Jackson about this club."

We all remembered Jackson's reaction to finding out about some of Noah's kinks, so we readily agreed it would be best to keep the club a secret from Olivia's dad. By the time the plane touched down in Sydney, no one had let the cat out of the bag yet, and thankfully, he didn't seem to notice the look Noah gave Olivia when he said how lucky we were to be going to the resort.

We had so much to look forward to over the next three weeks, I hardly knew what to get excited about first. It wouldn't be like any Christmas I'd had before, but I knew it would definitely be one I'd never forget.

~Cole~

Even by my admittedly exacting standards, the service we received from the hotel impressed me from the start. A concierge waited for us outside immigration and ensured we were comfortably settled into two air-conditioned SUVs, one for the older generation and one for the younger, before we left the airport and headed south to the city of Wollongong where we'd find our resort destination.

When I first shared the plans with him, Jackson asked why we didn't hold the wedding at one of the Stamer hotels in Australia. It certainly would have been simpler, but my reasons were twofold: first, it would be harder to keep things quiet if we held it in one of our own hotels.

One small leak to the press and Eve would have photographers lurking outside just like there had been at my own wedding. I hadn't been happy about that and I knew she wouldn't be either. She didn't want anyone making a fuss, which led directly to my second reason: although Julien had made significant progress towards accepting that wealth didn't have to be a negative thing, she still didn't want to flaunt it, and having her wedding in a hotel that she technically owned wouldn't help.

In short, I tried to see things from her point of view, and my gut told me my daughter would rather not get married somewhere with her name above the door.

The resort Noah suggested looked ideal. A short distance out of the city, on one of the many beaches that lined the coast, it had something for everyone. The younger crowd could go surfing or swimming in the ocean, while Gemma and Holly had been eyeing some of the hikes in the surrounding forests and hills, along with the top-of-the-line spa within the hotel itself. It definitely didn't feel like Christmas when we arrived, even with the decorations in the airport, but I had a plan to help counter that.

As I said, the hotel staff were very accommodating.

The drive went quickly as we all enjoyed the scenery and talked about what the next few weeks might bring, and further into the future as well. In the new year, I would be scaling back my hours at Stamer Hotels and officially passing the reins to Noah. Gemma liked to remind me that I had been running the business for many years by the time I reached Noah's age, and in the eight years he'd been working with me, he'd proven himself a capable leader and shrewd businessman. I knew the business would be in good shape with him at the helm, but that didn't make it any easier to accept the fact that I wasn't needed anymore.

"You're not falling asleep on me, are you?" Gemma teased, leaning into me and taking my hand as the Hanmers chatted to each other in the seats behind us. I must have zoned out for a moment looking out the window. "I thought you had big plans for tonight and here you are napping."

"I wasn't 'napping'. I don't need to nap." My reply came out more tersely than I meant it to, since I knew damn well that Gemma didn't mean it that way. It just rubbed a nerve after all the talk of retirement and getting older. When I saw the confused look in her gorgeous green eyes, I immediately apologized. "I'm sorry. I'm just feeling my age today, I guess."

"I understand," she quickly assured me. "Our baby's getting married. It's kind of hard *not* to feel it. For some reason, it's different than with Noah."

I had to agree. Eve had been able to take care of herself for a long time already, but I still liked being the one she could turn to if she needed help. Now, she had Julien for that. Both of our kids were moving on with their own lives and the business would move on without me too. It felt a little bit like we were getting left behind with no real direction anymore.

However, Gemma was the last person I wanted to take any of that out on. If anyone kept me feeling young, she did, especially when I imagined all the things we might get up to in that club later on. At least for a little while, we'd be able to forget all about getting older.

At the hotel, another member of staff greeted us and showed us to our rooms. Each of us had a large suite, not unlike the one I'd been staying in when I first met Gemma in London. The whole wing of the hotel was reserved for Eve's wedding guests, so we would have plenty of privacy.

"Oh, hello, everyone." As we approached our rooms, the door to one of the other rooms opened to reveal a man I'd known in passing for several years but would likely be seeing more of from now on: Julien's father, Julian Ribar. He gave me a warm smile in particular. "Nice to see you, Cole. How was your flight?"

"Fine. When did you arrive?" We'd offered to fly the Ribars down with us on our plane, but they thought it might be awkward to be cooped up for that long with Julien's mother. Although Julien had made peace with his father's family, apparently things between his parents were less amicable. In the end, Julien's mother didn't come with us either, not wanting to accept our 'charity'. We hadn't even met the woman in the flesh yet.

"Last night," Julian replied. "Everyone else is out on the beach already, I just needed to grab a few things. Will we see you out there?"

An afternoon of lying in the sun might actually put me to sleep after the long flight. "Probably not today, but we'll see you at dinner tonight."

He said goodbye to everyone and headed out while I opened the door to our suite, letting Gemma go in first. She hadn't taken more than two steps when she gasped.

"Look at it! It's Christmas!"

Her squeal of delight drew the attention of everyone else in the hall who were still getting their keys sorted out, and they all peered in to see what was happening.

"It's gorgeous!" Noelle exclaimed.

"Is our room like this too?" Olivia asked.

"I don't think so," Noah replied, shooting me an amused look. "I think this is 100% Cole Stamer."

He was absolutely right. I'd requested that the curtains be closed when we arrived to give the full effect. Coloured lights were strung around the room and wrapped around the tall, thick, real Christmas tree in the corner, next to the fireplace. Stockings hung from the mantle, boughs of garland were draped around the table, and, of course, a sprig of mistletoe hung above the door.

"Cole." Gemma gave me a look that was part reproach and part delight. "You didn't have to do this."

"You said you didn't need snow, but you didn't say anything about the rest of it. Does it feel like Christmas now?"

"It does," she assured me, planting a sweet kiss on my lips. "Thank you."

"Alright, to your own rooms now," I ordered everyone else. They all left still exclaiming over the decorations, making Gemma smile again as I closed the door behind them.

Our luggage hadn't arrived yet, but the hotel had left us a welcome package with everything we'd need to freshen up in the meantime. A brochure highlighted all the resort's attractions, and tucked behind it, another small pamphlet gave us the information we'd need for the club. Noah told me that everyone in our travelling party would be getting one except for Jackson and Holly.

The club was called Paradise, and though the brochure didn't give too much away, it promised that its patrons would find their own version of paradise within its walls. If visitors wanted to have sex with other patrons, there were some hoops to jump through, but since Gemma and I only wanted the playspace, we didn't have to do much other than pay.

The blood pumping through my body as I let my imagination take over definitely made me feel like a much younger man, and when Gemma announced that she wanted to take a shower before dinner, my dick practically leapt in anticipation.

"I'll join you."

I didn't phrase it as a question, and Gemma immediately slipped into her natural submissive role, responding to my tone. "If you like, Mr Stamer."

Our clothes hit the bathroom floor in near record time, and soon, I had her with her back against the wall in the large walk-in shower. "Hold your hands above your head, like they're cuffed there," I commanded. Without question, she obeyed, and I took the opportunity to run my hands over every perfect inch of her. My fingers slipped over her puckered nipples, across her stomach and along the curve of her waist, down her thighs and back up again, ending between her legs where they made her gasp in pleasure as they rubbed her clit before thrusting into her.

So many men my age, people that I'd worked with or competed with or those who were mere acquaintances, had ended their marriages and wound up with much younger women, but that thought never even crossed my mind. Even if I looked at things from a purely sexual point of view, no one would ever suit me as perfectly as Gemma did. No one else would excite me the way she did when she moaned my name, or look at me with such pure surrender and need.

She came on my fingers, trembling around me with her arms still held above her head, but when she asked if she could return the favour, I declined. "If you want me to come, you'll have to go to the club with me tonight."

"You drive a hard bargain," she teased me, still catching her breath. "Let's get through dinner first and then we can decide."

"In that case, I'll be choosing what you wear tonight."

The heat in her eyes told me she knew exactly what I had in mind, but she didn't refuse.

The night ahead looked very promising indeed.

~Gemma~

The dress Cole chose for me that evening was surprisingly modest. A floor-length floral dress with flowers that complemented my red hair, it looked completely appropriate for the mother of the bride... and could very easily be pulled up to my waist beneath the table if he so desired. I had no idea if he actually intended to, given that we'd be at a table with a dozen other people including our children, but the fact that he told me not to wear any underwear beneath it made it clear enough that he wanted the option.

Over the past few weeks, he'd started to get a little morose every time the subject of his impending retirement came up, even though he wasn't fully retiring. He would still have a position on the board and Noah would still consult with him regularly, but I knew the idea of giving up control didn't come easily to him. Hopefully, we could have enough fun on this holiday with our own particular type of control that he would see that having a bit more time to enjoy ourselves together didn't have to be a bad thing.

He'd been a brilliant CEO, a wonderful husband and an amazing father. Whatever came next, I had no doubt he would be just as successful, and I'd buoy him up as much as I needed to until he figured that out.

"Mom!" Eve's squeal of delight rang out across the hotel lobby as soon as I stepped into it, and in the next second, my little girl rushed into my arms. Not so little anymore, actually; she had a couple of inches on me in height, and in her grey wrap dress that ended mid-thigh, paired with high-heeled strappy sandals, she had the eye of every man in the room on her.

Including the one behind me. "It's good to see you, Eve."

"You too, Dad." She let go of me to step into her dad's embrace instead, while Julien came up behind her, a soft smile on his face as he watched his bride-to-be. His white shirt and khaki shorts showed off his tanned, toned limbs, and he turned to me as he approached.

"I see where Eve gets her ability to look incredible no matter how long we travel. You are radiant, Mrs Stamer."

He kissed both my cheeks as I tried not to blush. "And I see why Eve is marrying you. Very smooth, Julien."

He chuckled graciously before taking a step back and drawing another woman into the group. "May I introduce you to my mother? Emilie Labrecque, this is Gemma Stamer."

The woman at his side had the same brown hair as Julien, though hers had a fair amount of grey in it too, but the resemblance between them didn't go much deeper than that. Where he had an open, almost eager-to-please expression, hers looked sour. Her face seemed to naturally settle into a frown.

"Bonjour, Emilie," I greeted her, drawing on the French I hadn't used much since school to ask about her flight. "J'espère que tu as passé un bon vol."

Perhaps the long journey accounted for any grumpiness she may have felt. Her jeans and t-shirt looked like they might have been the ones she wore on the plane.

"It was exactly as I expected," she answered me in blunt, accented English. "Long, cramped and uncomfortable."

It wouldn't have been so cramped or uncomfortable if she came on our plane with us, but I kept that thought to myself. "Well, I'm delighted we're all here. I thought they were crazy when they said they wanted to get married in Australia, but this is really lovely."

We all glanced around the light, airy hotel lobby, a perfect mix of classy and casual. The ocean that sat just in front of the resort dominated the view out the floor-to-ceiling windows. Skylights in the vaulted ceiling made it feel like we were still outside while protecting us from the elements, and the natural wood furniture added to the earthy vibe. I'd have to find out who the design firm was.

"It's a waste of money for all of us to fly all the way here when they could have just come home," Emilie grumbled. "It isn't like Julien at all."

"Maman! Arrête ces bêtises!" Julien's sharp words clearly weren't meant for my ears, since I didn't understand what he said, but I knew that 'arrête' meant 'stop', so I had to guess he didn't appreciate her comment.

"Is there a problem?"

My back immediately stiffened at Cole's stern tone, even though it hadn't been directed at me. Julien gave him a somewhat pained smile. "No, everything's fine. Mr Stamer, this is my mother."

Cole said hello while Emilie just nodded at him, her lips pursing in even stronger disapproval.

While Julien went to introduce Emilie to the rest of the group, I pulled Eve aside and repeated her father's question, in my own way. "Is everything okay?"

She sighed, immediately understanding what I meant. "Madame Labrecque isn't happy about Julien's father being here. Julien told her that if she was going to complain the whole time, she didn't have to come. It appears she's decided to do both."

I supposed it might have been too much to hope we'd make it through both our kids getting married without some kind of wedding drama. "Where is she sitting tonight?"

"Between Julien and Aaron. Aaron's the person with a background closest to her own, so we figured he might be the safest bet. The Ribars are going to be on the opposite side of the table."

Hopefully, that would be enough of a separation. If Emilie didn't put her hurt feelings aside to let her son enjoy his wedding, I would have to step in before Cole did, but for the time being, we would start with just getting dinner.

A private room in the hotel's restaurant had been reserved for us, with an oval table to accommodate the whole group. Julien and Eve sat at the widest part, with Cole next to Eve and me beside him. On my other side were Noah and Olivia, followed by the Ribars, while Jackson and Holly sat next to Noelle and Aaron. More introductions were made until everyone had met everyone else, but Emilie refused to acknowledge the Ribars at all as she took her place.

"You look stressed," Cole murmured in my ear as the waiter came around to pour us all some wine.

"I'm worried about Julien's mother," I told him honestly. "I just want this to be perfect for Eve and Julien."

"It will be. Even if I have to get the hotel staff to 'accidentally' lock her in her room, it will be."

The calm, matter-of-fact way he said that made me laugh out loud, earning me a curious look from Noah. "What's so funny?"

"Nothing. You two aren't having any wine?" I asked, partly to change the subject and partly because I'd just noticed their empty glasses.

"No. Liv's stomach still isn't 100% and I'm keeping a clear head in case she needs me."

His consideration made me proud as a mother, but as I glanced around the table, I realized they weren't the only ones abstaining. Noelle's glass also sat empty, and Eve's too.

At least Holly was partaking, and she raised her glass to make a toast. "Eve, I know we're not blood family, but you're part of our family all the same, and we're so happy that you found someone who completes you so perfectly."

My skirt began to drift up my legs while she spoke, and though I kept my eyes on her and not him, I had no doubt Cole was responsible.

"Your lives are going to be one great adventure after another, I can tell, but the people at this table will always be your home. We're here for you, no matter what, and thank you for bringing us all here to celebrate together. Cheers."

"Cheers!" echoed around the table from everyone else as Cole's hand went to my now-bare thigh, his palm hot against my skin.

"Emilie, tell us what Julien was like as a boy," Jackson requested once everyone had taken a drink. "We've known Eve since the day she was born, but we're still getting to know Julien."

Julien groaned good-naturedly as everyone else called out their encouragement, while Cole's hand slid between my thighs.

Thankfully, Emilie not only agreed, the question actually put a smile on her face. "He was the best child. One winter, when he was seven or eight, he found a dog on the street. It was so cold out, he knew he couldn't leave it there, so he brought it home, and he made posters to hang around the neighbourhood for the dog's owner. When the woman came to get the dog, she gave Julien fifty dollars as a reward. That was a lot of money for us."

She threw that last line in as if she had to explain the value of money to us, and my lips tightened. In response, Cole's hand slid up, closer to my centre, close enough that he could brush my clit with his fingers if he wanted.

"I asked him what he wanted to buy with it," Emilie continued, "and he told me he wanted to donate it to the SPCA, to help any other dogs who might be cold that winter. He always thought of other people first, so it didn't surprise me at all when he decided to go into charitable work. That is the kind of boy he was."

Everyone made polite murmurs of appreciation, but I knew Jackson had been looking for something a bit more light-hearted than that, so I tried a different tactic. "Noah, why don't you share a story about Eve?"

My son's eyes lit up at the opportunity to tease his sister, while Cole's fingers pressed further against me, dragging slowly through the growing wetness.

"Eve never got along well with animals, except for horses. She expected to be able to boss them around and they'd do what she said but it rarely worked that way. My favourite story has to be when she got chased by a chicken in Trinidad after she told it to lay an egg for her."

"That's not what happened!" Eve protested while Julien laughed and Cole's finger pushed into me.

"Are you feeling more relaxed yet?" he teased as the conversation carried on around us, everyone but the two of us completely oblivious to the position my husband had me in.

"Better," I assured him. If nothing else, it became harder to concentrate on anything other than what his hand was doing, and that made it harder to be annoyed about anything either.

Cole brought me all the way to the edge of orgasm before backing off, leaving me squirming in my seat.

"Alright, Gem?" Holly asked from across the table after we'd finished our appetizer. "You look a bit flushed. I hope you haven't got what Olivia's got."

"I think that's impossible," Cole whispered to me. "But that doesn't mean I wouldn't love to see you pregnant again. You looked so fucking sexy."

Twice more, he worked me into a speechless state, and left me hanging right before the finish. "Are you enjoying torturing me?" I asked quietly when the dessert plates were being cleared away.

"I didn't think you'd want to come in front of everyone," he explained simply. "But if you're that unsatisfied, we could always go to the club and finish this there."

So, that was his game. Luckily for him, it worked. I wanted the orgasms he'd denied me, and I wanted to give him one too after he stopped me in the shower earlier. I wouldn't be able to sleep until I got some satisfaction, so I gave in.

"Alright. We'll go to the club."

Looking far too pleased with himself, Cole withdrew his hand from me and pulled my skirt back down. "I knew you'd come around, Gorgeous."

He didn't win any prizes for that. With him, I always came, again and again, and I couldn't wait to see what he had in store for me that night.

Chapter Two

PARADISE

~Cole~

The first words out of Eve's mouth when we ran into her in the lobby begged for my patience. "Don't give Julien's mother a hard time, alright? She's upset today but Julien swears it will pass. Don't make it worse."

"When have I ever made anything worse?"

She rolled her eyes at that, as I expected her to. "You know what I mean. If I need help, I'll ask for it, okay? Trust me."

I did trust her, and for the entire meal, I did my best to ignore Emilie Labrecque's digs at the wedding and our lifestyle. No wonder Julien had been wary of Eve's wealth when they first met if he had that woman as a role model. When Gemma expressed concern over it, I told her the truth: if I had to step in, I would, but for the time being, I left it in my very capable daughter's hands.

My own hands were otherwise occupied.

After teasing and edging Gemma through dinner, I couldn't have been happier when she agreed to go to the club that night. We both needed some distraction and Paradise should definitely provide it. We said goodnight to the others, pretending to be heading back to our room for an early night, as the Hanmers and Noah and Olivia were, but once inside, we slipped out the other door instead, the one that led out into the resort grounds.

Noah had told us that if we didn't know about the club's existence, we'd never find it, and I had to agree. Built mostly underground, patrons entered through a small, black, square building with no sign or any indication it might be anything other than a utility station or caretaker's shed. My firm knock on the door was immediately answered, and inside, we only had to give our room number at the resort for the next door to be opened for us, revealing a long, steep staircase made of black steps with red lighting. It drew us down as if we were descending into the depths of hell, or maybe just the depths of depravity.

Music grew louder the farther down we got, and when we reached the bottom, a final door opened, revealing a large, elegant bar. The air felt much cooler down there, probably to keep people from getting overheated during their various exertions. A couple of dozen people filled the room, sitting at the bar or at tables, chatting and apparently having a good time. Nothing about it screamed 'sex club' except for the topless bartenders, male and female.

"Welcome to Paradise." A handsome Australian man in his 40s appeared in front of us, making Gemma jump in surprise. I pulled her closer to me out of a possessive instinct, and the man grinned. "Sorry, didn't mean to startle you. My name's Derek. This is my resort, and my club. I'm a friend of Noah's."

Noah must have given him a heads-up that we might be stopping by. "Nice to meet you, I'm..."

"Cole Stamer. Obviously." He flashed a bright smile at us both. "And Gemma, it's a pleasure to meet you too. I'm a big fan of your work. The public areas of the resort were actually designed by an architect who promised to give me 'Gemma Stamer vibes' since I couldn't book you directly."

As always, hearing Gemma praised and appreciated for her work filled me with pride, and she accepted the compliment graciously. "I'm flattered, especially since I was admiring the lobby earlier. It's exceptionally done."

"That's very kind of you to say. I know you're here to enjoy yourselves, so let me get you a drink on the house and give you a quick overview of what you need to know."

He gestured to a nearby empty table, and Gemma and I accepted the offer, taking a seat while Derek pulled out an electronic menu.

"Since it's Christmas, we have a special seasonal menu of drinks, all based around flavoured eggnog."

"Really?" Gemma asked with a laugh, her eyes sparkling in that irresistible way they always did whenever Christmas was mentioned. "I thought eggnog only had one flavour."

"That's what they want you to believe," Derek joked, handing the menu over to us. "We've named them all after the kind of vibe you might want to explore here in the club. Matching the drink to the kink, as it were. You can stick with your usual flavour, or you can try something different. We're all about exploring and experimenting here."

"An eggnog experiment?" Gemma summed up, shooting a warm smile my way. "What do you think?"

I quickly cast a glance over the menu. At the top was the suggested drink for those who simply wanted a private room with no accessories: the vanilla eggnog.

The flavours and the kinks got progressively more daring, and it didn't take long to find the one I had in mind. "I think I'll give the blueberry a try."

Gemma leaned over to see where I pointed, and when she saw it listed as Bondage Blueberry, she couldn't hide her smile. "I guess that means I'm taking the strawberry?"

Submissive Strawberry for her sounded pretty damn perfect to me.

"Exactly what I would have guessed based on the pre-information you provided," Derek said with a laugh. "I've personally arranged a special room for you that should have everything you need. If you find anything missing, you can let me know personally. I'll take you there now and your drinks will be delivered shortly."

So far, Derek impressed me, as did the kink-positive vibe of the club. Maybe I should open my own club back in New York. It would give me something to do in my retirement, at least.

Several hallways led off the bar, like spokes on a wheel, and Derek took us down the one directly across from the staircase where we'd entered. Doors sat on either side of the hall, each with a keypad for entry, and when we got to the fourth one on the left, he stopped and keyed in an entry code, unlocking the door for us. "It's Gemma's birthday, the day and month," he explained. "In case you need to go in and out."

Simple and clever.

Inside, the room made an even better impression. Aside from the large bed with various restraints and the St Andrew's Cross, which I'd anticipated, it had a couple of swings and a few other chairs and apparatus as well. Though we had our own dungeon at home, it always interested me to see what equipment other people were using, and one piece in particular immediately caught my eye.

"You have a private ensuite bathroom through there, and a full range of toys and accessories in this cabinet here." Derek gave us the tour quickly, obviously understanding that we'd like to be left alone as soon as possible. "Anything you use, leave out and it will be fully sterilized at the end of the night. Any questions?"

"None. Thank you." I really did appreciate people who didn't overstay their welcome, and as the door closed behind him, I turned to Gemma, my dick already stirring in anticipation. "What are you thinking, Gorgeous?"

As always, we were on the same page. She immediately walked over to the 'fucking bench' I'd spotted and ran her hand lightly along its leather padding. She would lie on it, her chest, shins and forearms supported and held in place by the restraints. It didn't give me access to her breasts, but all of her holes were readily available. "This could be fun, if you have the energy after our long day."

"Don't worry about me. You're the one who's going to come until you forget which way is up."

"We're already on the other side of the world," she laughed. "How much more do you want to spin me around?"

"Just enough," I promised, but as I moved towards her, someone knocked on the door, and I groaned.

"It'll just be our drinks," Gemma guessed, and sure enough, when she opened the door, a topless waiter handed both of them over to her. One blue and the other red made it easy to guess which one belonged to which of us.

I'd never tasted a cocktail quite like it before, but I didn't hate it. The mix of the rum and eggnog and blueberry flavour felt rich and invigorating at the same time, and I drained mine in the time it took Gemma to take a few sips of hers.

"I'll give you more when you need it," I told her, taking the drink from her hand. "But first, you need to get in position. Strip for me and climb up on the bench. When you're in place, I'll strap you in."

"And then you'll fuck me?" she asked hopefully.

"What I do after that is up to me. You're going to take whatever I give you, aren't you?"

As always, the sweet, submissive look in her eyes made my dick harden. "I always do."

Yes, she did, and of all the many blessings in my life, that one easily topped the list.

~Gemma~

Cole always had the ability to make me forget about everything else. When we played together, nothing existed for me other than the two of us, my body and his, the pleasure we gave each other and the deep connection between us.

So when he told me to strip, I obeyed without question, removing not only the dress he'd chosen for me but all my worries and concerns as well. I put them all aside just as I let my clothing fall to the ground, stepping away from them until he decided we should rejoin the rest of the world. Until then, the only thing that mattered was enjoying ourselves and each other, the same way we always had.

The leather of the bench felt cool against my skin in the air-conditioned room as I pulled myself up onto it. It wasn't all that different from being on my hands and knees, except that rather than using my hands, my forearms bore my weight. It changed the angle, putting my ass slightly higher in the air, leaving me completely exposed as Cole circled me. Still fully clothed, he exuded power and control as he examined me.

When he spoke, his voice had that thick, husky quality that betrayed his arousal. "You look incredible. We might have to get one of these for our room."

Despite how turned on I was, I had to laugh. "Only if you get rid of something else. We don't have room!"

"We'll see," was all he said in reply.

Moving behind me again, Cole pushed my legs forward a tiny bit more, adjusting me to suit his height and his preference, and spread the leg plates a little wider before he began strapping me in. Methodically, he moved from my legs to my arms and finally to the straps across my back, tying each one tight enough that it fully restricted me, the pressure reminding me that I was at his mercy, but not so tight as to cause me any pain.

The pain would come later, I hoped.

When he had me in position, he went over to the cabinet Derek had pointed out earlier. From the bench, I couldn't see it or him, leaving me to try to guess from the noises I could hear what he might be looking at.

"Hmmm." His curious hum made my blood pump even faster as I imagined all the things that might have caused it, but I didn't ask. He wouldn't tell me even if I did.

More rustling built my anticipation even higher. Goosebumps spread down my arms while a steady pulse began between my legs as the possibilities multiplied in my head.

When he finally returned, I didn't get any further clues. In fact, he seemed to want to keep me in the dark, quite literally.

"I'm going to blindfold and gag you. Since you won't be able to speak your safeword, turn your head to the side if you need to stop. Alright?"

"Yes." I always answered him out loud when he needed to be clear on anything, and soon, a piece of soft fabric covered my eyes. Cole tied it firmly behind my head before moving onto the gag.

"It's a ring," he advised, and my heart beat even faster. We'd used a ring gag at home before, but not for a while. Although it restricted my speech like a regular gag, it also held my mouth open in an O shape, meaning he could make use of my mouth as he liked.

Apparently, we were going all out that night.

I opened my mouth for him in acceptance and he gently fit the ring into place before securing the gag behind the back of my head. It made swallowing a little more difficult, but not impossible.

With my arms, legs and chest tied down, blindfolded so I couldn't see and unable to speak, with all three of my holes exposed and ready for him to use as he saw fit, I couldn't have been any more vulnerable, and Cole knew it.

"Fuck, Gemma. Your body is perfection, but the way you trust me... *that's* the sexiest thing I've ever seen."

His words sent a rush of heat and pride through me. Trust lay at the very heart of our sexual relationship. I didn't let him dominate me because he was physically stronger than me. I did it because I trusted him to make the decisions that would benefit both of us, and in all the time we'd been together, he'd never betrayed that trust. He'd never even come close.

"You need to relax," he continued, and I could hear him digging around in the cabinet again. "I'm going to make you come so many times you forget your own name. For that, I'll need a little help."

The click of the vibrator startled me in the darkness caused by my blindfold, my body straining against the straps holding me as I became hyper-aware of the cool air on my pussy, all my attention focused there. Every nerve felt on edge as I waited for the touch I knew would be coming.

As soon as the toy made contact, I realized it must have been more than just a vibrator. Something hard and smooth slid inside me, with a rabbit-ear vibrator attached, and I moaned around the ring in my mouth as the ears found my clit.

The dildo didn't fill me as well as Cole did, but I suspected he was conserving his energy. He'd promised to make me come multiple times, so he would save his own orgasm for the finale.

"This slides in so easily," Cole commented in his deep, firm tone, pulling the toy out of me and thrusting it in again to prove his point. "You're so wet. You love me fucking you with it, don't you?"

I loved him fucking me with anything, but I didn't say that.

I couldn't.

I couldn't say anything at all.

"You also love me playing with your clit."

He pressed the ears against my clit more firmly and the vibration sent a jolt of pleasure through my body, letting him know without any words that he was right.

"You love it on your ass too."

Twisting the dildo around with it still inside me, he angled the ears to hit my back hole instead, and my body convulsed again. I loved every filthy thing he did, and I loved when he narrated it for me. My body pulsed and throbbed for him as he thrust the silicone cock into me, harder and faster.

"We're going to keep count tonight, Gorgeous. This is the first one. Right... here."

With just that word, my body surrendered, my first orgasm of the night washing over me in blissful release.

"Perfect," my husband assured me, his tone of voice leaving me in no doubt that he meant it.

It felt like an ending, but I knew the night had just begun, and it wouldn't take long before my body began to crave him again.

~Cole~

I never tired of the incredible sight of Gemma coming. The way she surrendered to it, the way she surrendered to *me*, somehow made me feel both powerful and humbled at the same time. In a life where I'd achieved just about every kind of success a man could have, her pleasure remained my greatest accomplishment.

Although my dick had been straining painfully against my pants since we walked into the playroom, I kept my clothes on, wanting to draw out the pleasure for both of us. I didn't have quite the stamina of my younger days but that night, seeing my gorgeous wife strapped down on the bench, gagged and blindfolded, I felt younger than I had in a very long time.

"Hold this tight for me," I instructed, pushing the dildo, now slick with her pleasure, back inside her. Gemma clenched around it to hold it in place while I returned to the cabinet to pull out the inflatable vibrating anal plug I'd noticed earlier. We'd done double penetration on her several times using a toy, but I'd never paired it with the ring gag before and at that moment, I couldn't remember why. That would soon be remedied, though. That night, I intended to fill her as completely as possible.

The lube felt cool on my fingers, and I could only imagine what it would feel like for her when I began to rub it around the rim of her back hole. Gemma's body clenched tighter in surprise, which pulled the rabbit ears of the dildo closer to her clit, and she moaned through her gag.

"Relax for me, Gorgeous," I instructed. "I've got you."

Instantly, her muscles loosened, and I set to work. With one hand, I began fucking her with the dildo again, and with the other, lubed one, I pushed my way into her ass, watching her carefully for any sign of discomfort or her nonverbal safe word. Only those muffled, gagged moans could be heard, so I kept going, fucking both her holes at once while my dick protested at its continued confinement.

When she came again, I switched out my fingers in her ass for the plug, inserting it with even more lube before gently inflating it. This particular model had a remote control for the vibration, which would be even more fun.

"That's two," I informed her, since I said we'd be counting her orgasms. "Does that feel okay?"

I rotated the vibrating part of the dildo slowly across her clit to help her forget any minor discomfort.

"Umm-phhhhh," was all the response I got, but since her head remained looking straight ahead, I took it as a 'yes'.

"Good. Hold it again."

Leaving the plug in her ass and the dildo in her pussy, I returned to the cabinet again. Gemma always enjoyed a bit of impact play, and over the years, I'd fine-tuned it to an art form. I knew just how much force to use and where on her body would give her the most pleasure, or the most exquisite pain.

For that night, I chose a simple flogger, something familiar among the barrage of other sensations she'd be feeling, and when I returned to her body, I dragged it up her legs, letting her feel the individual leather fronds as they trailed lightly over her skin.

Gemma shivered in anticipation, which only pushed the vibrator closer to her clit again, making her body jolt. Each movement brought a reaction, her whole body primed for me, and I hit the 'on' button for the butt plug at the exact moment I brought the flogger down on her ass.

"Gaaaahm!" Her unintelligible exclamation sent a rush of pleasure through me in response, my body responding to what she felt with no physical stimulation of my own.

"You're going to come on the third stroke. One."

I brought the flogger down on the back of her thighs, one of her favourite spots.

"Two."

Her lower back, just above her ass.

"Three."

As I hit her square on the ass again, her body contracted with her third orgasm of the night, and I finally gave into my own need by undoing my pants and pulling my painfully stiff dick out. Fuck, she turned me on.

Gemma's body continued to twitch with aftershocks of her orgasm, both the butt plug and the dildo still vibrating against her, while I tossed the flogger aside and moved around in front of her. Her head sat at perfect height, her mouth already propped open, so I didn't bother giving her any warning of my intentions as I pressed my hard dick through the ring opening and into her waiting mouth.

She hummed around me while I slid into her slowly, letting her adjust to the feel of me as she breathed through her nose while I filled her mouth. Her warm tongue along the underside of my shaft felt like heaven, especially after all the anticipation of the day, from the plane to the restaurant to everything we'd done since stepping into that room. It would have been easy to fuck her hard, pumping firmly into her until I came, but I wanted to savour it instead: the sight of my perfect Gemma tied down, all her holes filled, giving herself over to me entirely.

"You're going to give me a fourth one," I instructed, stroking her hair while I continued to fuck her mouth. "You're going to show me just how much you love my dick in your mouth by coming for me. Are you ready?"

She couldn't answer, but I knew her lack of response meant she was with me, and I reached down to plug her nose right as I thrust into her again, cutting off her air just for a second.

"Now."

Just as I expected, she obeyed, whimpering as she came again for me. As soon as she did, I immediately let go of her and pulled out of her mouth, reaching behind her head to release the gag as well for good measure. Gemma gasped for air in a dazed, satisfied way.

"You still good, Gorgeous?"

I knelt down to place a soft kiss of her lips and she pressed her lips back against mine, a little weakly but still intentionally. "I'm... good," she managed to get out.

"That's what I wanted to hear, because I know you've got one more for me tonight. I want to feel you coming on my dick before we go to bed."

A shiver of anticipation ran down her spine, even though she'd already come a handful of times. She always gave me just as much as I asked for.

Returning to the rear of the bench, I took out both the plug and the dildo, leaving her empty and ready for me. When I slid my hard dick into her wet pussy, it felt like coming home, no matter that we'd just travelled thousands of miles.

I kept my pace slow and steady to begin with, painting a picture for her with my words since the blindfold still blocked everything from her view. "In just a few days, you'll be standing up in front of everyone, the mother of the bride in your beautiful dress. None of them will know that a few days earlier, on this night, you let me tie you up and fuck you with anything I could lay my hands on."

"Oh, God," she whimpered, her hands clenching as I brought my hand down on her ass.

"They won't know how you begged me to let you come one more time, but I will. I'll still hear it."

"Please," she gasped, playing her part perfectly. "Fuck, Cole, come with me. Come inside me. Please."

Another spank, the sound of my hand on her skin sounding sharp in the rented room. "You're going to enjoy every minute we have here, but none quite like you'll enjoy this. Am I right?"

"Yes," she moaned. "Please, yes!"

Instead of spanking her again, my hand moved to her clit instead, reaching around her hips with one hand while the other rubbed her ass. "Anything for you, Gorgeous."

My eyes closed as my own release hit, and as soon as she felt me coming, Gemma let go too. We pulsed together, our bodies staying connected until I slowly took a step back, pulling out of her with a sigh.

"Give me one second." It didn't take long for me to clean myself up, tucking myself back into my pants before I set to work untying Gemma's restraints. The blindfold, I left until last, covering her eyes with my hands until she could open them without squinting. "Do you want to rest here or back at the hotel?"

By 'rest', I meant the way I always took care of her after we played together, and the room there at the club had several amenities I could use, but it didn't surprise me when she said she'd rather go back to our room.

After helping her dress, we let ourselves out of the club, climbing the stairs back to the real world, which hit us in the face with the warm, humid air as soon as the door opened for us.

"Was that a dream?" Gemma murmured, leaning against me as we walked slowly back to the hotel. "It hardly seems real."

"I promise it happened," I assured her. "And I'll never forget it."

Back in the room, I ran her a bath and sat on the edge of the tub to rub her shoulders while she let the warm water soak into her skin.

"I'm going to fall asleep any second," she mumbled as I moved on to massaging her scalp.

To tell the truth, I was starting to feel it too, but as I went to get her towel, her phone rang from the other room. "I'll get it," I quickly offered. "Wait here."

It took me a moment to locate the phone and when I did, the person on the other end seemed startled to hear my voice. "Oh, hello. I'm looking for Mrs Gemma Stamer. Is she available?"

The voice was British, and not one I recognized. "This is her husband, Cole Stamer. Can you tell me what this is about?"

"Mr Stamer, my name is Harry Woodward. I'm one of the solicitors for the Earl of Totnes."

That certainly got my attention. The Earl of Totnes was Gemma's brother, Thomas, who had inherited the title when her father died a few years earlier. I'd never met Tom, as Gemma referred to him on the rare occasions she spoke of him. Her family had completely cut off contact with her when we got married, and we weren't about to beg for acknowledgement.

"What is this about?" I repeated, since he still hadn't answered that question. I didn't want to give him access to Gemma if it would cause her any distress.

"It's about her inheritance," Mr Woodward claimed, which didn't make any sense to me.

"The Earl didn't leave her anything." I knew that for a fact.

"The previous Earl didn't," he agreed. "But Thomas passed away last night, and his will is a different story."

Gemma's brother died? So much for avoiding distress. She was going to have to deal with it, whether I wanted her to or not.

"Hang on, I'll get her for you."

Chapter Three

Old Friends and New Secrets

~Noah~

Tate walked into the hotel bar still holding his bags, which made him rather hard to miss.

"You could have checked in first," I pointed out as I got up from my spot near the end of the bar to greet him.

Tate gave me a wide grin, the same one he'd had since our college days. I'd long ago lost count of how many women I'd seen him win over with that smile. "I didn't want to miss a minute of this. Where's Liv?"

Unfortunately, I had to be the bearer of bad news on that front. "She's not feeling great so she's not joining us tonight."

"Aw, shit, I'm sorry to hear that." Dropping his bags on the ground, Tate pulled himself up onto one of the tall bar stools while I took my place again, my drink already half gone. The long bar had twelve high-backed stools, the reclaimed wood adding to the casual yet refined atmosphere of the whole room. Behind us, tables were set up at offset angles, with plenty of room in between for standing and mingling. During the day, the floor-to-ceiling windows made the room feel like an extension of the beach outside, and at night, the glass reflected the glow of the lights above our heads and the candles that flickered at every table.

As a man who spent a lot of time in hotels, I had to admit it was one of the most welcoming bars I'd ever been in, and it irritated me that it didn't belong to me.

Tate quickly came to the same conclusion as he looked around. "You going to try to buy this place?"

The thought had crossed my mind, but I didn't think it would be that easy. "I don't think Derek's looking to sell, but I'll definitely let him know that when he is, I'm interested. But we're not here to talk about work. How was the flight? And how are you?"

Although Tate worked for Stamer Hotels, my family business, with the corner office and the salary he'd always dreamed of, we didn't actually see each other that much. As regional operations director for Asia, his corner office was in Singapore while mine was in New York, and though we spoke regularly during management meetings, it had been too long since we'd had a chance to hang out in person. That was part of why I'd invited him to Eve's wedding when it turned out it would be happening on his side of the world.

The other part, naturally, had to do with the club on the resort grounds, the one we'd been hoping to visit that night. With Olivia not feeling well enough to join us, it would have to wait. She had to put her foot down to make me even agree to leave her alone long enough to meet Tate for a drink, insisting that I couldn't do anything to make her feel better even if I stayed.

That had become a recurring theme for us, and the helplessness had started to eat away at me even as we maintained our usual carefree facade for the rest of the world.

"The flight was a flight, and I'm fine," Tate answered me bluntly. "When did you get here? Has Tessa made it?"

Tate and Tessa had remained in touch ever since they met in Vienna the Christmas that Liv and I got together, but they hardly ever saw each other in person. With Derek also having been part of that amazing Christmas in Vienna, the week at his resort had started to feel like a bit of a reunion for all involved.

"She's here but she's having an early night too. She's laser-focused on the wedding, so we probably won't see too much of her until after it's done."

"So, I'm on my own for tonight," Tate guessed, and I had to nod.

"Sorry. Hopefully, Liv will be good as new tomorrow and we can check out Paradise then."

Although Derek's club catered to all kinds of kink, as a voyeur and exhibitionist himself, he'd given those particular kinks top billing. Since Tate and I happened to share those interests, we'd both been looking forward to exploring it for ourselves, but I never played without my wife. That rule, along with a couple of others, helped to keep any potential jealousy or doubts at bay.

"We'll have a drink first, though," I offered so he wouldn't feel completely abandoned. "Tell me what's going on with you."

Over our whiskey, Tate filled me in on his latest exploits. "I haven't been to a lot of clubs lately. The scene in Singapore is pretty small, but don't worry, I'm still getting laid. Somehow, I've got myself a reputation as the guy rich businessmen go to when they want to watch their wife get fucked by someone else."

"I can't imagine how," I teased him drily. I could picture the scene easily: Tate and a beautiful woman in some sleek, high-rise apartment while the husband sat to the side, stroking himself as he watched them. Some men enjoyed it as a form of degradation while others, like me, simply got off on watching their partner be satisfied. "Are you enjoying it?"

"It's definitely got its perks," he grinned back. "But I miss our clubbing days, the three of us."

I did too. Those seemed like much simpler times in retrospect: me and Liv and Tate spending the night at a club, watching each other and not caring about anything beyond that night. Tate always kept his eyes open for a woman who might turn our trio into a quartet, someone he could share his life with the same way Liv and I had each other, but he hadn't found her yet, ironically. I'd been the one not looking for anything long-term when the perfect woman landed in my lap, and Tate had been ready to settle down for years but hadn't met the right person yet.

The reminder of Liv made me pull out my phone, double checking that she hadn't tried to get a hold of me, and Tate rolled his eyes. "You'd obviously rather be looking after her, so go. I'll be fine. We can catch up more tomorrow."

I appreciated that, since I really did want to see how she was doing. "Thanks, Tate. You never know: maybe someone's been checking you out since you got here but was too shy to come over while there were two of us."

"Yeah, that's it." Tate's sarcastic tone made me smile as he glanced around the bar. "But actually, there *are* some gorgeous women here. Hopefully, some of them know about the club too."

My gaze followed his to a table where two pretty women sat with a big, good-looking guy, and my brow furrowed. "Hang on, I know those people."

"Seriously?" Tate asked with a laugh. "You just got here."

"So did they. Come on, I'll introduce you."

Not waiting for a reply, I headed over to the table and gave the small group a charming Stamer smile. "You all having a good night?"

"Definitely." The guy, whose name was Corey, I remembered, gestured to an empty chair. "Come and join us."

"Thanks, but I can't. I just wanted to introduce you to another of the wedding guests. This is my good friend, Tate. Tate, these are the groom's half-sisters. Maribel is married to Corey here, and Crystal is her sister."

"Half-sisters? Sounds like there's a story there." Tate's charming grin rivalled my own, and the people at the table instantly responded to it, as people always did.

"There is," Crystal assured him, pulling out the chair next to her. "Have a seat and we'll fill you in."

Tate dropped into the empty chair while I took my leave. "Have a good night everyone. See you tomorrow."

Feeling better that Tate wouldn't be completely on his own, I walked briskly out of the bar and back to my room to check on my wife.

~Olivia~

Although I told Noah to stay out as long as he wanted to, it didn't really surprise me when the door to our hotel suite opened less than an hour after he'd left.

"Liv?" He called out my name before he reached the bedroom, and when he walked in to see me curled up on my side with my e-reader, his handsome face broke into a soft smile. "What kind of monsters are getting fucked in this book?"

"Aliens," I admitted breezily, having no reason to hide my monster romances from my kinky husband. He loved hearing about them, and he'd even bought specially designed dildos that matched some of the more unusual cocks I'd read about. Noah had never been one to shy away from whatever turned me on, so I had to burst his bubble before he got too carried away. "Mostly humanoid this time, unfortunately."

"How boring." His grin left me in no doubt that he was teasing, but as he stepped closer, I could see the concern still clouding his eyes. "How are you feeling?"

"Better." It frustrated me that I'd been so nauseous all day, but it did seem to be easing, at last. We'd been so careful about planning the appointments around the wedding, but we didn't count on the side effects. "I think people are getting suspicious, though."

Though Gemma and Cole hadn't said anything on the plane, I could guess what they were thinking. Just like my own parents, they'd be thrilled if we announced we were expecting, but it wasn't that simple.

No matter how much we wanted it to be, it would never be that simple.

"It might be a good sign," Noah suggested tentatively, taking a seat beside me on the bed and reaching for my hand. "You weren't nauseous the other times."

No, I hadn't been. The first three embryo transfers, all unsuccessful, might have been emotionally draining, but physically, I hadn't felt anything at all. The nausea I felt this time *might* be a good sign, or it might just be a side effect of the treatment. We wouldn't know for sure until we took the pregnancy test.

Intellectually, logically, we knew we weren't the only couple to ever have trouble conceiving. The other women I saw at the fertility clinic were proof of that, but in our small circle, among our friends and family, no one else had struggled the way we had. Or, if they had, they'd never talked about it. If anything, they spoke about how easy it had been, like how Noah had been conceived by accident the one time his parents didn't use protection.

Maybe that explained why we decided not to share our ordeal with our families. Or maybe we were still just holding onto the dream of being able to announce a pregnancy just like everyone else, as if we hadn't gone through all the needles and medication and blood tests and hormones and endless, endless appointments.

At least we didn't have to worry about the cost of it, which was one blessing in the midst of all our stress. So many of the other women I'd met were using all their savings for their IVF treatment, and if it didn't work, they wouldn't be able to afford another try. On our side, we could afford to keep going for as long as it took from a financial perspective, but from the emotional side, I didn't know how much more I could take.

My body barely felt like my own anymore, poked and prodded and injected and studied, and when Noah first told me about the club at the resort that he wanted to visit, not only to watch but to perform, I thought he had to be joking. "Nobody wants to look at me right now. I don't even want to look at myself. I barely feel like a woman, Noah."

He cupped my face in his hands, looking down at me with a fierceness I rarely saw in his green eyes. "You're just as perfect as you've always been. Nothing has changed."

Those were easy words to say, but the reality felt quite different.

In any case, I didn't want to dwell on what might or might not be happening inside my body at that moment. The transfer had taken place twelve days earlier, so in two days, we'd be able to take a pregnancy test and find out if the embryo had attached. If it had, we could share the good news with our families. If not, we'd have to decide what came next.

It didn't help me to imagine either scenario until we knew for certain.

"How's Tate?" I asked, ready to change the subject as I moved my e-reader to the bedside table and sat up enough that I could curl up against Noah. "Did he bring anyone with him?"

"He's on his own, but I left him chatting with Julien's sisters so he had some company."

That hadn't been why I asked. "He didn't bring anyone for you guys to play with?"

I could feel Noah's grimace even though I couldn't see it. "I told you, Liv: I'm not doing a scene with anyone other than you. If you're not feeling up to it, we can just watch."

"But you've been looking forward to..."

"I've been looking forward to being with you," he cut me off. "That's all."

He meant to be supportive, but his refusal made me feel even worse. We'd always had an open relationship when it came to our kink. He liked to watch me with other men and I loved to watch him with other women. When we started trying for a baby in earnest, nearly three years earlier, we both agreed that I would stop having sex with other men, which only made sense to me. Even using protection, accidents happened, and if we had a baby, we wanted it to be Noah's.

On his own, he decided not to have sex with anyone else either while we were trying, which I found sweet at the time, but as the weeks and months went by, it began to feel like a burden instead. What we thought would take months at most stretched into years, with no end in sight. Not only was Noah not a father yet but his sex life had suffered too, and his insistence on sticking to his promise, even when I told him I didn't want him to, led to some of the few real arguments we'd had in all the time we'd been together.

Secretly, I'd been hoping that if Tate brought someone along that he was actually in a relationship with, Noah might feel comfortable enough to have fun with her, just like Tate and I used to with each other. But since Tate had arrived solo, it seemed like it would be just the two of us, putting all the pressure on me to get into the right headspace for a performance if I wanted Noah to have any fun at all.

Christmas had never been quite so stressful before.

~Noah~

A table had been reserved in the dining room for the wedding guests for breakfast in the morning, but when Olivia and I got there, we found it empty other than Noelle and Aaron, sitting next to each other at the long rectangular table, dressed in coordinating shorts and short-sleeved shirts.

"Where is everyone?" Olivia asked as she took a seat across from her sister and I sat down next to her. We were also dressed casually since nothing formal was happening that day and the forecast promised plenty of summer sun.

Noelle shrugged. "I'm not sure. Mom said she and Dad are having a lazy morning to adjust to the time difference and are going to have breakfast in their room. As for everyone else, I have no idea. The schedule said nine o'clock, so we got here for nine."

"There's a schedule?" I asked, completely deadpan, even though I knew exactly what she meant. I just wanted to see Noelle's reaction if she thought I didn't know about it, and she didn't disappoint.

"Of course there's a schedule! Didn't you look in your welcome pack? It has all kinds of important information and directions and..."

"Noelle." Aaron put his hand on hers as he gave her an affectionate smile. "He's teasing you."

"Oh." Noelle's sheepish smile always reminded me of Olivia's. Normally, they didn't look much alike, with Olivia taking after their mom with her blonde hair and more angled face while Noelle had Jackson's brown hair and approachable air, but whenever they got caught being a little over-competitive or over-pedantic, their expressions were identical. "Well, I assumed the jet lag affected everyone and that's why they're still in bed. How are you feeling today, Liv?"

Apparently, everyone really *had* noticed Olivia being under the weather the day before, but luckily, she felt a lot better that morning, and she told her sister so. "I'm absolutely fine. It looks like it's going to be a gorgeous day. What are you guys thinking about doing? Maybe we could go for a hike?"

While the two of them chatted about potential activities for later, I pulled out my phone to check on my family. They had all been in touch already, I just hadn't seen the messages yet. Eve said she and Julien were in a meeting for the wedding and were running late so to go ahead without them. My dad's message was a little more cryptic, saying that he and my mom had to go into Sydney to take care of something. He promised to fill me in later, and I trusted he would, but I couldn't help being a little curious about what would have come up that they would need to leave town for.

From Tate, I had nothing, so I sent him a quick text. *You alive?*

Barely, his reply came back. *You missed a great night. Your new in-laws-ish are pretty cool.*

Were they? I really hadn't spent much time with the Ribar family, so I couldn't say. *Breakfast?* I asked him instead.

Nah, but if you guys are doing something later, count me in.

"Sounds like Tate, Crystal, Maribel and Corey had a late night," I told the others. "And if I had to guess based on dinner last night, I'd say that Julien's mom and dad are both staying away because they think the other one will be here. So, I guess it's just the four of us."

Our waiter came over for Olivia and I to order food, and when he walked away, Aaron leaned forward across the table. "While we've got you alone, can we ask you about this Paradise club?"

Olivia nearly choked on her surprise. "Are you two interested in going?"

Even though Noelle's cheeks turned pink just talking about it, she nodded. "We thought it might be kind of fun, just to say we did it once, but we don't know what to do or if we'd be way over our heads. You know a lot more about it than we do."

That was an understatement if I'd ever heard one. "How did you even find out about it?"

I hadn't told them, and I knew Liv hadn't either, but I should have guessed the answer. "Eve told us. And don't worry: she made sure we knew not to tell Dad."

So, Jackson was still clueless, thankfully. "Well, there's no one-size-fits-all experience. It's literally meant to be *your* idea of paradise, but my advice to you for your first time would be to watch one of the performances on stage and have a private room booked for yourselves afterwards. Chances are the performance will turn you on, and then you can enjoy doing whatever it is you do in private."

Noelle and Aaron exchanged looks, having a whole conversation with their eyes before turning back to us. "It wouldn't be you guys performing, would it?" Noelle asked tentatively.

"No!" Olivia assured her with a laugh. "We know way too many people here to do a completely public performance. But we'll be going to watch for a while. If you want to come with us so you're not on your own, that would be fine."

It sounded like Liv definitely planned on us going to the club that night, which was music to my ears. She'd been so down on herself recently, and I was dying for a chance to remind her of just how amazing she was, baby or no baby.

"I think we'd like that," Noelle said, with Aaron nodding in agreement. "Maybe tonight, before we lose our nerve? There's nothing on the wedding schedule for this evening."

"It's a date," Liv agreed.

After breakfast, we all headed out to the hotel's terrace where we ran into Eve, Julien and Tessa just coming from their meeting. The morning sun already felt hot, especially after leaving the New York winter behind, but at least the breeze off the ocean helped to make it feel a little cooler.

"Is breakfast already over?" Eve asked in dismay, her hand going to her stomach. "I'm starving."

"Go and eat," I instructed. "You didn't miss much. Only the four of us were there."

Julien's lips tightened at that news. "I better go and check on my mother. Go ahead, Eve, I'll catch up with you there."

Olivia, Noelle, and Aaron decided to head back into the dining room to keep Eve and Tessa company, so I excused myself to go find Derek. I hadn't had a chance to say hello yet since we arrived, and I was soon shown into his office, a comfortable, relaxed space that felt light years from my own office at the Stamer Hotels headquarters.

"Good to see you, Noah," he greeted me, getting up to shake my hand as his assistant closed the door behind us. "I thought we might see you at Paradise last night."

"It didn't work out, but hopefully tonight. I've heard great things about it."

I meant in general, but he seemed to take my words more literally. "It was great to see some of your group there last night."

That only made me curious about who had already been to check it out, but I knew better than to ask. Discretion was key at a place like that.

"So, any plans to put this place on the market anytime soon?"

As I expected, he laughed, and we chatted business until Olivia texted me that everyone was ready to go for a hike. By the time I got back to the lobby, a sizeable group had gathered, though we were still missing the older generation. Tessa had arranged some cars to transport us to the top of Mount Ousley, and from there, we were promised a relatively easy hike for those still nursing hangovers or jet lag or both, with gorgeous views over the Wollongong coast.

Noelle and Aaron quickly regretted their decision to wear shorts as the spiky branches of some of the local bushes prickled against their legs, but once we got out into the open vistas of Brokers Nose summit, everything else was forgotten. The world opened in front of us with the forest, the city, the beach and the ocean all competing for our attention. We even spotted some kangaroos in the distance, which led to Noelle filling us in on all the kangaroo facts she'd read up about.

The fresh air and exercise seemed to do us all good and everyone was in high spirits as we set off back to the hotel.

I ended up near the back of the group on the return trip with only Noelle and Aaron behind me, and at one point, I turned back to say something to them only to find that they'd vanished. "Hold up!" I called to the rest of the group, and they all came to a stop as I headed back along the path to see where we'd lost them.

It didn't take long to locate them around the next bend, just off the track with Aaron holding Noelle's arm and rubbing her back while she hunched over a nearby bush.

"Is everything okay?" At first, I thought maybe she'd scratched her legs again, but as they both turned to me with a startled look and Noelle wiped her mouth, a much more likely explanation sank in, one that made my stomach feel like lead even as I pasted a smile on my face. "Are you pregnant?"

"How the hell did you jump to that conclusion?" Aaron grumbled. "It could be anything."

It could be, but from the look on Noelle's face, I knew I had it right even before she confirmed it.

"We didn't want to say anything until after the wedding," she explained with that sheepish smile, so like her sister's. "Can you keep it a secret until then?"

Fuck. Of course I was happy for them, but all I could think of at that moment was how Olivia would feel when she found out. If we had our own good news, that would definitely make it easier to take, so staying quiet for a couple of days wouldn't be an issue. At least it would give me some time to decide how to break the news to her before she heard it from anyone else. She could get all the complicated emotions out first so that only happiness remained when her sister told her she would be an aunt.

"I won't say a word," I promised.

Chapter Four

A RETURN TO FORM

~**Olivia**~

Noah seemed preoccupied on the way back to the hotel after our hike. When I asked him if anything was wrong, he gave me a somewhat forced smile. "I'm just curious about what's going on with my parents."

That didn't feel entirely right, since he'd been relaxed and happy on the mountaintop, but I didn't push it. With my nausea cleared and the stress of the flight behind us, I planned to put my worries aside as much as possible and enjoy Christmas with our families, even if we were on the beach instead of having snowball fights at Isabelle's farm.

As it turned out, Noah didn't need to wait for long to find out what had taken his parents to Sydney that morning. As soon as we returned to the hotel, Cole asked Noah and Eve to come to his and Gemma's suite. Naturally, Noah brought me and Eve brought Julien.

The winter wonderland that greeted us inside Gemma and Cole's suite made me smile, just as it had when I peeked in at it the day before. Cole would go to any lengths to make his wife happy, and luckily for me, Noah had inherited that characteristic. The Stamer men were truly something else.

"Have a seat," Cole invited us. He wore a suit, as he usually did, despite the heat, and Gemma wore a business-like dress too. Whatever they'd been doing, it must have been something official. "Does anyone want a drink?"

Eve and I both shook our heads, and Noah and Julien refused too, probably more out of solidarity with us than because they truly didn't want one.

Pouring himself a drink anyway, Cole took a seat on the sofa next to Gemma, leaning forward with his elbows on his knees as his piercing dark eyes took us all in. "You all know I hate unnecessary drama, so I'll get straight to the point: Gemma's brother passed away last night."

"Oh, I'm sorry," was my instinctive reply, even though I couldn't remember Gemma ever mentioning her brother. I knew from Noah that she had one, but Noah had never met him. They had no contact with Gemma's side of the family at all.

Gemma gave me a grateful smile as Julien also murmured his condolences. Noah's thoughts, however, headed down a different path. "He didn't have any children, did he?"

"No," Gemma answered. "Apparently, he was gay, which we also learned last night. He kept it hidden the whole time our father was alive because he knew the Earl wouldn't approve and he wanted to keep his inheritance. I know how it felt to live in fear of my father's judgement, and it saddens me that Tom put up with it for so long. In the years since my father died, I guess he'd been more open about it, but there were no children, biological or otherwise."

The talk of children set off that empty, aching feeling in my heart that had become commonplace for me over the last couple of years, but I ignored it to focus on what I knew Noah must have been thinking. "What happens to his title, then?"

Cole jumped back in. "That's what we've been talking about today. Apparently, with no heir of his own, Thomas left precise instructions that the title, lands and property should pass to Gemma and her children instead."

My mind whirled as I looked over at Noah, trying to take that all in. Apparently, not only was my husband the heir to the Stamer Hotels business, he stood to inherit a peerage too?

A peerage that would someday need heirs of his own.

Heirs that we didn't seem to be able to provide.

As if he could sense my thoughts spiralling, Noah grabbed hold of my hand before focusing back on his mom. "What does that make you?"

She gave an almost self-conscious shrug. "A Countess, believe it or not."

It didn't seem that odd to me. I'd always thought of Gemma as one of the most beautiful, graceful women in the world. Along with my own mom, I had no shortage of women to look up to.

"And what would you be?" Eve asked her dad.

"Earl Consort. The 'consort' gets added because Gemma's the one with the title, not me."

Briefly, I wondered how the dominant Cole Stamer would deal with getting second billing, but the supportive, affectionate look he gave his wife made it clear that even if he never deferred to anyone else, he would always put her first.

"So, you're accepting it?" Noah clarified. "This is really happening?"

"It is." Gemma answered for the two of them, giving Cole a warm smile. "I wish that my brother had got in touch and let me know he planned this, or tried to rekindle our relationship, but I believe he must have wanted the title to stay in the family and I'll honour that. In some ways, the timing is perfect. With Noah taking over as CEO, Cole needs a project anyway."

He certainly did seem more energized than he had in a while. "Running the Countess of Totnes' business affairs is more like a full-time job than a side project, but it's a new challenge I think I'll enjoy, and I agree with Gemma: as far as the timing goes, it makes sense."

"And you'll be moving to England?" I asked in some dismay. Having both sets of parents close at hand had always been a blessing for us, and I'd always imagined raising our kids with their grandparents nearby.

"At least part-time," Gemma conceded. "We won't be selling the New York apartment though. We'll have to see how things go. We just found out last night, so this is all new for us too. We can all figure it out together, especially since, as the oldest, Noah inherits the family's second title. That makes the two of you officially a Viscount and Viscountess."

Well, we certainly hadn't expected *that* when we woke up that morning.

"I remember you taking us to Wilby Park when we were kids," Eve said, her dark eyes shining as she smiled over at her mom. "You loved it so much. It's wonderful that you'll get to spend time there again."

"I love the idea of our extended family visiting there," Gemma admitted, her eyes dotting with tears at the mere idea. "Celebrating Christmas in those rooms where generations of my family did before would be very special. It means more to me than I thought it would. It's... well, it's a lot to take in."

By 'extended family', I knew that she meant her grandchildren, and again, my heart constricted. Noah's hand tightened around mine as he spoke up again. "Well, this is a really big change, but if you're both happy about it, then we're happy for you."

I nodded in agreement, and Julien gave his congratulations as well, though I suspected he felt a little bit lost about the whole situation. Eve would have to fill him in later.

After speaking with us, Cole and Gemma must have shared their news with my parents, because by the time we got changed and headed out to the beach that afternoon, everyone knew all about it. Between speculation about what it would mean for all our lives and catching up with Tate in between rounds of Noah and Tate trying their hand at surfing and coming back salt-stained but happy, the rest of the day flew by. Almost before I knew it, we were getting dressed to head to Paradise that night.

"Is it going to be weird to be there with your sister?" Noah asked me as he put on his suit. The dress code said to wear whatever made you comfortable, and for Noah, he felt most at home in his suit, just like his dad. Meanwhile, I wore a pretty sundress, trying my best to see my body as something desirable rather than something broken. I'd grown to almost hate the sight of a mirror.

"I'm honestly shocked that she even wants to go," I had to admit. "But I'm glad they're giving it a try. I hope they have a good night."

"I know I will."

The gleam in Noah's green eyes sent a zing of excitement through my body, just like it used to, and I took that as a good sign. Maybe things were turning around for us. Maybe Gemma's news would be the start of a lot of new things.

And maybe that night, we could forget all about it and just enjoy ourselves, the way we always had before, back when we were just Noah and Liv, two people lucky enough to find their other half in each other.

~Noah~

I'd been to a lot of clubs over the years, both before getting together with Liv and afterwards, and Paradise impressed me right from the start. The irony of descending rather than ascending into 'paradise', the tight security that didn't feel intrusive, and the way we were left alone to find our way but someone was always on hand if we needed anything, all contributed to an atmosphere where we felt in control and catered to at the same time.

"This isn't too scary," Noelle announced as we grabbed a table in the bar. "It looks like a regular club."

It did, except for the electronic menus with suggestive graphics and even more suggestive drink names. "They've got virgin versions of all their seasonal cocktails," I pointed out to Olivia since she'd been avoiding drinking while she went through her treatment.

"What do you think I should get?" she asked me, her blue eyes sparkling with anticipation. Seeing her excited instantly excited me too, and my dick twitched so hard in my pants, I had to clear my throat before answering.

"I think the Watch-Me Watermelon sounds right up your alley."

"And a Praise-Me Pineapple for you," Aaron suggested to his wife, his glasses slipping down his nose as he raised his eyebrows at her, making her blush.

"Virgin too, please," Noelle reminded me as I entered the order in, and my eyes darted to Liv, wondering if she would pick up on that and ask why Noelle wasn't drinking. She seemed otherwise occupied, though, glancing around the bar and taking it all in, looking relaxed and happy. It did my heart good to see her in her element again.

"And for you?" I asked Aaron.

He perused the menu thoughtfully for a moment. "What's Vimto?"

Noelle jumped in with the answer. "It's a fruit cordial. We used to have it in England when we visited my mom's family. I think it's mostly grape-flavoured with a few other berries thrown in."

"You want the Voyeur Vimto?" I asked him curiously. I'd been looking at that one myself, but I hadn't thought it would be Aaron's thing.

He shrugged. "Tonight's about experimenting, right?"

"Definitely." Adding our two drinks to the order, I put the tablet down and turned back to my wife. "This place looks great, doesn't it?"

"It really does," she agreed. "Look, there's Tate."

Our friend had indeed just walked in the door, with a familiar-looking woman at his side. I raised my hand to catch his attention and he greeted us as they came over to join us. "Hey, guys. You all know Crystal?"

We did know Julien's half-sister, at least by sight, but I hadn't anticipated that she would be joining us in the club.

Olivia seemed to agree, looking just as intrigued as I felt. "We obviously don't know her well enough. Come have a seat."

Crystal sat next to Olivia who peppered her with curious questions while I leaned over to Tate and asked a different question under my breath. "Is she into the club scene?"

"We came over for a little while last night," he explained. "She hadn't ever been to one before, but she loved it. I think she might be a natural."

Though he sounded as laid-back as ever, I could hear the undercurrent of excitement in his reply. It didn't take a genius to figure out why: a pretty, curvy brunette, confident and charming, from a well-connected family, if Crystal shared our kink too, she might be exactly the kind of woman Tate had been looking for. He didn't say those words out loud, and neither did I, not wanting to jinx anything, but I could tell we were both thinking it. Maybe coming to Eve's wedding would turn out to be a lucky break for him.

When we'd all finished our first drink and grabbed a second, we headed to the club's stage area. Smaller and more intimate than the clubs in bigger cities, the theatre probably only seated around a hundred, and only half the seats were full as our group made our way in and settled down in an empty section. Noelle and Aaron sat in the row ahead of us while Tate and Crystal sat next to me and Liv, just one seat separating me and Tate.

Onstage, a fully-dressed man had just started going down on his naked partner, a busty, tanned golden-blonde woman who kept her eyes on the audience, running her hands over her breasts while the man's tongue flicked across her clit. My hand immediately went between Olivia's legs, up the skirt of her dress, pressing against her to help mimic the sensations the woman on stage must be feeling and enhancing the visual aspect of the performance.

Ahead of us, Noelle slunk down further in her seat, as if she could make herself invisible, and I chuckled softly. "Looks like you got all the voyeur genes in the family," I whispered to Liv as my fingers continued to stroke her through the thin fabric of her panties.

Next to us, Crystal had her hand on Tate's dick through his pants, clearly not shy about it.

The soft moans from the stage, amplified by the microphones and speakers, drifted through the air around us, and when the man began to remove his clothes, he looked out over the audience, his gaze landing and lingering for a long moment on Olivia. No one could blame him; even in a crowd of beautiful women, she stood out, and my fingers slipped beneath her panties into the wetness waiting for me there. One of my fingers pressed inside her as the man on stage pulled his dick out.

"Noah." The soft, needy way she murmured my name had my own dick begging for release. It felt like ages since we'd had a moment like this, enjoying sex and our kink just for the fun of it. Our sex life had become scheduled, subject to Liv's ovulation cycle, and though I always wanted her, it did take some of the spontaneity and excitement out of it. Fuck, it felt good to just let go and be ourselves again.

As we watched, the man at the front of the room began thrusting into his partner, in a missionary position with one of her legs up over his shoulder, both of them looking into the crowd rather than at each other. Tate kissed Crystal's neck while she kept her eyes on the performance, while Noelle covered her face with her hands, peering through her fingers.

My movements stayed slow and steady, deep thrusts into Liv with my finger, as far as I could go, before pulling it back out and rubbing my wet fingertip over her clit. Her legs spread a little wider, craving more, as the couple on stage reached the climax of their performance. As soon as the woman came, her legs trembling around her partner, he pulled out and finished himself off on her stomach, the crowd applauding as he coated her body in his cum.

"Can we go now?" Noelle whispered, loud enough for us to hear her even as she kept her eyes forward.

"Absolutely," Liv agreed, giving me a heated smile as I removed my hand from her skirt. "This way."

As a group, we headed out of the room and followed the signs to the private rooms we'd reserved earlier. We pointed Noelle and Aaron into their own room while Tate, Crystal, Liv and I went into another one, all of us eager and ready to take the evening's fun to the next level.

~Olivia~

Something about being in the club that night made me feel more like myself than I had in a long time. Maybe it had to do with Noelle branching out to try new things. Maybe it had to do with Tate bringing along a woman that he knew outside of the scene, which had never happened before. Maybe it had to do with the man on stage who picked me out of the crowd to share his moment of pleasure with. Or maybe it simply had to do with the wonderful man next to me, my incredible husband who, even after everything we'd been through, still looked at me like I was the only woman in the room. It had never mattered to me whose body his hands were on because his eyes were always on me.

"I've never had sex in front of anyone before," Crystal admitted with a giggle as the door closed behind us, leaving the four of us alone in the private room with a king-size bed along one wall and a large, sectional sofa along the other. There were already top-ups of the drinks we'd been drinking earlier waiting for us on a side table, which made for a nice, personalized touch. Derek had done a great job with the club. I'd have to find a chance to tell him so later.

"You don't have to do anything you're not ready to do," Tate assured her, sliding his arm around her waist. "We can keep watching if you want. Noah and Liv look like they're ready to jump each other anyway."

Did we? I certainly felt that way, but I didn't realize it would be so obvious. My illness of the previous day was long forgotten as my body throbbed with need, fired up from the performance we'd just watched and the anticipation of having an audience for what we were about to do.

Still, I had to offer a disclaimer to the people who were going to watch. "I've got some bruises at the moment. It's not pretty."

The hormone injections in my stomach often left large, reddish-purple blots. The ones in my ass didn't bruise as much but they hurt more. I cried almost every time Noah had to give me one, and he hated upsetting me, meaning he ended up upset too.

"As long as Noah's not giving them to you, it's all good," Tate promised with a laugh. "You always look good to me, Liv."

"You look great to me too," Crystal agreed. "But if it makes you uncomfortable, we don't have to just sit and watch. We can have some fun too."

"Are you sure?" As much as Tate said he wouldn't rush her, he sounded like he just won the lottery when she proposed jumping in.

"Sure. Why not?" Crystal wrapped her arms around Tate's neck, bringing him close to her for a kiss, and her obvious hunger for him drove my own desire higher too. Luckily, Noah was on exactly the same page.

"You don't need to be self-conscious," he murmured in my ear before kissing his way down my neck. "No one's going to be looking at your bruises when there are so many other gorgeous parts of you. You've never looked more beautiful to me, Liv. Each bruise reminds me just how strong you are."

Sincerity bled through every word, and when our mouths collided, it felt like a weight inside me lifted, suddenly making it a lot easier to breathe.

I'd wasted so much time feeling sorry for myself that I almost lost sight of just how lucky I'd been that Noah Stamer fell in love with me. Not just because of the kink, which was amazing, and not because of his money or his new title or anything that came with it, but simply because he had stood by me every step of the way for the past three years and never once made me feel like a failure.

It had been killing me to feel like I let him down or held him back, but the desire in his kiss and the sparkle in his gorgeous green eyes told me that he'd never felt that way at all.

Maybe I had just needed to get out of my own head all along in order to see it.

"Crystal?" As soon as Noah and I broke apart, I addressed the other woman in the room. "What do you say we swap partners to get them warmed up?"

Noah's eyebrows raised in surprise but he didn't say anything, waiting to see what Crystal's response would be. If she said no, nothing else mattered.

However, she took a moment to consider it, looking Noah up and down as the possibilities played out in her head. "That's something you guys do?"

"It is. I love to see Noah enjoying himself, and vice versa. Only if you're interested, though."

She glanced back up at Tate, who shrugged happily, looking like a kid in a candy store. "Your call, baby."

Still thinking it over, Crystal stepped over to the side table and picked up one of the drinks. Her eyes on Tate, she drained it in one long gulp, reminding me of myself back when I first started in the scene and often needed a bit of liquid courage to get my nerve up. It had nothing to do with whether I wanted to do it or not, but just giving myself a little push to work past my inhibitions, and that seemed to be exactly where Crystal was. When she returned to us, she'd made up her mind. "Let's go for it."

Now would be the time for Noah to object if he didn't want to go ahead, but he simply kissed me again. "You're so sexy, Liv. I'm so fucking hard for you."

I believed him, but when Crystal and I dropped to our knees in front of the men, her with Noah and me with Tate, I got a chance to see it for myself. His cock pulsed with need, his eyes fixed on me as Crystal's lips wrapped around his head.

"Fuck, Liv." Those words came not from Noah but from Tate as I took him into my mouth too. Although I'd sucked Tate off before, it had been years since I'd been with anyone but Noah in any way, and I'd almost forgotten how different one man could taste from another. A touch of salty pre-cum made it clear Tate found the whole night just as titillating as Noah and I did, but I didn't look up at him at all. My eyes were on Noah, watching me even as he held Crystal's hair back while she deep-throated him.

It didn't take long for the men to tell us we needed to stop, both of them getting too turned on for how early we were into the evening. As Crystal and I got back to our feet, she surprised me by leaning over to kiss me, the taste of Noah on her tongue mingling with the drink she'd just had, and Noah and Tate both groaned in appreciation as the aching inside me got even stronger.

"Our turn," Tate announced as he and Noah both shed their clothes. Noah came back to me, naked while I remained fully dressed, but not for long. Gently, he lowered me onto the bed, lying horizontally across it, and undressed me item by item while Tate did the same to Crystal who lay next to me.

If anyone saw my bruises, they didn't mention it, and I forgot all about them too as Noah spread my legs and lowered his head to my aching pussy.

"Oh, fuck!" Crystal gasped from beside me as Tate's tongue went to work, and I grabbed her hand as Noah slid his fingers inside me, his tongue playing with my clit.

My entire world narrowed to that club, that room, that bed. All I cared about at that moment was the pleasure my husband gave me, the pleasure we shared with the other two people in the room, and the orgasm that he quickly built towards.

"Watch Liv come," he ordered the other two, his voice deep with desire as it rumbled from between my legs. "She's gorgeous when she comes."

Obediently, Tate and Crystal both turned to me, and their eyes on me with Noah's fingers inside me and his mouth on my clit sent me hurtling over the edge of my orgasm, my whole body trembling in release.

"That's not fair when you know exactly how to turn her on," Tate grumbled good-naturedly. "I've still got to learn all of Crystal's secrets."

"You're... off to a very good start," she gasped, her hand tightening around mine as he found a good spot.

It didn't take too long for Tate to get her there, and for Noah to give me a second orgasm, by which time the men were eager to move things to the next level.

"On your hands and knees, facing the other way," Noah instructed me while Tate simply grabbed hold of Crystal's hips and pulled her towards him, still on her back. From my new position, I had a perfect view of the other couple as Noah rounded the bed to take his place behind me.

Crystal's moan made it clear exactly when Tate slid into her, and Noah's cock thrust into me almost immediately after, filling me in the perfect way it always had. "God, yes," I mumbled, barely able to form the words among the pleasure that flooded every inch of me.

"Fu-uck," Crystal whimpered as Tate lifted one of her legs over his shoulder to pump into her even deeper. He looked up at me for a second, long enough to give me a wink, but his gaze quickly returned to the woman he was fucking.

"You're going to come once more for them, Liv, and then once for me," Noah murmured behind me. "Remember just how good it felt your first time with an audience."

My body jolted at the reminder, even before Noah's fingers found my clit.

"Remember how it feels to have everyone watching you."

My knees nearly buckled, but I managed to hold steady.

"Remember how I've been there with you every single time."

Those words were the ones that did it. I came hard on Noah's cock, and with a satisfied growl, he pulled out of me and flipped me over onto my back again. When he entered me that time, we were face-to-face and I could see nothing but him.

"I'll always be here for you, Liv. No matter what. I love you. Always you, and only you."

I knew exactly what he meant. Even if we never had the family we'd dreamed of, it would be okay. I was enough for him, and he had always been enough for me.

"I love you too, Noah."

At some point, the couple next to us must have finished, but I didn't even hear them. Every part of me was wrapped up in the man above me, sweat lining the brow of his dark hair, determination and adoration in his stunning green eyes, and his hard cock driving into me over and over again, until the world exploded.

Chapter Five

WATCHING

"Oh. My. God."

The words practically leapt out of my mouth as soon as Aaron closed the door behind us. My heart had been pounding ever since we walked into the theatre and saw the naked woman on stage. Despite the fact that no one else seemed to find anything strange about it, it still felt like at any moment, we were all going to get in trouble for... I didn't even know what, but surely, it couldn't be legal to sit there casually drinking eggnog and watching what we just watched.

"Is that a good 'oh my God' or a bad one?" Aaron asked. Behind his glasses, his hazel eyes watched me intently, as focused on me as always.

"They were just... there! Right there. Naked! Fucking!"

I couldn't even try to be eloquent. My power of speech abandoned me while my hands flapped uselessly as I tried to use them to punctuate my point.

Aaron's lips twitched as he answered me. "You knew it was going to be a live sex show. What did you expect?"

"I don't know! Just not... that. And the way they looked at us? I've never wanted to be invisible so badly in my life."

My hands pressed against my cheeks which burned in both first-hand and second-hand embarrassment, and Aaron chuckled as he stepped closer to me, wrapping his arms around me. "It's okay. It's over now and you were very brave."

"Are you patronizing me?" It definitely sounded like teasing but I didn't understand how he could be so calm about all of it. "You said you hadn't been to a club like this before either."

"I haven't, but that's pretty much exactly what I thought it would be like."

He still sounded remarkably relaxed. "Did you... like it?"

As always, he answered me analytically. "I found it interesting from an academic point of view to see what other people enjoy, but overall, I wouldn't want to make it a regular thing. Being alone with you is much more enjoyable."

His hands slipped beneath the back of my shirt, travelling lightly up my back and sending little shivers down my spine. Some of the tension in my body released with his touch, but my heart continued to beat faster than usual as I remembered that we were still in a sex club.

"No one can see us now, can they?"

"Of course not," he assured me. "This room is completely private. I made sure of it before we came. No one gets to see you except for me, Noelle. You're *my* girl, no one else's."

Those magic words relaxed me further, even as they excited me. Aaron always knew just how to make me melt.

For the first time, I looked around the room we'd ended up in. It looked a lot like our hotel room, with a bed, a sofa and a TV. On the coffee table, two drinks were waiting, which looked the same as the ones we'd ordered earlier, and I went over to take a sip of mine, relieved to taste no alcohol in it, just like before.

Olivia hadn't reacted at all when I ordered an alcohol-free drink, so it seemed like Noah really had kept his promise not to tell her. Honestly, that impressed me. I probably wouldn't have been able to keep something that big from Aaron, even if I gave my word.

"What do you think is on the TV?" I asked him as we both took another drink.

"Honestly? Probably something a lot like the performance we just watched. If you didn't enjoy that, I don't think you want to turn the TV on either."

My cheeks flushed again at the memory, and I leaned over to press my face into Aaron's shoulder. "You must think I'm such a prude."

His chest vibrated with laughter. "After all the things we've done together? I would never think that. You tried something new and it wasn't for you. That's not prudish and it's not cowardly either. I'm proud of you for giving it a chance and for knowing your own mind. You don't need to like something just because other people do. In fact, I'd like to give you a reward for choosing your own path."

The praise sent a flash of pleasure through me, my heart rate picking up again for a completely different reason. "What did you have in mind?"

"Something that we'll both enjoy. Come with me."

After taking the drink from my hand and putting it back on the table, Aaron led me to the bed. It smelled clean and fresh as he gently lay me down, my body sinking into the soft duvet while he removed my shoes. Though my pregnancy hadn't begun to show yet, the nausea sometimes made me dizzy, and sure enough, the change in position caused the room to start spinning. I closed my eyes to block it out.

Aaron had always been tuned into my body, but since discovering I was pregnant, he paid even more attention than before, and he picked up on my dizziness immediately. "You okay?"

"I'm good," I answered simply, blinking my eyes open again and giving him a smile to confirm it. "I'm just waiting for you to make me feel even better."

The challenge brought out his smile in return, and he pulled off his glasses before lifting my skirt and quickly discarding my underwear. "They call this place Paradise, right? That's how it's going to feel when I'm done with you."

A shudder of anticipation snaked its way through my body. "Yes, please."

The breathy words would have stayed in my head before I met Aaron, but he always encouraged me to say what I wanted, to speak it out loud and not hold back, and when I did, he grinned up at me in approval. "Good girl."

The pleasure those words brought me was immediately echoed in the feel of his lips on my pussy, the psychological and physical combining into something even better than the sum of its parts. He kissed me slowly and deeply, like we had all the time in the world as his tongue moved along my skin, tasting and teasing me. My legs spread wider as my hips tilted up towards him, craving his touch and the fulfillment it always brought me.

"Such a good, wet girl," he murmured between long strokes of his tongue across my clit.

"Only for you," I breathed out, writhing beneath his touch as my need grew stronger. "Please, Aaron."

"Please what?" He always wanted me to say the words, and I gave them to him, knowing they gave him just as much pleasure as his words did for me.

"Please make me come."

With a deep hum of approval, he got back to work, his pace increasing as he added his fingers to the mix. With the extra sensation, the pleasure of his praise, and the added titillation of knowing exactly where we were, it didn't take much longer for him to fulfill his promise of taking me to paradise, right there on that bed.

If being at a sex club meant feeling like that, maybe it wasn't so bad after all.

~Aaron~

It seemed I found the live performance at the club a little more excit-ing than Noelle did. It came down to simple biology: by and large, men were wired to be turned on by sexual imagery, and watching two people have sex right in front of us definitely created an image. However, it certainly didn't make me interested in the woman on stage, or give me any urge to get up there myself. All it did was make me crave the one person who fulfilled every one of my desires: my charmingly mortified wife in the seat next to me.

Whenever she got awkwardly nervous that way, it always reminded me of the week we fell in love and how unsure she'd been of herself then. I loved the more confident version of herself that I usually saw, but the throwback had its own charm too, especially while we were on vacation with Corey and Eve. Nostalgia combined with the very current passion I felt for her, culminating in the orgasm I just gave her on the club's bed.

Without my glasses, I couldn't see much else in the room, but it didn't really matter. Noelle was my focus, and as she panted my name, I didn't feel like I was missing a thing.

"That was perfect," I told her after running my tongue over her pussy one more time. "How many more do you think you have for me tonight?"

Noelle's sex drive had taken a bit of a dip thanks to her pregnan-cy-related nausea, while I found her sexier than ever since we learned she was carrying our child. From my reading on the subject, I knew her aversion would only be temporary, so I did my best to be patient and wait it out.

Thankfully, that night, we seemed to be on the same page. "At least one more," she murmured happily, peering down at me from behind her half-closed eyes. "I want you inside me when I come again."

I fucking wanted that too.

It didn't take me long to shed my clothes, tossing them indiscrimi-nately onto the floor behind me so that I could join her back on the bed as quickly as possible. As I moved, though, something caught my eye: the full-length mirror at the end of the bed.

An idea quickly popped into my head: we'd learned that Noelle didn't like watching other people have sex, but maybe it would be different if she were watching *us.* I already knew it would work for me, so I grabbed my glasses and put them back on, to Noelle's surprise.

"What are you doing?"

"I want to be able to see you for this," I told her honestly, grinning as that irresistible blush spread up her cheeks. "I need you to get up."

Still a bit confused, she did as I requested, and I took her spot on the bed, resting with my head on the pillows and my body at a slight angle so I could see the mirror.

"Now, you're going to be a good girl and climb on top of me, facing the mirror. We're both going to watch as you take my dick inside you."

Noelle shivered at my words as she glanced between my body, my dick hard against my stomach, and the mirror at the end of the bed. We'd done a reverse cowgirl position many times before, but never with the mirror there. If it looked as good as it already did in my imagination, we might have to rearrange our bedroom at home.

When she hesitated for just a moment, I did my best to bolster her confidence. "You're going to look amazing riding me. I love seeing you take control and set the pace. I love watching you when you know just what you're doing to me."

Flush with my praise, Noelle got to work. On her knees, she straddled me while I reached down to lift my dick up, running the head back and forth across her pussy to coat it in her wetness. Her sweet moans and the way she bit her lip at the sensation sent another rush of blood straight to my dick, and when I gave her hip the slightest downward pressure, she immediately sank down onto me, taking every inch into her as I groaned in pure ecstasy.

Fuck, that never got old.

She never got tired of hearing my thoughts either, so I shared them with her freely. "God, I love your ass. The perfect shape of it bouncing up and down on top of me. I love watching my dick disappear inside you at the same time I feel it. And now, I can see you in the mirror too. I can see your perfect breasts bouncing too, and that sweet stomach that's got our baby inside it. You couldn't be any more beautiful to me if you tried, Noelle. Do you see it?"

Still blushing, she looked tentatively into the mirror, and to her surprise, she seemed to like what she saw. "We look good."

"Damn right we do."

Reaching down, I slid my finger inside her along with my dick the next time she took me in, getting it nice and wet before I slid it down to her back hole.

"Do you want me here too?"

I never did anything anal without asking her first. Sometimes she wanted it and sometimes she didn't, and I trusted her to tell me.

That night, she nodded, her hands cupping her breasts as she watched me through the mirror, watching her. "I want you everywhere."

Anywhere other than the bedroom, I would have called her out for the impossible nature of her statement. I couldn't be everywhere, but in bed, her wish was my command, so I did my best to comply. The next time she sank down onto my dick, my finger pressed into her ass at the same time. Her happy gasp sounded like the sweetest music to my ears.

"Such a good girl, taking me so well. Keep going. Ride me hard. Ride me until you come."

Craving the praise along with the orgasm, Noelle did as she was told. With each rise and fall of her body, my dick grew harder, my pleasure growing until it seemed to take over every part of me. Nothing existed but the sight of my beautiful wife, my favourite person in the world, and her gorgeous body, working to please us both.

"Are you close?" My words sounded strangled as they came out since I didn't know how much longer I could hold off. She had me at her mercy, hanging onto her every move.

"Almost," she confirmed, and I knew exactly how to turn that 'almost' into a 'yes'.

"Let me feel you come, Noelle. Come all over my dick for me. You'll make me feel so good. I know you can do it."

Those words were just the push she needed, and as her body began to tremble with its orgasm, I let myself go too. In hard spasms, I emptied myself inside her, each spurt accompanied by a wave of pleasure that washed over me.

"Fuck, you're fantastic."

I didn't even mean to speak those words out loud, but Noelle giggled happily when I did, climbing off me to come and curl up next to me on the bed, both of us happy and sated.

"That guy up on stage tonight was way too quiet," she said after a minute or two of post-coital silence. "It would have been sexier if he were more vocal. More like you."

"Sexier to you, maybe. I don't know if the rest of the crowd would agree."

The guy had been a tanned, muscled bodybuilder by the looks of it. I had no illusions that most people in the club would prefer a guy like him over a guy like me, but I honestly didn't care. The only woman who mattered to me had chosen me, and that made me feel like the luckiest man in the world, every single day of our lives.

~Noelle~

The morning sun had already begun to filter through the curtains of our hotel room when I woke up to the smell of fresh coffee. With a long, languorous stretch, I blinked my eyes open to find my husband standing next to the bed, placing a breakfast tray down on my bedside table.

"Did I miss breakfast?" I gasped as I quickly sat up. "The schedule said nine, is it past nine? It must be. Why did you let me sleep in?"

Aaron gave me an affectionate smile, reaching down to caress my head. "Relax, Noelle. Hardly anybody else showed up, just like yesterday. I told Eve you'd meet her at the spa for your girl's day in an hour. You haven't missed anything."

He seemed to have everything under control, and the firm touch of his hand relaxed me almost as much as his words did. "Did you already eat?"

"I did. We're leaving for the golf course soon."

The day before the wedding had been divided up by gender with the men going golfing and the women using the hotel's spa. The activities didn't particularly represent either Julien's or Eve's interests, but Olivia's friend Tessa had gone ahead and booked them when she couldn't get a hold of the engaged couple to confirm what else they might want to do. Eve and Julien didn't care all that much about the details, they just wanted to get married and for their guests to have a good time.

I certainly didn't mind. Spending a day being pampered with my best friend sounded pretty good to me.

Aaron, on the other hand, had only recently taken up golfing, and I knew he felt a little self-conscious about going to play with my dad, Cole, and all the other men who'd been golfing for years.

I tried my best to reassure him. "It's just for fun and you'll be great."

"I wouldn't count on it," he contradicted me with a grimace. "But at least Julien says he's terrible too. We can be terrible together."

With that optimistic thought, he gave me a kiss before leaving me to have my breakfast and get ready.

An hour later, precisely, I met Eve and both our moms outside the door to the spa. "Good morning!" I squealed as I gave my best friend a hug. "Can you believe it's your last day as a single woman?"

Eve's laugh sounded as elegant as always. "I haven't felt single since the day I met Julien. This is just making it official, that's all."

"That's kind of how I felt about marrying your dad, since we already had a baby and everything," Gemma said. "But it meant more to me than I thought it would. It might for you too."

At the word 'baby', my hand instinctively started to move to my stomach, but I caught it in time. I knew very well how it felt to have the spotlight on someone else, and I had no intention of stealing Eve's thunder on the day before her wedding.

Trying to change the subject, I glanced around at the otherwise empty waiting area. "Where's everyone else?"

"Michelle, Maribel and Crystal Ribar are already inside, starting the day with some mimosas," my mom explained with a laugh. "Olivia said she'll be here soon but to go ahead without her."

"And Julien's mom?" I asked tentatively. I hadn't had a chance to find out from Eve exactly what was going on with her soon-to-be mother-in-law, and she grimaced when I brought her up.

"I'll tell you about it when we're in there. Massages are up first, and you're with me, Noelle."

When I heard we were doing massages as part of the day, I sent a message to the spa privately to let them know about my pregnancy, just in case there was anything on our schedule that I shouldn't be doing, and they assured me they would take all necessary precautions without making it obvious that they were treating me any differently from the rest.

Inside the spa, we broke off into groups of two, with Crystal on her own for the time being since Olivia hadn't arrived yet. Maybe she wore herself out at the club the night before? Aaron and I didn't try to find the others before we left, so I had no idea how late they stayed.

As soon as Eve and I were alone, she brought up the club while we stripped down for our massages. "Did you end up going to Paradise last night? How was it?"

"The performance wasn't for me," I answered honestly. "But afterwards, we went to our own room and had a good time. Just being there made it feel different, even though we didn't really do anything we wouldn't have done at the hotel."

"Context can make a big difference," Eve agreed, lying down on one of the massage tables and covering herself with her towel. She made it look so easy, but when I tried to do it, I kept getting one end or the other too high or too low, leaving part of me exposed, until eventually, Eve stood up to arrange it for me before returning to her spot. "Julien and I are hoping to go tonight, if I can get him to stop worrying about his mom."

She'd promised to explain the situation to me, so I asked for more details. "What's going on with her?"

The door to our room opened and two rather buff men entered, introducing themselves with Australian accents while I did my best not to catch Eve's eye, knowing that if we made eye contact, I would start laughing at the idea of these two men with their hands all over us for the next hour.

As the men got to work on our massages, Eve filled me in. "She and I have actually gotten along okay for most of this year, so we weren't expecting this attitude when she got here. It's partly to do with Julien's dad being here, and partly because we didn't get married in Québec in a Catholic church like she would have liked. I think it's almost like she's finally realizing that Julien's a grown man who's about to start his own family, and she feels left behind. I can understand it to a point, but we're literally doing everything we can to include her. I don't know what else to try and Julien's at his wits' end. While you were having fun at the club, he was in his mom's hotel room making sure she didn't get on a flight back to Canada."

I hated that the situation was causing Eve any stress, and I did my best to come up with a solution. "Maybe we could ask my parents to keep her company tonight. My dad can get anyone to warm up to him, and at least it'll give you the evening free to have some fun of your own."

I could tell the idea appealed to her. "That might work. I'll talk to Julien about it when he gets back from the golf course."

"Aaron told me that Julien's just as bad at golf as he is," I giggled. "Is that true?"

"I've never seen him play anything other than hockey, so it probably is," Eve had to agree. "I hope my dad doesn't make them feel bad. But hang on: you need to back up a second and give me some more details about exactly what happened at the club last night. You kind of skipped over all that, don't think I didn't notice!"

I could hardly say anything about it with the masseuses in the room, and Eve knew that, giggling as I blushed bright red with her teasing. Thankfully, she let me off the hook and we chatted about the wedding and life in general while firm hands worked all our stress away.

Sometimes, life was pretty damn good.

Chapter Six

COMPLICATED

~Aaron~

The idea of golfing with Cole and Noah Stamer had been giving me nightmares.

Yes, Noah was my brother-in-law, which technically made Cole family too, but although we saw each other at family events like this, I knew Cole much better as the CEO of Stamer Hotels, where I'd been working ever since I graduated from college. In the office, he had almost mythical status, and even if Noah intimidated me a little less, I still didn't relish the idea of making a fool of myself in front of either of them on the golf course.

Thankfully, all my worry came to nothing when we arrived at the golf course after lunch and Noah suggested splitting our group of seven into two smaller groups. "Dad and I can play with Mr Ribar and Corey, and Julien can go with Jackson and Aaron."

"*Dieu merci,*" I heard Julien mutter under his breath and I had to smile. *Thank God indeed.*

"You didn't want to play with your father and father-in-law?" I guessed after the other group had left and the remaining three of us picked up our rented clubs. The golf course in Wollongong looked beautiful on the sunny, warm December afternoon. Despite the dry weather, the course was bright and green, a testament to the care of its staff, and it looked even nicer with the pressure I'd subconsciously put on myself lifted.

"No, not really," the groom admitted, giving Jackson a sheepish smile. "They both seem pretty competitive."

Jackson laughed good-naturedly. "You're not wrong, at least about Cole. I've golfed with him for years and it still drives him crazy when I win. I'm not sure what Julian Ribar's like, but the four of them can fight it out and we can just enjoy the stroll."

That sounded perfect to me.

Jackson kept up a steady stream of small talk as we played the first holes, talking about the resort and the city, the wedding, Julien's work and my work too. He had an ability to set people at ease that I'd always admired, but when I asked about his plans after Cole's retirement, he grew uncharacteristically somber.

"I'd love for Holly and I to both retire and enjoy ourselves but she's not ready to give up her work yet. I love her passion for it, don't get me wrong, but I'm not quite sure where that leaves me. I think I'll drive her crazy if she's working and I'm not."

My father-in-law had never been quite so frank with me about his relationship, like he actually wanted some advice, and I tried my best to say something helpful. "Could she cut back her hours, at least? I mean, Noelle's doing great running the day-to-day side of the business, so Holly doesn't need to be in the office all that much."

I could never resist the chance to praise my wife. Where Olivia had joined Stamer Hotels to work with her husband and dad, Noelle went to work for her mom instead and in just three short years, she practically ran the place. She was ready to take over completely as soon as Holly decided to go, even if she sometimes still had the odd moment of doubt about whether she could handle it.

I had no such doubts.

At that moment, though, we were talking about Jackson, so I brought the conversation back around to him. "She could work from anywhere if you guys wanted to go travelling. Maybe you could even work together on things if you want to spend more time together?"

Jackson laughed at the last suggestion. "You haven't seen me try to colour-coordinate anything. Design is definitely not my forte, and working together might not be great for us either. I know some couples do it well, but it could potentially go wrong. What do you think, Julien? How does it work for you and Eve?"

Julien had been lining up his next shot, and Jackson and I watched as he made a rather nice drive just shy of the green before he turned back to the two of us. "Honestly? It's got pros and cons. We're never short of things to talk about, but it makes it harder to separate our work from our leisure time. Sometimes, it feels like we're always working unless we both make a conscious decision to focus on just us instead."

"That'll get even harder when you have kids, if you do," Jackson warned as the three of us set out towards the green. "Some of those early years when the girls were small are just a blur. A wonderful, joyous blur, to be sure, but it goes so fast, if you don't carve out a bit for the two of you, time can slip away."

That was good advice for me given my impending fatherhood, but I noticed that Julien winced when Jackson mentioned having kids. "Do you guys want children?" I asked him bluntly, trying to figure out what caused his reaction.

"Oui. I mean, I would be happy to have them soon, especially since I'm already thirty and feeling a bit of a ticking clock, but Eve isn't as sure. She thinks it'll be too complicated while we're still travelling so much with work. On the other hand, I think there will always be complications and we will deal with them when we need to."

I could see both points of view. Raising a child on the road would bring its own challenges, but if they waited for the 'perfect' time, it might never come.

"You have time to figure it out," Jackson suggested. "Thirty is still young! Some might even say that fifty-five is young too."

He puffed out his chest as Julien and I both laughed, but Julien's face quickly turned more serious again. "We might not actually have much time, or much of a decision to make. Eve might already be pregnant."

Neither of us were expecting that, and I glanced over at Jackson to follow his lead on how to respond. He always knew what to say, and he didn't hesitate a moment, though he must have been just as surprised as me. "Congratulations!"

"Thanks." Julien's half-smile managed to look both proud and concerned at the same time. "Like I said, we don't know for sure yet. She took a test and the positive sign was very faint. She did another sample this morning that the hotel is going to send to a doctor to confirm it for us. I shouldn't have said anything until we know for sure. I don't know why I did."

I could relate. Jackson had a way of drawing things out of me I didn't intend to say out loud.

"We won't tell anyone," I quickly assured him, and Jackson nodded in agreement. "Eve isn't happy about it?"

Again, my thoughts were with Noelle, and how excited she would be to go through pregnancy with her best friend, even on opposite sides of the world, but if Eve wasn't thrilled, that could put a damper on things.

"I think she's just overwhelmed," Julien explained. "The work with the charity has been all-consuming, as I said, and we didn't plan for this right now. I'm excited, but her feelings are a bit more mixed. When we know for sure if she's pregnant or not, we'll have a better idea."

"Between that and getting ready for a wedding, you *both* must be overwhelmed," Jackson said sympathetically. "Is there anything we can do?"

"If you could magically make my mother have a good time, that would be a good start," Julien joked, but Jackson didn't laugh, his lips pursing thoughtfully instead.

"I'm sure that's possible. Leave her to me tonight. Holly and I will have a good time with her if it kills us."

We all laughed again and turned to lighter talk as we carried on golfing, but my thoughts kept drifting back to Eve and Julien's potential baby, and my confirmed one. Things were going to change for all of us soon, it seemed. This wedding would only be the beginning.

~Noelle~

Normally, a soak in the hot tub or a steam in the sauna followed the massage in the spa's bridal package, and I'd been trying to come up with a plausible reason why I didn't want to do either without revealing my pregnancy, but in the end, I didn't have to. Eve said she'd rather skip it and no one argued with the bride. Instead, we went to get manicures and pedicures, all of us seated in a circle with the nail technicians in the middle so we could chat with each other while being pampered.

"I think Julien's rubbing off on me," Eve admitted as we soaked our feet in preparation for our manicures, relaxing in our bathrobes, our bodies feeling looser after the massage. "This all feels a little excessive."

"Don't let anyone make you feel bad about treating yourself," my mom replied firmly. "I went without little luxuries for a lot of years, saving every penny I could, and it didn't help anyone, including me. Life has enough hardships, so enjoy the good times when you can."

"He doesn't try to make me feel bad," Eve protested, perhaps realizing she'd given the wrong impression. "Trust me, I'd put him in his place if he did. It's more that with all the places we've been this year and the things we've seen, sometimes it feels like a completely different world. I guess I can just understand his point of view even more now than I could before. There's nothing wrong with enjoying life, but it's unfair that some people never get that chance."

None of us could argue with that, but I had no idea what to say in response.

Luckily, someone else did. "Tell us about some of the people you've met," Gemma encouraged her daughter, giving her a warm, proud smile.

While our feet were taken care of, Eve told us several stories that had us all laughing or crying or sometimes both at the same time. We heard about mishaps with animals, incredible resilience through natural disasters, misunderstandings over customs and extraordinary generosity from those who could least afford it. The strength of some of the people she'd met left me in awe, but the last story she told hit particularly hard.

"A few weeks before we came here, a woman came into the office of the charity we were visiting. She had these three adorable but rather sad-looking kids with her. Apparently, the woman heard there was a young, childless couple visiting, and she hoped we would take the children home with us."

My gasp was echoed by just about everyone else in the room. "She wanted you to take her children?"

Eve quickly shook her head. "That's the thing: they weren't *her* children. They were her nieces and nephew, her sister's children. Their father died a couple of years earlier and their mother passed away just a few weeks before our visit. This woman is the only family they have, but she already has six children of her own. She didn't know how she could take care of them but the country's adoption system is overloaded. If she gives them up to the state, they might be neglected. If they stay with her, they might not survive. She was desperate. She even tried to give us the little money that she had to take them with us. It was awful."

Eve's eyes filled with tears as she spoke and mine weren't much better. A quick glance around the room showed me we weren't the only ones getting emotional about it.

"What did you do?" Maribel asked, on the edge of her seat just like the rest of us.

"What *could* I do? We couldn't take them. We had to send her away. I gave her a bit of money and I passed on her information to some of the other charities we know, but it didn't feel like enough. I can't stop thinking about what's going to happen to those kids and it makes me feel like having my own child would be completely selfish when there are so many others who need help."

Before I could stop it, my hand went to my stomach almost defensively, trying to protect the little life growing there from all the cruelties of the world, and an uncomfortable feeling of guilt began to creep in. Was it wrong to be excited to have my own baby? It had never occurred to me to think of it as selfish before.

Without me having to ask it out loud, Gemma answered my question, addressing her daughter. "There's nothing selfish about it. Yes, some people are born much luckier than others. Unfortunately, that's the way the world is, but if those of us who are lucky enough to be in those positions raise thoughtful, dedicated children like you who want to make the world a better place, then maybe someday, gradually, it will all be a little less unfair. You're literally giving all you can, Eve, and if you and Julien want to have a baby of your own, no one would think there's anything wrong with it."

"What does Julien think about all of this?" I asked, still not sure whether he was responsible for Eve's frame of mind or not.

Eve gave me a wry smile through her tears. "He agrees with my mom, actually. He says we need to pick our battles and that we can't adopt all the needy children in the world. He also thinks having a child of our own, created out of our love, would be a wonderful thing."

A chorus of appreciative 'awww's filled the air, and I inhaled in relief, both to know that Julien hadn't been planting these ideas in Eve's head, and that no one else in the room seemed to think getting pregnant was something shameful.

"I think both are equally beautiful: having your own child or adopting a child who needs a loving family," my mom added. "There's no right or wrong when it involves love."

"Well, I'm not ready to have kids yet, no matter how they arrive!" Crystal declared, almost instantly lightening the mood. "There's still an awful lot I want to do first."

How much of that included the kind of things she'd been doing in the club the night before with Tate, I wondered? I glanced over at Olivia to see if she was thinking the same thing, but she was looking off into the distance, her eyes unfocused and her face pale, her thoughts clearly a long way away.

"Are you alright, Liv?"

Though I tried to say it quietly, everyone immediately turned to my sister to see what I meant, and she quickly looked down at her hands. "I'm fine. Just thinking about what pattern to get on my nails. What are you having done, Eve?"

Just like that, the conversation moved on, but I knew my friend. Eve would still be harbouring her guilt long after the others had forgotten about it. Somehow, I'd have to get her alone to talk things through more thoroughly, especially since I had to tell her about my news soon.

Who would have ever thought that announcing a pregnancy would be so complicated?

~Aaron~

As soon as we got back to the hotel, Julien, Noah, and Cole headed directly to the front desk to check for messages, leaving me and Jackson behind, watching in bemusement.

"They don't exactly look like men who are on vacation," Jackson commented wryly. "The Stamer men have never been very good at relaxing."

It seemed he considered me more like himself than them, and I didn't mind that assessment. Jackson and I spent more time together than I did with my own father. "I'm going to head back to our room. Noelle just texted me that they're finished in the spa so she'll be there soon. Do you want me to say anything to her about Holly and the business?"

I hadn't forgotten what Jackson said about his disagreement with Holly over her retirement, and maybe if Holly had any concerns about leaving things in Noelle's hands, my wife might be able to allay those fears.

However, Jackson shook his head. "Thank you, but no. Don't worry about it. It's something Holly and I need to work through together. You two focus on enjoying yourselves, just like you have been. Where did you end up going last night, anyway? I saw you all heading out."

Shit. Noelle said we weren't supposed to mention Paradise to Jackson, but I didn't want to lie to him either, so I settled on a compromise before excusing myself as quickly as I could. "Just a nearby club that Noah knew about. See you at dinner."

Noelle managed to get back to the room before me, and I walked in to find her in her underwear, surveying two potential outfits to wear that evening. The time in the spa seemed to have done her good. Her hair hung down, curling naturally over her shoulders, her makeup light and unobtrusive on her glowing skin, and her nails polished and painted as she tapped them absent-mindedly against her crossed arms.

"Hey," she murmured as caught sight of me, her attention still focused primarily on the clothes. "Which one do you think I should... oh!"

Her question got cut off as I strode over to wrap my arms around her, capturing her lips in a firm kiss. Her surprise only lasted a moment before she melted into my embrace, her arms going around my neck and her sweet mouth moving against mine, sending a thrill through my body just as strong as the very first time we kissed.

"What was that for?" she gasped when we finally took a breath.

I offered a few explanations, all of which only scratched the surface. "You look incredible. You smell amazing. I missed you. Take your pick."

"I missed you too," she murmured back before kissing me again. My dick had already begun to harden against her when she pulled back apologetically. "I'm sorry. I'd love to keep going but we don't have time right now. I invited Eve to stop in before dinner."

"Why?" I groaned in frustration, but I took a step back too, giving my body a chance to cool itself down.

"She seems upset," Noelle answered vaguely. "I want to talk to her about it. How was Julien today?"

I did actually have some information from Julien that I knew would be of enormous interest to Noelle, but I'd promised him I wouldn't say anything about his unintentional slip. On the other hand, Noelle and I didn't keep secrets from each other, and when I hesitated over my answer, she immediately called me out on it.

"Something happened, didn't it? What is it?"

"I'm not supposed to tell you," I replied honestly. "I mean, I'm not supposed to tell anyone."

"I'm not 'anyone'," she argued, her arms crossing again even as her blue eyes shone with curiosity. "I won't tell anyone else, but if it's something about Eve, I need to know."

After all our time together, she knew I couldn't resist when she stood up for herself, demanding what she wanted, and it worked that time too. I caved remarkably quickly. "Eve might be pregnant."

"What?!" Her shriek nearly burst my eardrum as her eyes went wide with surprise. "But she said... that must be why... ohhhh. I think I get it now."

Noelle began pacing, clearly putting something together in her head, but I had no idea what it might be. "Don't tell Eve I told you," I reminded her, since it seemed like she was formulating some kind of plan. I knew the look.

"I won't," she promised. "But we have to be quick and change for dinner so we're ready when she gets here."

Reluctantly, I watched my beautiful wife put her clothes on when I'd much rather have been taking them off, and I swapped my golf clothes for pants and a dress shirt that evening. We were all having dinner together as a group before the wedding the next day, but since the bride would be with us, we couldn't technically be late.

When Eve knocked at the door soon afterwards, she wasn't alone. Julien came with her, giving me a nod as he closed the door behind them while Eve marched straight up to Noelle, her face pale but determined. "I have something to tell you."

My wife looked equally resolute. "I have something to tell you too."

"I'm pregnant."

The words came out of both of them with the same force, at almost exactly the same time, and Julien and I both had to laugh at the stunned looks on their faces. A second later, they both threw their arms around each other, exclaiming in a shorthand language only they seemed to understand.

I couldn't add much to their conversation, so I went over to shake Julien's hand instead. "You got confirmation, then?"

He nodded. "We did. The message from the doctor was waiting for us when we got back."

That must have been why he ran to the desk as soon as we returned. Noah and Cole were probably checking on Stamer Hotel business, but Julien's business had been personal.

"You kept a good poker face this afternoon," he added. "I had no idea."

"We didn't want to steal focus from your wedding."

"It's a little late for that," Julien said with a laugh, looking pleased and overwhelmed all at once.

"And Eve's okay with you guys expecting?" I asked quietly, looking over to where our partners were still hugging each other, laughing and crying.

"Yes, I think she is." He sounded relieved. "Now that it's for sure, she wants to make the best of it. We didn't intend it right now, but sometimes, life has other plans."

I definitely knew how that went. Once upon a time, I had been certain Eve was the woman for me, but fate gave me a firm push in Noelle's direction instead. Things had definitely worked out for the best then, and hopefully, they would for Eve and Julien too, and the new children we'd all be welcoming into our growing extended family very soon.

Chapter Seven

EXHAUSTED

~Cole~

"What's wrong?" I asked Noah bluntly on the way back to the hotel from the golf course. As much as I enjoyed winning, he hadn't even given me a challenge. Corey came close, but Noah had been way off his game. "You haven't golfed like that since you were ten."

"Must be the jet lag," he tried to claim, but he didn't look me straight in the eye when he said it, a clear giveaway that his words weren't entirely true. "Or the heat, maybe."

My kids rarely felt the need to hide anything from me, which I considered one of the greatest successes in my life, so it concerned me that he wouldn't just tell me what was bothering him, since something obviously was. "Does it have anything to do with your mom's new title? It doesn't have to change anything for you and Liv if you don't want it to. At least not right away."

"It's not that," he assured me quickly, and that time, I believed him. It had to be something else, then, but I couldn't guess what. I never liked being left in the dark, but I had to accept that my son had a right to privacy if he wanted it so I didn't push any further.

When we reached the hotel, I went to the front desk to check for messages for Gemma since we were waiting to hear from the lawyer with some formalities about her brother's will. "Any messages for Mrs Stamer?"

"I'm expecting a message for Mrs Stamer," Noah practically echoed, speaking to one of the other receptionists at the front desk. At the far end of the desk, Julien also spoke to someone, too quietly for me to hear.

The three employees all went to their files and one of them came back holding up three pieces of paper and looking a bit sheepish. "I have three messages for a Ms or Mrs Stamer, but without opening them, I'm not sure which is which. I'm so sorry, we had a new member of staff working earlier and they didn't write the guest's first name or room number on the envelope."

That was a frustrating oversight from a hotel that had been performing pretty flawlessly up to that point. "Does it list who the message is from? My wife's message should be from a law firm."

I assumed neither Eve nor Olivia would be consulting with a lawyer, and the receptionist quickly proved me right as he pulled out one of the sealed envelopes and handed it to me. "There you are, Mr Stamer. I'm afraid, though, that the other two are from the same sender."

Noah and Julien exchanged surprised glances, both of them looking unsure what to do next. "Who's the sender?" I had to ask.

Noah and Julien held each other's gaze a moment longer before Julien nodded, giving his agreement for Noah to answer me, and my son turned to me. "An obstetrics clinic."

It took a moment for my brain to process that, but finally, the penny dropped. "Test results?"

They both nodded mutely as I tried not to smile. Keeping a poker face had always been one of my strongest skills, but the possibility of getting not one but two grandchildren all at the same time tested me more than I'd ever been tested before.

"Why not let him open one?" I suggested, gesturing to the uncomfortable-looking man behind the desk. "He doesn't need to look at the results, only the name."

They both considered that, but in the end, Noah shook his head. "I'd rather not get a stranger involved. No offense."

The man quickly assured him he took none.

"What's your suggestion, then?" I asked Noah.

He exhaled sharply, and gave me a nod. "You can look."

"I might not be able to stop myself from looking at the result," I warned him frankly. Even if I didn't mean to, it would only take a stray glance.

"I know. It's okay."

I looked over to Julien for his permission. "What do you think?"

"Eve will already kill me for not keeping my mouth shut, so why not?" he said with a sheepish shrug.

They both looked more nervous than excited, which concerned me, but I didn't want to put them on the spot any further when I could simply put them out of the misery of not knowing. I held out my hand for the envelopes from the receptionist, who quickly walked away when he was no longer needed. Randomly, I chose one, and broke it open, my heart beating faster than it had in a long time.

The name at the top was Olivia's, I saw at a glance, but my eyes took in the entirety of the message in one fell swoop, since it was only one sentence long beneath her name.

This patient is not pregnant.

A strong wave of disappointment hit me, but I did my absolute best to give nothing away as I folded the paper back up again. I had no idea if Noah wanted the result to be positive or negative, so I didn't want to project anything onto him. Although I'd unexpectedly gotten involved, this wasn't my news.

"This one's yours," I told him, handing him the opened envelope and Julien the unopened one.

"Merci," my soon-to-be son-in-law said gratefully, taking his envelope and heading towards his room, where he and Eve would likely open it together. They would tell me soon enough which way it went, I had no doubt, but at that moment, my attention was entirely focused on Noah whose fingers twitched over the seam of the letter, not moving any more than that.

"It's negative, isn't it?" he said quietly, so quietly that I needed to lean in closer to hear him.

"Why do you think that?"

He gave me a half-smile, a mirror image of my own usual smirk. "You're not quite as good an actor as you think you are."

As soon as the words were out of his mouth, his smile began to falter, and I knew in an instant: this wasn't good news. He wanted it to be positive.

"Come with me."

Guiding him in front of me, I led him quickly to my own room, and once inside, I pulled him into a hug, my arms tight around him. My grown son, the soon-to-be CEO of Stamer Hotels, held me back just as tightly, his shoulders beginning to shake as he cried against my shoulder for the first time since he was a little boy.

"I'm sorry, Noah." My voice sounded raw and distant, and it took me a second to realize there were tears in my eyes too. "How long have you been trying?"

That kind of despair didn't come from a one-time test. Clearly, more had been going on than I knew about.

His reply came back so muffled that I had to ask him to repeat himself. The second time, I thought I caught the answer: "Three years."

Three *years*? Why the fuck hadn't he said something before then?

"Have you been to a doctor? Specialists?"

"Yes, Dad." With a deep, shuddering breath, he pulled back from me, wiping his hands roughly across his cheeks to erase his tears, though droplets still clung to the eyelashes framing his green eyes, so much like his mother's. "We've tried it all. I don't know why, but I really thought this time was going to be it. Liv is going to be devastated, especially with everyone else..."

He trailed off there, but I thought I understood. Eve and Julien couldn't have been trying very long, if they'd even been trying at all.

I knew better than anyone that sometimes, it just happened, whether you wanted it to or not, but I'd never once imagined Noah and Olivia struggling in that way.

"What can I do?" I asked him next. There had to be something. What was the good of money and connections if you couldn't help the people you loved?

Noah, however, shook his head. "Nothing. I know it's hard to believe, but not even Cole Stamer can fix this. I need to go talk to Liv. Don't say anything to Mom yet, okay? I'll tell her myself."

Keeping secrets from Gemma had never been one of my strong suits, but for my son, I'd do it. "I won't say anything to anyone. I love you, Noah."

"I love you too." With tears threatening his eyes again, Noah headed out the door, leaving me feeling more helpless than I'd felt in a very, very long time.

~Olivia~

As soon as I finished changing back into my clothes after the spa treatments, I headed back to my room to see Noah and find out if we'd heard back from the doctor's office yet. That morning, the home pregnancy test had been negative, but Noah had a feeling it might have been a false negative.

"The home tests aren't as accurate this early as a clinical test," he reminded me. "Let's get a formal one done, just to be sure."

With the negative test clutched in my hand and the familiar, hollow feeling inside me, I already felt pretty sure, but I agreed anyway. He wanted to keep the hope alive a little longer, and I didn't have the heart to say no, even though I suspected nothing would change once we got the clinical results.

We still didn't know exactly why we couldn't conceive. Noah's sperm counts were normal. My ovulation cycles seemed normal too, and so did my reproductive organs. Nothing jumped out at the many doctors who had run tests. Sometimes, it just happened, they said, which was frustratingly vague. As advanced as medical science was, it didn't have all the answers, so we just kept trying.

But as I sat there, listening to Noah on the phone making arrangements for a urine sample to be taken to the clinic in town, I felt strangely detached from the whole thing. Maybe because we weren't at home, or maybe because of the night before, when I'd felt more like myself again than I had for years, but I didn't feel as devastated as I usually did when the test came back negative. I mostly felt... numb.

"Liv?"

I hadn't quite made it back to my room when my mom called out my name from behind me. I turned around to find her hurrying towards me, on her own. "Yes?"

"Do you have a minute? Your dad's not back yet, you can come to our room."

I didn't, really, since I knew Noah would be back any minute and would want to open the results letter with me, but my mom rarely asked to speak to me in private. It seemed important, so I agreed.

"What's up?" I asked her as soon as we were inside her room.

"That's what I want to know. You've been very quiet today. Is everything alright?"

Prying into my personal life had never been my mom's style. She was always open and willing to talk if I wanted to, but she very rarely inserted herself without being asked, which told me that she must really be worried.

Had I been quiet? I'd been thinking about things a lot all day, about the test result, about the club the night before, about Tate and Crystal and the excitement of their new relationship, and especially about the conversation we'd all had in the spa about pregnancy, when Eve suggested having children in the world these days could be considered selfish.

There were things I needed to talk about, but with my husband rather than my mom, at least for the time being. "I'm okay, Mom. I appreciate your concern, but it's something I need to work out on my own, at least for now."

That answer clearly didn't satisfy her, her eyebrows drawing together in concern over her bright, blue eyes. "It's not Noah, is it? Is everything okay between you two?"

On that point, I could answer more firmly. "Noah and I are solid. Always."

Hearing the certainty in my voice, she took a step back. "Alright. I won't keep you, but remember, I'm here for you. So's your dad, and Noelle too."

"I know." My family had always been one of the greatest blessings of my life. Maybe that explained why I wanted a family of my own so badly.

Giving her a quick hug, I left the room and headed to my own room instead.

"Noah?" The last I'd heard from him, he'd just arrived back at the hotel, so he might have gotten there before me. I called out his name as soon as I got inside.

"In here." His voice came from the bedroom, but when I reached the door, I stopped short in surprise. My strong husband, usually so in control, sat on the end of the bed with red eyes, his face drawn and sad. It took me a moment to notice the open piece of paper in his hands and put the pieces together, and even though I'd expected the negative result, the familiar heartache came back anyway. Worst of all was the feeling that I'd let Noah down, and the tears that refused to come that morning pushed their way to the surface.

"I'm sorry," I whispered as I sat down next to him.

Immediately, his strong arms wrapped around me. "Don't apologize, Liv. Ever."

His voice sounded so raw and his body shuddered against mine as he held me, making me suspect there was more to his reaction than just the usual disappointment. It also struck me as odd that he'd opened the letter without me. We'd made a point of doing every part of this together. "What else is wrong?" I asked him simply.

Noah took a deep breath. "My dad knows. It's a long story, but he opened the letter. I asked him to. And I told him how long it's been. I'm sorry, I know we weren't going to tell anyone, but..."

"Don't apologize," I quickly repeated back to him. "I'm not upset that you told him."

"You're not?" He pulled back to look at my face, his eyes registering his surprise. "I thought you didn't want people to know."

"I didn't, but that was when I thought we still had a chance."

Dismay crossed his face, mingling with all the other emotions on display there. "We're not giving up. Are we?"

I shrugged, brushing the tears from my eyes. "I don't know how much longer I can do this, Noah. It's consuming us. I've had a lot of time to think about things today, and I think... well, I think maybe we need to change course."

"To what?" He shuffled a little further back, turning so he could face me directly.

"To *us*. Last night was wonderful. It felt like just you and me again, like we used to be, before it all became about hormones and schedules and cycles."

Noah's sigh sounded like an agreement, so I kept going.

"And as much as I want the experience of being pregnant and having a 'normal' path to parenthood, we know that's not the only way out there. Maybe we need to seriously consider other alternatives."

We'd talked about both surrogacy and adoption before, but as a very firm plan B, only when we'd exhausted our other options.

At that point, I felt exhausted.

"Are you sure?" Noah's eyes searched mine curiously.

I nodded as firmly as I could. "I'm not happy about it, obviously, but we can't keep doing this, Noah. It's wearing on us both, and the truth is, there are kids out there right now who need a home. We could give them one. Eve was just telling us about a family who needs help, and it made it feel a little more real to me than it ever has before. These kids already exist. There would be no more appointments. No more waiting. No more disappointments."

He thought that over carefully before nodding slowly. "Alright. If that's what you want, let's go talk to Eve."

I blinked at him in confusion for a second, not understanding exactly what Eve had to do with anything, until the penny dropped. "Hang on, I didn't necessarily mean *that* particular family. I just meant..."

He didn't let me finish. "You said no more waiting, right? These kids need a home now? What's the harm in talking about it?"

I supposed there wasn't any. We could get a bit more information, at least, and Eve or Julien would probably have at least a basic understanding of what would be involved in adopting from another country.

A little flicker of hope and excitement flared to life in my stomach, even as I warned myself not to get carried away. We were only going to talk about it. There was a long way between that and the family I'd always dreamed of, but maybe, after all this time, we were finally heading down the right road.

Chapter Eight

REHEARSAL DINNER

~Eve~

As Julien and I left Aaron and Noelle's room, I thought the biggest emotional upheavals of the day were behind us. After a few days of feeling a bit queasy and not even being able to enjoy some drinks with our guests at our pre-wedding events, I finally gave in and took the home pregnancy test that morning. When the positive sign appeared, I couldn't do anything but stare at it in disbelief.

"We weren't even trying," I managed to stutter to Julien who sat next to me on the bed, watching my reaction carefully. I took my birth control regularly, but with all the travelling and the changes in time zones and the occasional food-related illness emptying my stomach, I couldn't claim to have been one hundred percent on top of it at all times.

"Sometimes, it just happens," he pointed out with a shrug, sounding much more relaxed about the whole thing than I felt. "Maybe it's fate. Like how we met."

That felt like a false equivalency. Julien and I meeting the way we did was so unlikely that I had to consider it some kind of good fortune, but getting pregnant unexpectedly felt much more like bad luck. The charity was still getting off the ground and we were meant to be travelling for another six months in remote parts of the world with spotty medical care. My work was important to me and I didn't want to have to delegate it, but if the test was accurate and we really did have another person to consider, it could change everything.

That was even before taking into account all the mixed feelings and guilt I'd been having since the conversation with that desperate woman and the three orphaned children. Julien may have been able to put it out of his mind, having more experience with seeing that kind of need close up, but for me, it all felt very fresh and new. Every time I closed my eyes, I still saw their sad little faces.

"Maybe the test is wrong," I suggested, clinging to any last hope of sticking to our original plan. "They're not totally accurate, are they?"

"I think they're more likely to be falsely negative than falsely positive," Julien countered gently. "But if you want to be sure, I can get a test done at a clinic. That way, we'll know for certain."

I quickly agreed, happy to put off any kind of decision for even a few hours longer, and he went off to make the arrangements before leaving for his golf game with the men while I went to the spa with the women. Although I didn't intend to say anything, I couldn't help blurting out some of my feelings during the manicures, and my mom and Holly's assurances that there was absolutely nothing wrong with having my own child in such an unfair world did actually help to ease my fears a little.

By the time I got back to the room and found Julien there with the results paper, waiting for me to open it together, I managed to step out of my own head long enough to take a good look at the man in front of me.

A year on from the night we met, he'd grown more handsome to me with each passing day. While travelling, he often grew his beard a bit longer, but for the wedding, he'd shaved, leaving him with only a five o'clock shadow that highlighted his strong, firm jawline. The south Pacific sun had bronzed his skin, and his kind brown eyes looked over at me with such love and hope that I suddenly realized what I'd failed to see that morning.

Julien *wanted* the test to be positive. He wanted this for us, even if the timing sucked, and knowing that made me feel much more open to it. For him, I would always be willing to compromise.

"Would you rather have a boy or girl?" I asked him as I took a seat next to him on the sofa, even before we opened the envelope. We'd talked about having children before, as something we'd do sometime at an unspecified date in the future, but we'd never really talked about the details.

He answered me honestly and eagerly, as usual. "I would love either, but if I got to pick, I would choose a girl. A strong, independent girl, just like her mother."

"She'll have you wrapped around her finger," I warned him.

"*Mais oui.* Just like her mother."

We shared a smile full of affection and understanding before I gestured to the envelope in his hands. "Go ahead. Open it."

His fingers trembled as he did, but I felt strangely calm. Although I'd been the one to try to deny it that morning, I knew even before his eyes raised back to mine, full of joy, that it would confirm what the test that morning had already said: we were going to have a baby.

Many things in life got decided for us, out of our control, but this one, even if I wouldn't have chosen it at that particular point in time, was a blessing. As Julien's arms wrapped around me, I let myself embrace it fully, putting my doubts and guilt to the side. "I love you, Julien. You'll be a wonderful father."

His chuckle echoed warmly in my ear. "I hope so. I don't have much of an example of fatherhood to go on from my own childhood, but I will follow your lead. This child will have parents who love each other and them, not to mention grandparents and aunts and uncles. A whole family, ready to welcome them."

A whole family, all of whom were right there, ready to celebrate our wedding day. Now, we would have two things to celebrate.

"I have to tell Noelle," were the next words out of my mouth.

Julien grimaced as he pulled back from me. "About that..."

I knew that tone of voice. "What did you do?"

He'd never been much good at hiding anything from me, and he didn't even try, admitting the truth to me freely. "Some people may already know that it's possible."

"Who are 'some people'?"

He ticked them off on his fingers: "Aaron, Jackson, Noah, and your dad."

"What?!" How had he managed to tell that many people in such a short amount of time?

Julien winced, but I didn't press him for an explanation. It seemed if I wanted the chance to tell anyone myself, I better not wait much longer.

"Never mind. Come on, we're going to see Noelle and Aaron as soon as we're ready."

Noelle had already invited me to stop in before dinner, so as soon as we got changed, we went to her room and I told her my news only for her to share *her* news at the same time, and in an instant, we were in each other's arms, laughing and crying together.

"How long have you known?" I demanded.

"A couple of months," she admitted, wincing as my jaw dropped. "I wanted to tell you in person, but not until after the wedding. I didn't want anything to distract from your special day."

"Well, it's a little late for that," Aaron joked, giving Julien a nudge. Both men looked rather pleased with themselves.

"How far along are you then?"

"Three months," she told me. "We're going to announce it to everyone after the wedding. You're the first one to know... other than Noah."

"Why does Noah know?"

Julien said Noah knew about *our* pregnancy too. How did my brother get mixed up in everything?

"He came across Noelle being sick on the hike and figured it out," Aaron explained.

"He and Olivia might be expecting too," Julien supplied. "They also got a message from the obstetrics clinic this afternoon. That's how he knew we might be."

Noelle and I looked at each other in disbelief. Could we *all* be pregnant at the same time? What were the freaking odds?

As if he'd heard us talking about him, my phone buzzed with a text from Noah at that exact moment.

We just went looking for you in your room. Do you have a minute? Liv and I want to talk to you and Julien.

"Speak of the devil," I told the room, holding up my phone. "He wants to talk to me and Julien right now. Maybe we'll be getting the news now."

"I'd say there was something in the water if we hadn't been on the other side of the world for the last six months," Julien laughed, taking my hand to lead me to the door. "Congratulations, both of you. We'll see you at dinner."

They both agreed, Noelle still wiping her eyes dry, while Julien and I headed back to our room to see exactly what my brother and his wife had to say.

~Julien~

Eve's hand in mine felt solid and reassuring as we returned to our room to meet with her brother. The heightened emotions of our wedding, the stress of dealing with my mother's unhappiness, and the turbulence of Eve's unexpected pregnancy had all come at us at once, buffeting us like the rocks that stood just offshore being pounded by the relentless waves, but with Eve beside me, excited and happy about our future just as I was, it felt like nothing in the world could knock us down.

Noah and Olivia didn't give anything away as we let them into our room, the four of us taking a seat around the coffee table in the suite's living area. Each of the hotel rooms were larger than many of the houses Eve and I had stayed in during our travels, and it still amazed me how she could seem equally at home in both settings. No matter what life threw at her, Eve always met it head-on.

Even so, she seemed as startled by Noah's opening line as I was.

"Liv said that you told her about a woman who had some children in need of adoption. Tell me about them."

That wasn't at all the conversation we expected, and I hadn't realized Eve had mentioned it to anyone at all. Was it still weighing on her mind that heavily?

"There's not much more to tell than what I already said," Eve told him, giving Olivia a sympathetic smile. "It's hard to imagine, isn't it?"

"Tell me about the children," Noah insisted. "How old are they? Boys or girls?"

I actually had those details, even if Eve didn't. Unbeknownst to her, I'd been checking up on them after she told me about them, hoping to be able to share with her when they'd found a new home. It hadn't happened yet, so I hadn't mentioned it, but I answered Noah's question anyway. "There are two girls and a boy. The older girl is four, the younger is not quite six months. The boy is three."

Eve looked over at me in surprise. "How do you know that?"

Meanwhile, Olivia and Noah exchanged glances. "Three under the age of five? What do you think?" he murmured.

"I've got my sources," I told Eve gently before turning to Noah. "Why are you interested?"

Perhaps he and Olivia were interested in providing some money towards their upkeep if Eve's story had touched Olivia's heart. I still didn't know my soon-to-be brother-in-law all that well, but I knew that, like Eve, he had a genuine compassion for other people. The Stamers weren't at all the kind of self-absorbed people I'd imagined them to be before I got to know them.

"What would be involved in adopting kids like that?" he asked, not quite answering my question.

His query took me by surprise, but assuming that perhaps he knew someone looking to adopt, I gave him the explanation I usually provided in that situation. "Assuming the potential adopter meets the eligibility criteria, they would go to an agency in their own country or an international agency. It would need to be determined that the children can't find a safe home in their own country in order to be eligible for international adoption. Once matched, the adopter would go to the country and meet with the child they wanted to adopt. There's legal paperwork to be filed in both countries, immigration permissions to get, and once that's all complete, they can take the child home. It's a process, but a worthwhile one in the right circumstances."

"What about *these* children in particular?" Noah pressed, holding onto Olivia's hand tightly. "Is there a way to expedite it? You said their aunt couldn't afford to look after them."

He addressed the last question to Eve, who was giving her brother a shrewd, concerned look. "Noah, what's going on?"

I wouldn't have asked it quite that bluntly, but I was also interested in his answer. His curiosity on the subject seemed both intense and completely out of the blue.

He glanced over at Olivia again, who gave him a small, encouraging nod, and with a deep breath, he explained it to us.

"Liv and I are having trouble conceiving, so we're considering whether adoption might be right for us."

Olivia's message from the obstetrics clinic suddenly took on a whole new meaning, and Eve stared at them both blankly for a moment, uncomprehending. "But... sometimes, it takes a while, right?"

Noah's lips tightened to a disapproving look very similar to his father's. "I know that, Eve. It's *been* 'a while'. We wouldn't be asking if we weren't serious about this."

"How serious?" I asked, jumping back in to talk specifics since Noah seemed to want to focus on practicalities.

He gave me a grateful nod, understanding me perfectly. "We'd want to meet the kids, obviously, but assuming everything goes well, we could start the process right away."

"It's a huge decision," Eve pointed out, looking over at Olivia to try to draw her into the conversation too. "Don't get me wrong: any of those kids would be lucky to have you, but..."

"All of them," Noah interrupted her. "We wouldn't break up their family. We'd take them all."

Again, Eve looked to Olivia for some input, and that time, Olivia smiled over at both of us. "Forgive him. It's been three years of feeling like there's nothing we could do but hope. Now that we might actually be able to *do* something, he's a little eager."

She and her husband shared a tender look between them while Eve and I smiled at each other too. We could both relate to that. Neither of us were very good at waiting around either.

"Well, if you're serious, we could set up a meeting with the charity that's supporting them as soon as you like. You could meet them first before you start the rest of the process. I'm sure with your resources, things could be sped up."

Normally, I wouldn't approve of paying extra to skip a line, but the sooner those kids got into a loving home, the better. My principles could bend a little when the outcome was for the best.

Eve had helped me realize that.

"Next week?" Noah asked, and Eve laughed.

"You really *are* eager." Though she was teasing, I could see the affection behind her smile. "I'm sorry you've been struggling with conceiving, but I think it's amazing you want to do this. I can't tell you what a difference it would make to those children, or their aunt."

"Or us," Olivia added, leaning over to rest her head on Noah's shoulder.

We couldn't help everyone, that was a sad truth I'd had to accept when I got into charity work in the first place, but sometimes, you could change everything for the people you did help, and if Noah and Olivia went ahead with this, it would certainly change their lives forever, along with the lives of those children.

A shrill ringing interrupted the sweet moment as our room phone rang out. Quickly, I jumped to my feet to silence it. "Sorry, I'll get it. Hello?"

I'd barely gotten the word out into the receiver before my mother's voice echoed in my ear, in rapid-fire French. "Where are you? I'm sitting here at dinner, all by myself. I don't know why you wanted me to come if you were going to leave me on my own the whole time. I'm going to go back to my room now."

The irritation that I'd done my best to control all week threatened to bubble up again as I responded to her as calmly as possible. "I'm sorry, Maman, we got held up. We're coming now. Don't leave: you need to eat, and it's our final dinner before the wedding. I'll be right there, I promise."

Without giving her a chance to respond, I hung up, giving Eve an apologetic shrug. I didn't need to say more than that: she knew who I'd been speaking to by the fact that I'd spoken in French. With a sigh, she got to her feet.

"We better go. We can talk about this more later, alright?"

She gave both Noah and Olivia a hug before we all left the room together. We hadn't told them about Eve being pregnant, but maybe that was for the best. They already had a lot on their minds, and Eve and I still had a wedding to get through. Once we made it through without my mother throwing a tantrum or walking out, then we could move onto sharing our good news with everyone else.

At that point, just getting through the next twenty-four hours felt like an uphill climb.

~Eve~

Life certainly never stood still. In the span of a day, we'd found out we were expecting a baby, that my best friend was also pregnant, and that my brother had been keeping a secret about his and Olivia's attempts to have a baby of their own.

It didn't seem fair that they'd struggled so much while I got pregnant without even trying, but life wasn't always fair. Two years of charity work around the world had certainly taught me that, and getting upset about it never did much good. All I could do was try to make a difference where I could, and if that meant helping my brother and his wife adopt those sweet children, it just might help alleviate two injustices in the world at the same time.

That would be a pretty good day in the grand scheme of things.

I wanted to get started right away, just as eager to move forward as Noah had been, and my fiancé knew that. Julien always understood and embraced my take-charge qualities, so he stopped just before we got to the restaurant. "Send an email to the charity now. I can go get the dinner started without you."

"Are you sure?" I felt bad about leaving him on his own for the start of our rehearsal dinner, especially with all the drama with his mother. As much as he supported me, I always wanted to be there to support him too.

"Will you stop thinking about it until it's done?" he teased me gently. When I shook my head honestly, he smiled. "Then go and take care of it. No one will mind waiting for the beautiful bride, and I will manage everything until you get back."

He gave the back of my hand a sweet kiss before heading into the restaurant, while I found a quiet spot in the lobby to draft and send an email to the charity director. Julien's notes and files were meticulous, as always, so it didn't take me any time at all to locate the contact information in our shared documents.

When we started working together, Julien quickly assessed where my strengths and weaknesses lay, and he naturally filled in the gaps to better complement me. I'd always been an ideas person, sometimes skipping over the smaller details, so Julien stepped in to make sure those details got taken care of. His submissive nature shone through in the way he supported me in every situation, not just the bedroom, although that part of our life had only grown more fulfilling in the time we'd been together.

Not a doubt existed in my mind that he would be an amazing husband, and after the news of the day, a wonderful father too. Very different from my own father, certainly, but absolutely amazing all the same.

When I finally headed in to join the dinner, the last one to arrive, Julien got to his feet to welcome me, kissing me on the cheek and sliding his arm around my waist, touching me as if we had been apart for fifteen days rather than fifteen minutes.

"Fashionably late, as always," my mom chided me with an affectionate smile.

"We used to call it 'Eve time'," Noah told the assembled group, looking relaxed and comfortable as he leaned back in his chair, his drink in one hand and the other arm around the back of Olivia's chair. "No matter what time zone we're in, Eve's always got her own clock."

I could have pointed out that I was only late because of him, but I took the ribbing in good humour. "This is my wedding. If there's one time I'm allowed to be on my own schedule, this is it."

Most around the table gave me indulgent smiles, but Julien's mother, Emilie, muttered something under her breath. Though I didn't catch it all, I definitely heard the word 'typique'. Even if Julien hadn't been helping me learn some French, I could recognize that word based on its English equivalent.

"Typical of what?" I asked her straight out, putting her on the spot. Julien had been beyond patient with her over the past few days, but *my* patience was wearing thin. She'd been nothing but miserable since arriving and Julien deserved better.

Her startled look made it clear she hadn't expected to be called out, but as soon as she realized everyone was looking at her, Emilie jutted out her chin in defiance. "Typical of rich people, to think your time is more valuable than anyone else's."

"Maman, ce n'est pas le bon moment," Julien said, telling her the time wasn't right for this discussion, but I disagreed. We'd been humouring her far too long, and I wasn't the only one who thought so.

"Emilie, this has to stop." I half-expected the words to come from my dad, but they didn't. *Julien's* dad said them instead, and everyone went quiet as the two former lovers faced each other properly for the first time in thirty years. "You're here to watch your son marry the woman he loves. I assume you're happy for him, but it's only an assumption, because every time I've seen you, you look like you're at a funeral instead. Is this attitude because I'm here? I imagine if you're always this sour, he wouldn't have invited you at all."

Noelle's eyes went wide across the table and Corey shifted forward in his seat, clearly ready to back up his father-in-law if needed. Everyone's gaze immediately went to Emilie, waiting for her response.

She didn't hold back, getting straight to the heart of her complaint. "You have no right to be here. You rejected him before he was even born."

That was unfair and she knew it. Yes, Julian had obeyed his father and cut ties with Emilie when she got pregnant, but he made several efforts afterwards to be part of Julien's life, which she blocked at every turn. I had my mouth open to point that out, but Julien's hand on my arm stopped me. When I glanced over at him, he shook his head just slightly, asking me to let them handle it themselves. Beside him, I could see my parents in an almost identical position, my mom's hand on my dad's arm to hold him back.

"I made a mistake," Julian agreed bluntly. "But Julien has chosen to try to move past that. He invited me, and that's why I came. You don't have to forgive me and we don't have to be friends, but you should respect that your son made that choice."

That made perfect sense to me, but Emilie still disagreed. "You should respect that I raised my son all on my own, and we should be able to celebrate without strangers here."

She gestured at Julian's wife and children with distaste, and that seemed to be the final straw for my fiancé.

"Maman, that is enough. I have told you before: having the Ribars as part of my life doesn't diminish your role in it. Look around this table. For so many years, it was only you and me. Now, we have my father's family, and Eve's family and friends. No one here is a stranger, and everyone has come here to share in my happiness with the woman I love. I want to enjoy it too. If you can't be happy about that, I don't want you to come to the ceremony tomorrow."

Noelle couldn't stop her gasp, and everyone else looked equally surprised. Julien rarely took such a strong stand, but I had seen him do it before, back when he decided that he and I weren't right together. Just like that time, his words weren't spoken in anger but in quiet certainty, which made them all the more devastating.

Then, I disagreed with him vehemently, but this time, I believed he had it right and I hoped with all my heart that his mother would see reason.

Instead, after staring at her son in hurt and disbelief for a moment, she got up and walked out of the room without another word.

Chapter Nine

In Control

~Julien~

Everyone shuffled in their seats after my mother stormed out of the room, no one entirely sure what to say next, but as she so often did when I needed it most, Eve immediately took charge.

"Well, what's a wedding without a little drama?" she asked with a laugh, raising her non-alcoholic drink in a toast. "Who had mother-of-the-groom in the 'dramatic exit' pool?"

Eve's dad chuckled and everyone else tittered too, a little nervously but doing their best to relax and put the awkwardness behind us.

"One of Holly's nephews peed in the bouquets before our wedding," Jackson offered to lighten the mood, and that helped even more as everyone laughed genuinely.

"You weren't supposed to tell anyone about that," Holly admonished her husband, laughing as much as anyone. Soon, people around the table were exchanging funny stories from other big occasions, moving on from the subject of weddings and mothers entirely.

While the conversation carried on around us, Eve leaned over to me, speaking quietly into my ear. "Are you alright?"

I could reassure her on that front. "Oui. I don't regret what I said."

Ever since we'd arrived, I'd done my best to try to soothe my mother's hurt feelings over events that happened thirty years earlier, but at some point, she needed to take responsibility for her own reactions. My patience was considerable, but not without limits, and I wouldn't let her ruin my wedding day, nor Eve's.

"Good," my beautiful fiancée praised me. "Maybe I can take your mind off it tonight?"

Desire lurked in her dark, expressive eyes at the mention of the evening's plans. We had a private room booked at the hotel's secret club, since Eve figured we would be too tired after the actual wedding the following night to celebrate in the way she had in mind. That night, after the rehearsal dinner, was meant to be our unofficial wedding night, the night we declared our intention to devote ourselves to satisfying each other for the rest of our lives.

After the surprise pregnancy news, I hadn't been certain she still wanted to go ahead with those plans, but in her gaze, I could see that the thought still appealed to her just as much as it did to me. No matter what else might be going on in our lives, my desire for her would never be in any doubt. Every single thing about her turned me on. That was her superpower, and I would happily play sidekick to her, as long as she'd let me.

"I would love that, Madame E."

As always, that name for her confirmed my willing submission, and the confirmation sparked another level of heat in her eyes. "In that case, let me make sure you're ready."

Her hand slipped beneath the table, into my lap, where she found my cock already stirring within my pants simply from her words. The pressure of her fingers against it sent a rush of blood to the spot, leaving me straining within my clothes. While she chatted easily and happily with our family and our guests over dinner, her hand stroked me through the fabric, keeping me in a constant state of semi-arousal that I could do nothing to satisfy until she decided the time had come to do something about it.

"Are you nervous about tomorrow?" Jackson asked me sympathetically from across the table. "I found the waiting the hardest part."

"It is hard," I confirmed, trying not to gasp as Eve's hand pressed against me harder, my cock twitching beneath the weight of her palm. "But I'm sure it will be worth the wait."

She teased me that way for over an hour, edging and baiting me, until the last forkful had been eaten and she suddenly tapped her knife on her glass to get everyone's attention. "Julien and I are having an early night tonight. We'll see you all tomorrow."

No one dared to argue with the bride. Eve got to her feet easily and gracefully while I stumbled to mine, trying to hide the bulge from my semi-erect cock as I wished them all a good evening. "Bonne nuit, everyone."

Their good wishes followed us out of the room while I winced as soon as my back was turned.

"You're not thinking about your mother anymore, are you?" Eve teased, taking my hand and leading me out the back door of the hotel, towards the club's secret entrance we had been shown earlier.

"Not one bit," I promised. My thoughts were entirely focused on the fiery redhead at my side and what she might have planned for me that evening. Although we were always creative when it came to implementing our dynamic in the bedroom, living out of a suitcase in less affluent parts of the world meant that we didn't have a dedicated playroom or toys to work with most of the time. Getting to play in a club dedicated to our kind of pleasure would be a rare treat, and I didn't intend to waste a second of it thinking about anything other than the two of us.

I would put myself in Eve's hands entirely, just as we both wanted.

"Good evening, Ms Stamer," the hostess greeted us once we'd made our way down the darkened staircase to the club's bar. It had been a long time since I'd been to a sex club. I used to go frequently when I first started exploring my kink and would meet dommes there, but work obligations took over, and I got more selective in my dommes. Since meeting Eve, I'd had no need to meet with anyone else. "We have the bridal suite ready to go for you. Drinks are on the house."

"Take us there." Eve's firm instruction was obeyed by the hostess just as quickly as I would have hurried to do it myself. Everything in her tone and stance suggested she was a woman used to getting her own way, and people naturally deferred to her. I saw it every day, but only I got the chance to please her in private. It made me feel incredibly lucky.

On top of that, the room we walked into nearly made my body weak with desire. Eve had obviously made some specific requests when she booked it, and I could already guess what she had in mind even before she picked up the special eggnog cocktail menu and chose her beverage for the night.

"I think Pegging Peach sounds pretty good, don't you?"

I could only bow my head in agreement as my cock throbbed in anticipation. "It sounds perfect to me."

"Good. Then strip, and get on your knees."

~Eve~

Julien's fingers fumbled over his buttons in his haste to get undressed, his brain throwing out instructions faster than his body could follow. After the scene with his mother earlier, I didn't know if he'd still want to play together that evening, but his reaction to my order made it clear he wasn't just humouring me. He wanted it as much as I did, and after our unexpected news earlier, Noelle's news, Noah's revelation *and* the confrontation with Julien's mom, I wanted the escape that the evening promised more than ever.

With so much I couldn't change, I wanted to feel in control. I *needed* it, and Julien knew exactly how to give me that feeling.

He made me feel powerful in a way nobody else ever had, which meant that the power actually rested equally with him. We needed each other to find the fulfilment we craved, and that night, we would find it, I had no doubt. Everything in the room was designed for exactly that purpose.

When he had removed his clothes, his cock already stiff with anticipation from my actions during dinner, and knelt on the floor in the centre of the room as I'd ordered, I slowly circled him, surveying his body in open appreciation. If anything, in our year together, he'd gotten even better looking. Our time abroad made an active lifestyle more of a necessity than a choice, and his lean body had become even firmer because of it. With his defined muscles and his long, thick cock, he looked every inch a virile, strong man, which only made the way that he submitted to me even sexier.

A knock at the door signalled the arrival of the drinks I'd ordered. Still fully clothed, I went to get them myself, putting Julien's on the table in the room, in his sight but out of reach, until I decided he'd earned it. My virgin version was thicker and sweeter than I expected, but not unpleasant. Eggnog cocktails were certainly different, and I had to give the club points for creativity.

"You don't need your hands for this," I told him when I'd finished taking a long, slow drink. "Put them behind your back."

He obeyed without hesitation, and I grabbed a pair of handcuffs from the table, next to our drinks. I hadn't known exactly what inspiration would strike me in the moment, so I'd requested quite a few different things, giving us a lot of different options. Besides the table and a bed, the room also contained a St Andrews Cross, a couple of different benches, and even a human-sized cage. My instruments to choose from included items for bondage, impact and sensation play. We'd never been in a playroom together, at least not counting the one in my parents' apartment that I took him to simply to show it to him, and I wanted to make the most of it.

When Julien's hands were secure, I walked back in front of him, letting him watch me as I slowly removed my clothes. The appreciation and desire in his eyes made me feel just as sexy as I had the first time we were intimate with each other, the first time I realized that our dynamic suited us both perfectly. He kept quiet, as he knew I wanted him to, but he couldn't entirely hide the way his breath caught as I removed my bra, or the subtle intake of air when I bent over. Methodically, I removed each item of clothing until I stood completely naked in front of him except for the high-heeled shoes on my feet. Besides turning him on, they kept me at the perfect height for what I had in mind next.

"You're being so good, waiting so patiently," I praised him. The concrete floor of the playroom must have been hard on his knees, but he hadn't so much as twitched. He craved the slightly painful sensation, so I intended to make him stay there a little bit longer. "For your reward, you get to make me come."

"Thank you, Madame." His breathy reply was completely genuine, the anticipation in his eyes supporting the sentiment as I walked over to him, bringing my pussy directly in front of his face. With a groan of appreciation, he leaned forward, his hands still tied behind his back, and inhaled deeply. "You are so good to me."

"Because you're good to me," I reminded him, a short gasp interrupting the words as his tongue connected with my clit. Instinctively, I leaned forward even further to make it easier for him, craving his tongue and his lips as much as I ever had. He was good at oral, without question, but what made it even better was how much pleasure he got from it, how he truly viewed it as a reward to be able to please me. He would stay there as long as it took, restrained and bent, until he achieved his goal of making me feel good.

It wouldn't take all that long, though. The sight of him added to my arousal, his eyes closed in pleasure as his mouth worked between my legs. His tongue knew just how to tease my clit, swirling around it with the perfect amount of pressure before dipping down into my pussy. Julien groaned happily as he tasted me, allowing himself that moment's pleasure before he returned to his task, and the sound of his enjoyment drove my need even higher. My body throbbed for him, my bare nipples stiffening above him and my legs beginning to tremble in their heels as he buried his face as fully as he could between them.

When he clamped down on my clit, sucking it hard and firmly, I couldn't resist any longer. I really didn't want to. Whispering his name, I came on his face, sighing and shuddering against him as he groaned again in appreciation. His tongue lapped up as much as he could before I took a step back and he smiled up at me, his lips glistening and his sweet brown eyes showing nothing but satisfaction. "Thank you, Eve."

I should be thanking *him*, but that wasn't our style. Instead, I simply nodded my approval before gesturing over at one of the benches in the room. "On there. On your stomach."

Awkwardly, with his hands still tied behind his back and his cock nearly hard enough to act as an extra limb, Julien got to his feet and went to the bench. A wide central beam supported his torso while thinner padded beams down either side let him rest on his knees, putting his ass on perfect display for me. His stiff cock pressed against the end of the bench, hanging down between his spread legs.

While he got into position, I stepped into the strap-on dildo I'd requested that the club provide. In our travels, we didn't take many toys with us, but one we couldn't leave behind was the strap-on Julien bought me a year earlier, on our first Christmas together. It was meant for him to use, a way to achieve double penetration for me without including another person, but I'd used it on him as soon as I opened it, and over the course of the year, I'd used it on him many more times. Pegging had become one of our favourite activities in the bedroom: a perfect way for him to demonstrate his submission, a way for me to feel even more powerful and in control, and a way to draw out our satisfaction, delaying his orgasm while still bringing him pleasure.

Twice, we'd had our bags searched at customs in different countries, and the men rifling through my things always stopped short when they got to the toy. Julien would blush and avoid eye contact with them, but I always held my head high. I liked having it used on me and I loved using it, and I refused to feel any kind of shame about that.

That night, though, I'd requested a size up from the one we usually used. Thicker and longer, the silicone cock jutted out from my body as I finished doing up the straps, giving me an immediate rush of anticipation. Though I would never know exactly what it felt like to have that appendage attached to me and the sensations it brought with it, this came close. I could bring Julien pleasure with it, and that satisfied me fully.

His muscles flinched, his ass tightening involuntarily as my fingers with the cold lube on them slid between his cheeks. "Relax," I whispered, using my other hand to stroke the underside of his hard cock, distracting him from any temporary discomfort. "You're going to take what I give you, aren't you? You're going to let me fuck you before you fuck me."

"Oui, Madame. Je le veux."

He always slipped into French when he was turned on, as if his brain couldn't function well enough to make the necessary translations, but I'd learned enough of the language to know he said he wanted it, that he gave me permission to go ahead, as I knew he would.

My fingers played around the rim of his hole, sliding gently inside with the lube, being careful not to scratch him with my newly-manicured nails, and when he felt relaxed and ready, I applied a large helping of the lube to the cock on my hips. The bench was the perfect height for me to line the dildo up with his ass, and Julien groaned as the thick head pressed against the opening.

"I'm going to fuck you hard," I warned him, smiling as a shudder worked its way down his spine. "You're going to stand up tomorrow in front of our friends and family, promising to love me, body and soul, but here's where you prove that your body is mine."

"It's yours, Eve," he grunted, his voice strangled as I pushed my hips forward, filling him up. "Tonight and always, I'm yours."

~Julien~

Though I had been doing a pretty good job of keeping my mother out of my thoughts thanks to Eve's excellent distraction, I couldn't entirely stop myself from wondering for a brief second what she would have thought if she saw me at that exact moment: naked, handcuffed, getting fucked in the ass by my gorgeous fiancée, and loving every second of it.

It served as a good reminder to me that we never truly knew anyone quite as well as we thought we did.

Pegging suited my submissive side perfectly, but for a long time, I struggled to find a domme who brought the right mix of domination and respect to it. Degradation worked really well for a lot of subs, but it never appealed to me. Neither did I want an excess of praise or to be called a 'good boy' like many others did. My personal sweet spot fell somewhere in the middle, and Eve had found it naturally, with very little direction from me.

I wanted her to peg me not as punishment or reward but because she loved me, and she did exactly that, making it just another part of our sex lives rather than something unusual or unconventional. Everything between us was equal in its own way. I fingered her, she jacked me off. I went down on her, she went down on me. I put my cock in her and she put hers in me. We enjoyed each and every way of being intimate with each other.

In short, we did it because we both enjoyed bringing each other pleasure. It really was as simple as that.

"Ah, crisse," I groaned as Eve pushed deeper into me, the silicone cock rubbing against my prostate in a way that made my toes curl. She knew exactly what angle would stimulate it best, and a warm heat began to spread through my body with each thrust of her hips. She'd also grown so used to me swearing in French during sex that if I ever tried to say 'fuck' instead, it made her laugh. Therefore, I stuck to doing what came naturally.

My stiff cock pressing against the cold end of the bench caused a slight pinching pain which, honestly, I needed. Without it, there would have been almost too much pleasure and I would have been in danger of coming before I could get my cock in her as she'd asked me to. Disobeying my domme was the worst sin I could commit in the bedroom, and especially on the night before our wedding.

However, Eve knew exactly when I was getting too close and she slowed right down, scraping her pretty nails down my back and over my ass as she drew out her movements, pressing into me much more slowly, inch by inch, letting me feel each and every one. Letting another person inside you was an act of intense trust, and doing it myself only made me respect women more, especially the beautiful one currently focused on my pleasure.

I meant it when I said my body was hers. That promise came easily because I knew she knew exactly what to do with it and how to make me feel good by giving me the chance to please her.

In order to have that chance, she needed to stop before I came, and she did exactly that.

"Over to the bed," she ordered as she pulled out of me entirely, her throaty voice telling me she'd enjoyed that just as much as I had. "On your back."

I did as she commanded, shuffling awkwardly off the bench with my hands still tied behind my back and over to the bed while Eve removed the strap-on. She kept it in her hand as she joined me, and I soon realized why.

"Roll over on your side."

As soon as I obeyed, she pushed the dildo back into my ass, filling me up again before unlocking the handcuffs. The slight pressure of her hand told me to roll onto my back again, and when I did, she raised my hands over my head to tie me to the bed.

"Perfect," she assessed, her eyes roaming over me from my cuffed wrists, down the strained muscles of my arms and chest, to my painfully hard cock lying against my stomach and the large dildo sticking out of my ass. "You look incredible. So fucking sexy."

Not every woman would have thought so, but somehow, I got lucky enough to find one that truly meant it. Not to mention I was pretty sure there was barely a man alive who wouldn't let her tie them up that way if it meant she would straddle them, as she did to me then, and fill herself up with my aching cock.

"Fuck yes," she moaned as her head fell back when she bottomed out on top of me and her hands skimmed over her perfect, full breasts. My fingers twitched, itching to touch her too, but with my hands cuffed to the bed, I could do nothing but watch as she touched herself, knowing exactly how to turn herself on as she rose and fell on top of me. At that moment, my body was a tool for her pleasure, and I was happy to let it be so.

The pressure of her riding me made the dildo in my ass move too, just enough to tease me and remind me it was there. I'd been turned on before, but with the combination of sensations she provided then, I felt right on the edge and it wouldn't take much to push me over.

Obviously, Eve knew that, because when she got close, her hands moved into a different position. Her right hand went to her clit, rubbing against it with her hips still grinding into me, and her left hand reached behind her back to grab hold of the dildo base beneath her. She didn't move it much, just pushing it in rhythmically, in time with the bucking of her hips, but it did the trick. My orgasm built quickly as the dildo pressed against my prostate, adding to the incredible feeling of my cock inside her and the sight of her so completely in control of both of our pleasure.

"Eve. Please." I groaned out her name, begging her for mercy, and as it often did, the sound of my control breaking served to break hers. She shuddered into her orgasm as I gratefully let myself go, coming long and hard inside her, my arms straining against their restraint as the rest of my body blissfully surrendered.

For a long moment afterwards, neither of us spoke. Panting breaths gave way to sighs of satisfaction as Eve climbed off me and began to get dressed, leaving me still handcuffed to the bed.

"There's so much we didn't get to do," she groaned in regret as she looked over the assorted accessories and equipment. "But I think we really need to get some sleep before tomorrow."

"You're right." There would be other nights and other playrooms, but only one wedding day. "At least I'll sleep well tonight."

By that, I meant that she had successfully taken my mind off the situation with my mother, and she understood that as she came over to release my restraints. "Good. There is one more thing I want you to do for me, though."

"Anything."

I meant it; whatever she asked, I would agree, and when she picked up one of the toys from the table and held it up, I had to smile.

"Wear this tomorrow, during the ceremony."

The silver butt plug had a wedding ring on the end of it, which felt rather appropriate. "I will. I promise."

As we made our vows to each other, it would serve as a reminder of everything we'd found in each other that only the two of us could truly understand, and I honestly couldn't wait for the chance to proclaim to the world that I planned to devote the rest of my life to the incredible woman who had chosen me.

Chapter Ten

THE PRIVATE CLUB

~Jackson~

Cole held it together very well until Eve and Julien walked out of the room after dinner. However, as soon as they'd gone, my best friend's face instantly transformed, his features tightening into a fearsome scowl that would have had me cowering if I didn't know him as well as I did. "I'm going to murder that woman. Who the fuck does she think she is, trying to ruin my daughter's wedding?"

None of us needed to ask who he meant by 'that woman,' and Gemma placed her hand on his arm in support. "Murder isn't necessary, but we could always kidnap her, tie her up and send her on a cargo plane back to Canada tonight."

Holly laughed in surprise at Gemma's uncharacteristic suggestion, but I hated seeing either of them upset at what was supposed to be a happy occasion, so I tried to offer an alternate perspective. "She's obviously got a lot of unresolved feelings over the situation with Julien's father. I feel sorry for her that she can't move on after all this time."

"You're always looking for the good in people, but she's out of order," Holly chided me. "Her feelings should be secondary to what makes her son happy, just like you were able to put Liv's feelings ahead of your own when it came to Noah."

My reservations about Cole and Gemma's son marrying my daughter hadn't been a secret from anyone, and Holly was right: once Olivia made it clear that she chose Noah, I made a concerted effort to put my own feelings on the subject behind us. Maybe Emilie Labrecque just needed someone to help her figure out how to do the same.

"I promised Julien I'd try to help his mother have a good time tonight," I admitted. "Obviously, that was before the scene at dinner, but I'd still like to try. What do you say, Holly?"

"Why did I have to marry such a nice guy?" Holly complained, rolling her eyes in mock disappointment as the Stamers smiled. "I'd much rather stay here and get drunk with everyone else."

"Better that you try to talk some sense into her than us," Gemma pointed out. "I think she already feels a little insecure about Cole's wealth, since she refused to accept our offer to join us on the flight, and I can't guarantee Cole won't lose his temper."

She had a point, though I found it funny that she referred to it as 'Cole's' wealth. After thirty years of marriage where they had shared everything, not to mention the title and properties she'd just inherited in her own right, Gemma was every bit as rich as Cole. However, she never considered herself wealthy because of him, which was part of what made her so perfect for him in the first place.

"Ugh, fine." Holly gulped down the rest of her drink before placing it firmly down on the table in front of us. "But we're getting drunk at the wedding tomorrow!"

"Deal." Drunk Holly was one of my favourite versions of my wife, especially as she'd gotten older and had even less filter than before, though there weren't any versions of her that didn't appeal to me in some way.

After wishing our friends and daughters a good night, Holly and I headed to Emilie's room while I tried to decide how to start the conversation with her. If it felt like an ambush, she might just dig in deeper, so I'd need to find a way to make it seem less formal and more like a legitimate, friendly conversation.

"What do you want?" was the greeting that we got when she opened the door, immediately crossing her arms as if she anticipated a fight.

Though she must have been around our age, she certainly looked older than Holly. Her brown hair had been pulled back into a severe bun and deep lines around her mouth gave her a perpetually unhappy look, even without the sour expression she put on top of it.

"Bonsoir, Emilie," I said in reply, wishing her a good evening with my rusty high-school French and supplementing it with a smile that I hoped would soften her even if my words didn't. "We were wondering if you'd like to join us for a drink?"

Her eyes darted suspiciously between me and Holly, as if the invitation might be some kind of trap. "Did Julien send you?"

"No," I answered honestly, and it almost looked like that disappointed her. Maybe she still hoped he'd change his mind about having his father at the ceremony, but I felt pretty confident he wouldn't. If anyone's mind would be changing, it would have to be hers. "We'd just like to get to know you better."

Holly smiled encouragingly beside me, but left the talking to me.

"I don't want to go to the bar," Emilie protested next. "*He* might be there."

So, we needed to avoid even the possibility of running into her ex. "How about taking a taxi into the city, then?"

"No. I don't want to be out that late."

She seemed determined to shoot down any suggestion I made, but there was one other option that might work.

"We could go to the private club here at the hotel instead?"

Holly looked over at me in surprise. "What private club?"

I hadn't had a chance yet to tell her about the conversation I'd overheard between the Ribar daughters before dinner, while I waited for Holly to arrive. They didn't realize I'd walked in, and I didn't want to interrupt. "Apparently, it's a members-only club but hotel guests can use it too. There's a secret entrance in the garden, and you can even request a private room, so if anyone you don't want to see is there, you can avoid them."

Crystal gave her sister full instructions on how to get in, so I felt pretty confident I could find it. She also said she'd had the best night of her life there, which sounded like a ringing endorsement to me. It should address Emilie's concerns about running into Julian Ribar, but also wouldn't involve leaving the property.

"It sounds a little strange, but I like strange," my beautiful wife laughed. "What do you say, Emilie? No wedding stress, no billionaires. Just a drink and a chat."

Though she still looked a little wary, her expression softened when Holly said we wouldn't be talking about the wedding, and we wouldn't. Not directly, anyway. "Alright. One drink."

Honestly, I hadn't even been sure we'd get that much, so I pounced on the offer before she could change her mind. "Wonderful. This way. Drinks are on me, you only need your room key."

We kept the door open to make sure she didn't bail while she grabbed her key, and soon, the three of us were walking through the garden in the late evening sunshine. It didn't take long to find the structure that Crystal had described as the entrance, though I certainly never would have suspected it of being anything other than a storage shed.

"Are you sure about this?" Holly teased me before giving Emilie a friendly nudge. "Maybe he's just going to force us to do yard work."

Emilie seemed a little bemused by Holly. Perhaps she couldn't fully understand her British accent, or maybe she just enjoyed her energy. Either way, her lips pulled upwards, which was the closest I'd seen her come to a smile since we arrived.

With as much confidence as I could muster, I knocked on the door of the outbuilding, and it quickly opened for us, revealing a man dressed all in black and holding an electronic device. "Name?" he asked me politely.

"Jackson Hanmer."

He typed it into his device and scrolled for a little while, the furrow in his brow growing deeper as he did. "I'm sorry, Mr Hanmer, I don't have you listed."

That was odd. "Are you sure? We're guests at the hotel. We're with the Stamer/Labrecque wedding."

Instantly, his expression cleared. *Those* names, he obviously knew. "Oh, it must just be an oversight, then. Please, come in."

He stepped back to open another door that led to a deep, dark staircase, descending beneath the hotel gardens.

"Well, this is exciting!" Holly declared as she took the lead. "Like an old speakeasy, or a magical pub from a novel."

Emilie looked a little less excited, but she followed my wife anyway while I gave the man at the door a friendly nod before bringing up the rear. Now, I just needed to get Emilie to confide in me. Hopefully, this night would be just what we needed to turn things around for her.

~Holly~

It didn't take me very long to realize Jackson's mistake.

From the get-go, it struck me as odd that nobody had mentioned this private club to us before. The fact that we weren't on the list also seemed strange, but when they let us in anyway, I was willing to let it go. At least we got Emilie Labrecque out of her room, and hopefully a drink or two would loosen her up and we could get to the bottom of her foul mood. If anyone could talk her out of it, Jackson could.

However, as we reached the bar at the foot of the stairs, my sense that something wasn't quite right got even stronger. I couldn't put my finger on it right away, but the dark booths along the wall contrasting with the brighter tables in the middle felt odd, as if it were designed for people to either watch or be watched, and so did the open stares we got as the three of us walked into the room.

Jackson, however, seemed oblivious to anything out of the ordinary as he pulled out a chair from one of the tables for Emilie to sit down, as gallant as ever. "Please, have a seat."

She did, and I took the chair next to her, so it wouldn't feel like we were ganging up on her, while Jackson sat across from us.

"I wonder if we need to go to the bar or if there's table service," he mused, looking over in the direction of the scantily-clad bar staff that seemed rather risqué for a members' club, unless it catered to a certain *kind* of member.

"Someone's coming over," I pointed out, having spotted a man in a suit walking over to us. Blond, tanned and toned, he flashed us all a bright smile as he greeted us.

"Hello. My name's Derek, I'm the owner of the club and the hotel. I understand you were left off our guest list somehow, and I'd like to apologize. Your drinks are on me tonight."

He offered Jackson an electronic menu, but a gut feeling told me that Jackson getting a look at that menu might not be the best idea, so I reached out and snatched it out of Derek's hand. As I remembered it, we'd come to the hotel because Derek was an old friend of Noah's, and I was starting to get a pretty good idea of where exactly the two of them had met.

"Why don't you let me choose?" I offered, giving Jackson a wink to try to make my stealing the menu out of his hand seem like flirty fun.

"Sure, if you'd like to." His brow knitted together in uncertainty for just a second, but he quickly turned his attention back to Derek. "I'm Jackson Hanmer and this is my wife, Holly. We're friends of the bride's family, and this is Emilie Labrecque, she's the mother of the groom."

Derek's eyes sparkled in delighted surprise. "Well, I love when new families can all get along and enjoy themselves together."

There definitely seemed to be a double meaning behind those words but Jackson missed it entirely.

"If there are any particular needs you have for tonight, just let a member of our staff know," Derek added. "Otherwise, enjoy yourself in Paradise."

He gestured to the room around us with a flourish before taking his leave, and Jackson gave me a bemused smile as he looked around. "I'm not sure this is how I would decorate a club called Paradise. I think it needs the Holly Hanmer touch."

Oh, good God. My husband might have been the sweetest man on the face of the earth, but he could also be incredibly naive. Charmingly, adorably naive, and his idea of paradise apparently differed from most men on earth.

"Why don't I get us some drinks?" I offered, tapping on the screen to turn on the menu. Sure enough, my suspicions about exactly what kind of club we were in were quickly confirmed when I saw the names of the drinks but I did my best not to react in any way that would alert Jackson to anything suspicious. "Any allergies, Emilie?"

When she confirmed she had none, and before Jackson could get a look at the screen, I ordered three and turned the menu off, placing it face down on the table as I gave Emilie the brightest smile I could muster.

"So, how exactly did Julian Ribar screw you over?"

"Holly!"

Jackson had obviously intended to be more discreet in our conversation, but as I saw it, we had to move fast before he figured out exactly where we were. It might not be possible for someone to die of embarrassment, but he would certainly feel like he wanted to if he realized what kind of establishment he'd brought us to, and I loved him enough to want to spare him that discovery. "What? If she didn't want us to know about it, she wouldn't have said anything at dinner."

"She's right," Emilie interjected, siding with me to my surprise. "I don't mind talking about it. I have nothing to be ashamed of. He's the one who behaved shamefully."

While our drinks arrived and we all sipped on the tasty cocktails, she told us the whole story about how she and Julian fell in love, how she got pregnant and how Julian's father forced Julian to leave her behind. Surprisingly, I found I could relate quite well; although I'd thankfully never ended up as a single mum, I'd had plenty of men pass me over because I didn't fit into the life they imagined for themselves, and I knew exactly how worthless it could make a person feel.

"So, you think he's going to steal Julien from you?" I guessed when she'd finished explaining the past and got back to the present.

"Non. Oui. I don't know." She shook her head to confirm her confusion. "I know he's grown now and he can't be stolen, not like when he was young, but it doesn't seem fair that Julian got everything he wanted, at my expense, and now he gets to have his son too."

"He didn't get everything," Jackson disagreed softly. "He missed out on Julien's whole life. As a father, I can tell you that I can't imagine anything worse. He's suffered, Emilie. I promise you he has."

"But you've suffered too," I pointed out. "You've stayed stuck in that hurt when you could have been living your own life. Was there never anyone else who caught your fancy in all these years?"

The far-away look in her eyes made it clear without her saying a word that there had been, in some capacity, but she shook it away with another shake of her head. "I had to put Julien first."

"When he was young, maybe, but for the last fifteen years? You've been wearing your loneliness like a badge of honour, and trust me, I know what that's like. When I met Jackson, I told him I was never going to love anyone again. I thought it made me strong but it didn't. What's strong is opening yourself up again after you've been hurt that deeply."

Jackson took my hand across the table, his eyes shining with affection, but his smile soon turned to a grimace. "I'm really sorry to break up this conversation, but I need to use the restroom. These drinks were pretty strong."

They were, but rather tasty too. I kind of wanted another, but the smarter thing to do would be to wrap this up while we were still ahead, so I sent him off while I tried to figure out how we could get out of there before it was too late.

However, as soon as he'd gone, and before I had the chance to say anything else at all, Emilie turned to me. "Look, I appreciate you taking the time to listen to me, and I'm very flattered, but this just isn't something I'm interested in."

"Excuse me?" Maybe the drink had been even stronger than I realized because her words didn't make any sense to me.

"I saw the drink you ordered," she said, as if that explained anything. "And this place..."

As she gestured around us, I realized that perhaps the drink *did* explain things. I'd ordered all of us the Ménage Melon off the special eggnog cocktail list, but only because it seemed like a pretty safe choice. I certainly hadn't meant to imply anything by it.

"It's not what you think. It was a drink, nothing more."

Emilie didn't look entirely convinced. "Then why did your husband bring us to a sex club?"

So, she'd picked up on that too.

I could only be honest. "Because he doesn't know it's a sex club. He genuinely thinks it's just a regular club."

Disbelief still lingered in her eyes, so I gave her another shrug.

"He was a virgin when we met. He's never been with any woman other than me and he couldn't be farther from a swinger. This is just a misunderstanding, but please don't tell him. He'll be mortified."

She continued to stare at me, trying to decide whether to believe me or not, but eventually, her lips began to twitch. "Seriously?"

A grin spread across my face as the ridiculousness of the situation fully set in. "Seriously. Men aren't all pigs, Emilie. Some of them are sweet and slightly clueless golden retrievers instead."

A laugh bubbled out of her, and I couldn't hold mine in anymore either. Fuelled by the alcohol in our blood, we both dissolved into giggles, and it actually felt, surprisingly, like we might be on our way to becoming friends. Not much bonded you to someone quite like accidentally going to a sex club with them.

Now, we just needed to get my husband out of there before he figured it out for himself.

~Jackson~

Just as it felt like we were starting to make some progress with Emilie, I glanced up and saw two familiar faces entering the room, heading straight in our direction. Although Emilie needed to talk to her son, we weren't quite there yet, and a too-early confrontation could work as a setback to what we'd accomplished so far.

With that in mind, I quickly excused myself, claiming to need the restroom, and set off to try to intercept the bride and groom.

"Hey." Their startled faces seemed almost *too* surprised when I suddenly appeared in front of them, but I got right to the point. "Julien, your mother's sitting just over there. You might want to avoid letting her see you for now."

"My... mother? Here?" His eyes darted over my shoulder to find the woman in question as the colour drained from his face.

Eve looked just as shocked, though her eyes remained on me. "Uncle Jackson, what are *you* doing here?"

"We brought Emilie here to talk. It's going well, but I don't think she's quite ready to see you yet."

"You... brought her... here." Julien just repeated my words back to me, still looking utterly bewildered.

"Are the two of you alright?" They were acting very strangely, and it crossed my mind that they might have been drinking or worse, which wouldn't be great the night before their wedding. Hadn't they said they were going to have an early night? I wondered what made them change their minds.

"We're fine," Eve assured me, making an obvious effort to take control again. "What do you suggest?"

"If you go along the back wall where it's darker, she won't see you. You should be getting some rest before your big day anyway."

"Yes. We should." Eve grabbed Julien's arm, whispering something to him in French that I couldn't make out before giving me a slightly strained smile. "Thank you, Jackson."

"Anytime."

They snuck away as I'd suggested, but the encounter left me feeling rather unsettled. Why were they so surprised to see me, and why, if they knew about this place, hadn't they mentioned it to the rest of us? I had to be missing something, but I had no idea what it could be.

Trying to stay out of sight myself, I glanced back over at the table where my wife and Emilie sat while Eve and Julien made their escape. From that distance, they seemed to be having a good time, talking and laughing together. They were *really* laughing about something, actually, seeming to get along better than they had all evening, and I didn't want to interrupt them too soon. So, as soon as Julien and Eve made it to the stairs, I turned around and headed to the restroom instead, for real that time.

It didn't take long to find the men's room down a short, dark hallway, but the room itself came as a surprise when I opened the door. Rather like a high-class change room or locker room, there were curtained booths, storage cupboards, and a seating area to one side, along with the more typical urinals and toilets. One of the booths had its curtain pulled, and a man washing his hands gave me a smile that almost felt flirty as I walked past him. I could have been imagining things, though. In a different country, things could often be interpreted in a different way, and we *had* been drinking.

The noises coming from inside the curtained room were harder to explain. Grunts, groans and the odd muffled laugh filtered out from behind the curtain, but having lived in New York most of my life, I'd learned long ago to mind my own business in public places. That got a little harder to do when the curtain opened just as I'd finished zipping my pants back up and two men walked out, also fiddling with the zippers on their pants. Both younger than me, they were both tanned and good-looking, and not at all self-conscious about what they'd obviously just been doing.

"How ya goin'?" one of them said, coming over to wash his hands next to me.

I'd never entirely figured out the correct way to respond to that Australian greeting, so I simply gave him a nod and stuck with a simple, "Hey."

Even though I only said the one word, he picked up on my accent immediately. "Where are you from?"

"New York. Is it that obvious?"

He and the other man exchanged grins. "You sound like a Yank alright. What's your scene?"

"My what?" I figured that had to be some kind of Australian slang I didn't know since the word didn't make any sense to me in that context.

"Your scene," he repeated with a laugh, mimicking my New York accent. "Your kink. What are you here for?"

The question still confused me. Maybe those drinks had been stronger than I realized, or maybe the culture gap was wider, but I tried to answer anyway. "I... uh, I'm here for a wedding."

He looked confused for a moment too before laughing good-naturedly. "That's a new one on me, but whatever turns you on, man. Have a good night."

"Yeah, you too."

The two of them walked out the door, and I followed shortly afterwards, still with a lingering feeling that something was just a little bit off. The club wasn't really at all what I'd expected, and the longer we stayed, the stranger it felt. Maybe we should go back to the hotel and finish our conversation there.

Before I could get back to the table to make the suggestion to Holly, a young couple stopped me. Close to Olivia and Noelle's age, they stepped directly into my path, leaving me with no choice but to stop.

The woman stuck her hand out, looking up at me in a way that suggested she definitely wasn't looking for some fatherly advice. "Hi, I'm Sheila, and this is my boyfriend, Bruce."

"Hi." I glanced over at Holly, who had seen me by that point. With wide eyes, she started to get up from the table. "Can I help you?"

"We sure hope so." Sheila giggled as she looked up at her partner. "We'd love to have you join us as a third if you're interested."

Once again, I felt lost. "A third what?"

I'd been to Australia several times before, and I'd never had so much trouble understanding people before.

The couple exchanged bemused looks. "A third in our..." the man started to say, but before he could finish, Holly reached up and practically threw herself between me and the others.

"Sorry, he's already spoken for. Excuse us."

Taking my hand, she pulled me away as the couple shrugged their shoulders and moved on, but after a few steps, I stopped too, pulling Holly to a halt beside me. "What was that about?"

"Nothing," she tried to claim, gesturing back towards the table. "Look, Emilie's feeling a bit better, so why don't we get out of here? We can head back to the hotel and have another drink in our suite."

"There's something you're not telling me." Though I may not understand everything else going on, I'd always been able to understand Holly. "What is it?"

She tried to laugh it off, but I could see genuine concern in her eyes. "This place is just... it's for a certain kind of clientele, Jackson, and we're not it. We'll be more comfortable back at the hotel."

She glanced back over at the table, and I followed her gaze to where a man had taken her place next to Emilie. He had his arm around the back of Emilie's chair as he spoke into her ear in a very familiar way.

"Who's that?" I looked back at Holly for an explanation, but she could only shrug. "What kind of clientele are you talking about?"

With defeat in her eyes, my wife looked back over at me. "I didn't want to have to tell you. I know you didn't know when you brought us here."

It felt like I really might start to go crazy if things didn't start making sense soon, but something in her affectionate expression did the trick. Things started to click into place: the secrecy, the guest list to get in, the things Derek said, the way Eve and Julien reacted to seeing me there, and most of all, the two encounters I'd just had and the way Holly intervened.

My stomach dropped painfully hard. "Oh, shit."

Chapter Eleven

A WORK OF ART

The look on Jackson's face when he realized exactly where he'd brought us both tugged at my heart and made me want to giggle. *Really* giggle. My laughter with Emilie earlier had already broken the dam, and it took every ounce of strength I had to keep my amusement inside as my sweet husband put all the pieces together.

"We have to get Emilie out of here," he said, his eyes darting frantically around the room. "That man she's talking to might say something and she'll know..."

"She already knows." It couldn't get much worse for him than it already had, so I might as well tell him the whole truth. "She figured it out all on her own. Besides, I think she might be in for a much better night than any of us anticipated."

The sour look on Emilie's face had completely vanished as she chatted with the man who sat down beside her. Maybe a good shag would help improve her mood even further? It certainly couldn't hurt.

"She... but... the hotel owner... and Julien and Eve?"

The revelations had started to spiral, and I quickly directed Jackson to an empty table to sit down. He honestly looked like he might pass out, so I gestured to one of the servers standing not far away at the bar.

She brought over two new drinks for us, since Jackson looked like he could use it. "What about Julien and Eve?"

Taking a long drink, Jackson swallowed hard, his Adam's apple bobbing in his throat. "They were here. I saw them here."

I hadn't realized that, but neither did it come as a surprise. "Does that really shock you? I don't know anything about Julien's tastes, but Eve is Cole's daughter and Noah's sister."

Bringing up Noah was a mistake, since that made Jackson think of Olivia in a way he definitely didn't want to be thinking about his little girl. Even if she *was* thirty years old. "Do you think they're here too?"

He glanced around nervously, as if he might see them having sex right there in the bar

"I don't know if they're here, but if Julien and Eve know about this place, I imagine the others do too."

It only took him a second to understand what I meant. "They kept it from us on purpose."

"That's my guess. You were never meant to overhear anyone talking about it. If you hadn't, we could have gone home none the wiser."

He drained the rest of his drink, wincing at the sharpness of the alcohol, or maybe just from his wounded pride. "They all think I'm a complete prude, then."

Having seen the more adventurous side of my husband many times, I would never use that word for him. "That's not true." When he raised his eyebrows in disagreement, I elaborated further. "They think you're a little more conservative when it comes to sex, sure, and you are. It's nothing to be ashamed of. I think it's sweet."

I leaned in to give him a kiss, and though he accepted it, I could tell it didn't really help. "Is that why you're not ready to give up work yet? Because all I can offer you is 'sweet' instead of anything exciting?"

Where in the world did *that* come from? "What are you talking about? You're always exciting to me, Jackson."

He shook his head, his shoulders slumped and low. "Never mind. Forget I said that. My head is all over the place right now."

Though he tried to deflect, I had seen the flash of doubt in his eyes, and I grabbed his hands so he couldn't turn away. "Don't 'never mind' me. Something's bothering you, so what is it?"

His lips tightened as he looked back over to the table where Emilie sat, where the man next to her had somehow gotten even closer to her. "Shouldn't we see if she's okay?"

"You think the woman who slagged off the father of her child in front of the whole wedding party is going to have trouble telling a stranger to fuck off if she's uncomfortable? She's fine, but we're not going to be if you don't answer the question."

My tone left no doubt that I meant it, and Jackson sighed in defeat. "It's not a big deal, but... it feels like everyone's moving onto the next phase of their lives, you know? Eve's the last one to get married. They're all going to start having kids soon. Gemma and Cole are retiring and maybe moving back to England to be aristocrats! I don't need anything *that* crazy, but I'm ready for us to move on too."

My heart tugged again at the idea that I'd disappointed him in any way. "What's so bad about our current life? You've enjoyed it up until now, haven't you?"

He gave my hands a squeeze, still holding onto me tightly. "Of course I have. And there's nothing wrong with it, but there's nothing wrong with a little change either. You've worked hard, Holly. You've accomplished so much and you deserve to take a break and enjoy yourself. This is the best time of our lives. We can travel, spend time with our kids and hopefully our grandkids soon too. We can spend time *together*. We've got enough money put away that we don't need to worry. It sounds amazing to me, and I don't know why you're not as excited about it as I am. Is the thought of spending more time with me really that boring?"

He smiled as he asked the last question, trying to make a joke of it as we so often did between ourselves, but I knew better. He actually thought that might be the case, and since we were being honest, he deserved the truth from me too. "Actually, it's the opposite."

His brow furrowed as he thought that over. "You think it'll be *too* exciting?"

"That's not what I mean." I swatted his arm in recognition of his teasing before getting serious again. The words didn't come easily, but I needed to say them since he couldn't be further off the mark. "For our whole marriage, I've always been Holly the designer. Holly the businesswoman. From the night we met at the hotel that I designed, it's always been part of who you know me as, and I'm... well, I guess I'm afraid that without it, you'll find me boring."

"Holly." His warm hand cupped my cheek, holding my head up so I couldn't avoid his gaze. "That will never, ever happen. I've been obsessed with you since that very first night. You're the only woman I've ever fully given myself to, the only one I've ever wanted to. I'm in love with Holly the woman, Holly my wife, and Holly the mother of my children. Not anyone else or any other version of you. After thirty years together, do you really think I'm going to change my mind?"

Unexpected tears sprang to the corners of my eyes as I realized he'd just hit on the very root of the problem, seeing into my heart as clearly as he always did. He'd helped me overcome my fear of commitment and fear of abandonment when we met, but maybe those feelings never fully went away.

And like I did whenever things got too serious, I tried to lighten the mood with a joke. "Maybe the last thirty years have been a fluke?"

He smiled as he always did in response to my humour, but the look of determination in his eyes made it clear he didn't plan to let this go with a joke. "Maybe we both like to play it safe sometimes, but that doesn't mean we can't spice things up too."

As he glanced around the room as if he were looking for something in particular, my skin began to prickle in anticipation. "What exactly are you suggesting?"

When he turned back to me, his smile had grown much more heated, making my stomach flip just as much as he ever had. "We're in a sex club, aren't we? Maybe we should do something the rest of them would never expect, and make the most of it."

~Jackson~

Despite my confident smile, I actually had nothing in particular in mind when I suggested to Holly that we make use of the club's facilities. However, when she smiled back at me, her eyes lighting up in a way that made it clear she was more than willing to experiment a little, I knew I had to come up with something good.

"You go make sure that Emilie really is okay," I suggested, and when she looked set to protest again, I held up my hands to stall her. "I need to go and make a few arrangements. I'll be back as soon as I can."

"Don't keep me waiting too long." Her words sounded like a purr, content and full of anticipation as she leaned in to give me a kiss, and if I hadn't already been excited about the chance to prove to her just how irresistible I found her, that would have done it. Holly had been it for me, right from the start, and if she truly believed I would ever find her boring, I'd obviously done something wrong.

That night, I would make it right.

The club's owner, Derek, had said to let the staff know if we had any 'particular needs', and though I hadn't understood what he meant at the time, it made a lot more sense now. With that in mind, I made my way straight over to one of the women at the bar. "Who can I speak to about getting a room for me and my wife?"

At least, I assumed they had private rooms, and thankfully, she didn't contradict me. "I can help you with that. What kind of accessories would you like?"

That was the big question. Many years ago, Holly and I snuck into Gemma and Cole's playroom and tried a few things out, but although we had fun, it hadn't really been natural for us. When Olivia accidentally emailed me Noah's 'fuckit list', I learned much more about kinks than I had ever particularly wanted to know, but nothing on it really stood out to me as something I wanted to try either.

What I needed was something to show Holly that I loved her for exactly who she was, but that we could also continue to grow and evolve. We could be *us* and still have it be exciting too.

As I looked around the room, hoping for inspiration, I remembered how I said to Holly that the place could use her special designing touch, and at last, an idea came to me.

"I'm not sure if you'll have this stuff," I started, but the woman simply laughed.

"I've worked here for three years and it's only happened twice where we didn't have something. In both cases, we could get it within the hour. Try me."

With that assurance, I explained what I wanted, and she promised it would be no trouble. "Give us five minutes and we'll have the room set up for you."

I couldn't help but be impressed. Maybe my request wasn't quite as out-of-the-box as I thought. "Thank you. Do you need my room number at the hotel or something to bill me?"

Honestly, I had no idea how any of it worked.

Again, the employee smiled. "You're with the Stamer party, right? Mr Stamer is handling all of it."

Of course he was, and of *course* Cole knew about this place. Part of me wanted to thank him for it the next morning, while the other part thought it would be funnier if he just got the bill at some point and saw my name on it without me ever saying a word.

I got back to the table to find Holly there on her own, sipping on another drink. An extra cocktail sat on the table in front of her, the same flavour as before, and she pushed it over to me as I sat down next to her. "These are good, aren't they?"

"They are," I agreed, glancing around for any sign of Julien's mom. "What happened to Emilie?"

"She decided to go have a 'private drink' with that very handsome and horny man," Holly giggled. "She might have a better night than we do."

"Don't be so sure about that." My hand went to her thigh beneath the table as I leaned over to whisper in her ear. "This is going to be a night we won't forget."

"It already has been," Holly assured me, still laughing, but I noticed the way her body leaned into mine and the way she tilted her head, the subtle signs I'd learned a long time ago that told me she was getting turned on. I knew exactly what worked for her and what didn't, and to me, that familiarity made things more exciting, not less.

We drank a bit more and teased each other some more until the same woman I'd spoken to earlier came up to me. "Your room is ready. Here's the keycard, and you'll find the supplies you requested in the closet. Have a good time."

I gave her a grateful smile as I took the card with one hand and wrapped my other arm around Holly's waist. "Have you seen this woman? How could I not?"

"Jackson!" Holly stifled another giggle, but despite her attempt to laugh it off, I could tell she appreciated my public appreciation of *her*.

Maybe I needed to do that a little more often too.

We both drained the remainder of our drinks before setting off to our assigned room, my arm still around her waist and hers around mine too. We must have looked like newlyweds, unable to keep our hands off each other. Just the idea of doing something different had made us both almost giddy.

"Shall I guess what's inside?" Holly asked when we reached the door. "A pool filled with Jell-o, maybe?"

Her exuberance made me laugh even as my body heated from its contact with her. "Is that sexy?"

"I think you could find a way to make anything sexy." Her eyes shone with so much excitement that I couldn't wait any longer. Taking her face in my hands, I pulled her into a deep, lingering kiss, right there in the hall. Sure, no one else was around, but there *could* have been. Anyone could have walked by at any second, and from the way Holly's cheeks flushed as we separated, I knew the thought crossed her mind too. Still, we both preferred our privacy. "Let's go inside."

After all that build-up, I started to worry my actual idea would be a let-down, and sure enough, Holly's face registered only confusion as I opened the door for her and she walked in to find a regular room with dark walls and dark hardwood floor. The only visible piece of furniture was a large King-size bed covered with an even larger grey canvas.

"This is... nice?" She gave me a quizzical look, not quite disappointed but certainly not impressed either.

"It will be, when we're done with it. You know how you're always asking me to add my own personal touches when you redesign the house?"

With the door locked behind us, I pulled my shirt loose from my pants and began to undo the buttons.

Interest sparked in Holly's pretty blue eyes as she watched me undress. "Yes, and you always tell me that you'll never improve on what I can do."

"Right." Pulling my shirt off, I moved onto my pants, my hands brushing against my dick as I pulled the zipper down. I was already half hard, and with the way she looked at me as I pulled the rest of my clothes off, it wouldn't take me long to get the rest of the way. "Well, this is my contribution for the next time you want to change things up."

"I don't understand." Holly's eyes had drifted away from my face, devouring the sight of me as if it were the first time she'd seen me naked rather than the five thousandth... give or take.

"You will. But first, you need to be naked too."

Stepping over to her, I kissed her neck as I began undressing her. It didn't take long: one zip down the back of her dress loosened it enough for me to drop it to the floor. My lips moved down to the swell of her breasts as I undid her bra, and then down to her stomach as I pulled her panties down. I lingered there, on my knees, as she offered me one foot and then the other to remove her high-heeled shoes.

"Now what?" she asked, all traces of humour gone from her voice. Lust echoed in every word, the same way that I felt.

"Now comes the fun part." Sliding the closet door open, I found exactly what I'd asked for: multiple tubes of coloured body paint. With a grin, I grabbed a few tubes and held them up to Holly for her inspection. "Now, we make some art."

~Holly~

The pride on Jackson's face as he held up the paint tubes melted my heart, but I still didn't completely understand what he had in mind. "We're going to paint on each other?"

"To start with." He walked back over to me, leaning down to kiss me again before continuing his explanation. The force of his kiss and the hunger in it left me nearly dizzy with my own desire, his playfulness and his confidence just as attractive to me as they'd always been. "First, we can decorate each other, and then, we use our bodies to paint the canvas."

Glancing over at the bed, things finally clicked into place. "We're going to have sex on there? And you want to hang it up in our house afterwards?"

Jackson's blue eyes twinkled mischievously. "Why not? We have tons of art on the walls. No one else would know exactly where it came from."

The more I thought about the idea, the more I liked it, and I could see why it appealed to Jackson too. Our family and friends who all thought he was too vanilla for this club would come and sit in our living room beneath a literal artistic expression of our sex life, and have no idea.

People always said the best revenge was a life well-lived. Maybe in this case, it should be a wife well-fucked, and I would be happy to play my part. "In that case, let's see just how colourful we can be."

The tube I grabbed out of Jackson's hand happened to be blue, and he chose a yellow one for me. "Like your hair," he claimed.

"Maybe once upon a time," I laughed. "These days, it's a lot closer to that grey canvas!"

"Let's fix that, then." With a wink, he squirted a large dollop of paint in his hands, rubbed them together, and ran them through my hair before I had a chance to react. My indignant squeal got cut off when his hands curled around my hair, tightening his grip as he leaned down to kiss me again, claiming my mouth with his, his tongue tangling with mine until I could barely breathe.

Fuck. As much as I enjoyed our sex life normally, and I definitely did, this side of Jackson had my pulse racing in a way that made me feel much younger.

I still held the tube of paint in my hands, and I managed to flip the lid open behind his back. After squirting some into my hand, I reached down and grabbed hold of his firm, perfect ass, making him groan into my mouth.

"I'm going to look like a Smurf, aren't I?"

He could always make me laugh. "Maybe a little. But I don't mind." Kneading my fingers into his muscle, I tilted my hips against his, pressing his erection between us. "Is this stuff safe to use everywhere?"

"The paint?" he clarified, his breath sounding shorter than before. "Yeah. It's non-toxic and...uh, edible, too."

Well, that certainly opened up a few more possibilities.

"So, I could do this?" My hand left his ass and slipped between our bodies, circling his cock instead. The wet paint provided a natural lubricant as I slowly stroked his length. "And then this?"

The sight of his blue cock as I took a step back made me grin, but only for the time it took me to drop to my knees in front of him. Jackson groaned again as I took him into my mouth, no doubt turning my lips blue in the process.

"I have no idea why that's so sexy, but it really fucking is," he breathed, his hands going to my hair again as I took him in deeper, keeping my eyes on him.

My hand moved down to his balls, painting them blue too while I sucked him slowly and steadily. My tongue knew just where to flick to make his cock twitch and my hand knew just how to tug to get him to inhale in that way that sent pure need through me.

"If you keep doing that, there's going to be nothing left for the canvas," he said after another minute, letting out a shaky laugh as he gently pulled back from me. "Besides, we need more colour."

He grabbed green next, running his hands over my breasts and gently pulling my nipples. I turned my back to him while I got some pink, giving him a chance to pull me back against his erection before I wriggled back to rub my hands over his chest, my fingers running through the hair there as Jackson's hands moved lower.

"What colour should I use down here?" he teased, trailing his fingers lightly across my pelvis.

"Anything but red."

Jackson's deep chuckle echoed through the room before he drove his fingers deep inside me. My laughter choked into a gasp as he curled his fingers to find my g-spot, exactly where he knew it would be. Did anyone else laugh with their lover quite so much while still finding them irresistibly sexy? I didn't know for sure, but I knew I never had with anyone else, and after all these years, I wouldn't want it any other way.

I forgot about painting him, gripping his shoulders tightly instead while he worked his fingers in and out of me, his thumb circling my clit at the same time in a way he knew would drive me crazy. His head dipped to my chest, sucking one of my green nipples into his mouth as his fingers fucked me, worshipping me until I couldn't take anymore. I came hard on his hand, my thighs clenching around his arm as he held me upright.

When my eyes flitted open again, Jackson's handsome face was right there, his eyes dark with lust. "Turn around." Even his voice sounded darker than usual, and I obeyed immediately, still catching my breath as he applied more paint to my back and the back of my legs. Soon, my whole body was covered, and when he told me to do the same to him, I didn't hesitate. Red splashed across his back and purple on his legs, with a dash of black in his hair.

As soon as we were completely covered, he threw the tubes down, sending them skittering across the floor while he picked me up to carry me over to the bed.

"Are you going to clean that up afterwards?" I teased, my body already aching for him again.

"Cole's paying." His self-satisfied smirk made me laugh, at least until he tossed me down onto the canvas-topped bed. "The only thing I'm worried about getting dirty tonight is you."

Grabbing hold of my ankles, he pulled me back towards him, the paint on my back soaking into the canvas beneath me. He'd never manhandled me quite this way before, but I rather liked it, especially when he flipped me over onto my stomach and my sensitive nipples rubbed against the bedding.

"On your knees," he instructed, lifting my hips into the air but leaving my upper half flush against the fabric. Again, I obeyed, spreading my arms to try to get some leverage as he lined his hard cock up against my entrance and pushed firmly in.

"Oh, fu-uck." The words stuttered out of me with the slam of his hips against my ass. My whole body slid forward, the paint making everything slippery and adding another layer to the picture we'd already begun creating. Trying to get my bearings, my hands clawed at the canvas while Jackson continued to thrust into me, holding my hips steady. Just as I got myself oriented, he raised one leg onto the bed, changing the angle, and a deep moan echoed from my chest.

This definitely didn't feel like a man who found me boring.

Using his leg to help steady me, he reached down and found my clit, sending another shiver of electricity through me. My hips lifted higher, almost on their own, wanting him deeper, harder, and he read all my signals, picking up his pace while he rubbed around my clit, just the way I liked it.

"Jackson!" I gasped out his name as my body contracted in another orgasm, and I heard him swear softly from behind me as his motions slowed, not wanting to overstimulate me. When I stopped shuddering, though, all bets were off.

"My turn," he announced as he pulled out of me and dove onto the bed next to me with his full weight, making me bounce into the air. My giggles only lasted a few seconds before he pulled me to him, rolling us over, and then over again, covering the canvas until I ended up on top of him. With his hands on the back of my knees, he parted my legs around him before reaching up to get his cock in place again.

When he pulled me down, filling me once more, I had a pretty good idea why they'd named the club Paradise.

He'd already made me feel so good that I knew exactly how to finish him off. Still sitting on him, I planted my feet on either side of him and reached down to grab hold of his shoulders. With my thighs squeezed tight together, I began to ride him hard.

"Fuck. Yes. Holly." Each word came out as a gulp, wrapped in bliss, and as his eyes closed, his head rolling back, I knew he'd found his paradise too.

Maybe we always would, as long as we were together.

Chapter Twelve

FAMILY MEETING

~Gemma~

Although Cole suggested another visit to Paradise the night before the wedding, I had to decline. After everything that happened with Julien's mother, Eve might want some support, and Noah had been preoccupied too, though I didn't know why. My mother's intuition told me I might be needed, and I wanted to make sure I remained clear-headed and available, just in case. My children might be grown, but I would never really stop worrying.

Besides, we still had plenty of time after the wedding to enjoy ourselves, when both my head and heart would be completely in it.

As he always did, Cole deferred to my wishes. Though it might seem to a casual observer that he held all the power in our sexual relationship, it had always been more complicated than that.

It seemed my gut feeling was wrong anyway, since nobody came to our door that evening. We had a relatively early night in, which turned out to be the right call when a knock came just before seven the next morning.

"You don't need to start getting ready already, do you?" Cole grumbled, rubbing his eyes as we both sat up.

I had to laugh as I got out of bed and threw on one of the hotel's robes over my nightgown. "I hope not. I don't look that bad, do I?"

"You're perfect, just as you are." His heated gaze made it clear that, playroom or not, he would be happy to spend the morning in bed together until our wedding duties called us away. The idea appealed to me too, but first, I needed to see who was at the door. Hopefully, nothing had gone wrong already.

When I opened it, however, it wasn't Eve or Tessa, or anything to do with the wedding. Noah stood there instead, giving me an apologetic smile. He looked like he'd been up for a while already, dressed in a golf shirt and khakis. "Sorry, I know it's early."

"That's alright. What's up?" He clearly hadn't come just to say hi.

"Could you and Dad get dressed and come to our room? There's something Liv and I want to talk to you about."

"Is it about the wedding?" I couldn't guess what else would be so urgent on the day his sister got married, but Noah shook his head.

"No, it's something else. I promise I'll explain it all when you get there."

After agreeing, I closed the door and turned around to find Cole standing in the bedroom doorway, having heard every word. "Do you have any idea what that's about?"

"I might," he admitted. "But let's see what they have to say."

We got dressed in casual clothes, intending to change for the wedding later, and made our way to Noah and Olivia's room, arriving at almost exactly the same time as Jackson and Holly.

"They want to talk to you too?" Holly asked curiously. "What's going on?"

"I have no idea. I hope everything's okay."

It had started to feel like a big deal, but I honestly couldn't guess what it might be. It occurred to me they might be expecting, which would be wonderful news but didn't really require a summit on the morning of Eve's wedding. Similarly, if they were breaking up, heaven forbid, it wouldn't make any sense to announce it then.

In the end, I came up blank.

Noah opened the door to the four of us, and we found Olivia sitting on the couch in the living room of their suite, dressed in a pretty sundress and looking *very* nervous. My confusion only grew deeper as Noah asked us all to sit down.

"We're sorry for the secrecy, and for doing this on the day of the wedding. We won't keep you any longer than necessary."

"What's going on?" Jackson sat almost on the edge of his seat, leaning forward with his elbows on his knees, his eyes fixed on his daughter. "Are you alright?"

"We're fine," she answered him quickly, but her fidgeting fingers suggested otherwise. "Noah will explain."

All eyes in the room moved back to my son, who took a seat next to his wife, taking her hands in his. "We've asked you here because we're about to have a video call with someone who might change our lives."

That certainly sounded dramatic, and Holly and I exchanged quick, furtive glances, both of us still completely in the dark.

"They've told us that we'll need to provide character references, and we thought that having our parents here with us would be a good start, to show that we have a stable and supportive extended family."

Nothing that he said made the situation any clearer.

"Character references for what?" Cole asked bluntly.

Noah and Olivia exchanged glances before Noah answered his father. "For adoption."

None of us expected that word, and no one seemed to know exactly what to say. Even Cole remained silent, which gave Noah the space to keep going.

"Liv and I have been trying to conceive for almost three years. We tried on our own for a while, and when that didn't work, we tried with doctors. We've been tested and medicated and Liv's gone through several excruciating rounds of IVF, and it's still not working. It seems like it's just not meant to be for us."

The pain in his voice tore at my heart, and I could see Holly shifting in her seat too, obviously wanting to go and comfort her daughter. Olivia's lips pressed tightly together as Noah squeezed her hands, and I couldn't begin to imagine what she must have been through. How could this have been going on for three years and we had no idea? Why hadn't they shared it with us before now?

Unaware of my internal questions, Noah kept going. "However, Dad always taught me that a Stamer never gives up. Our goal isn't simply to have a baby, but to have a family, and there's more than one way we can do that. Adoption is something we'd talked about before in a general sort of way, as a possibility, but yesterday, we found out about some particular kids who are in need, and it felt like that might be a sign for us that the time had come."

Holly put things together much more quickly than I did. "Do you mean the kids Eve told us about?"

Olivia nodded as Jackson looked between the two of them in confusion. "What kids?"

"There are three young children that Eve met during her work," Olivia explained, taking a deep breath when her voice came out a bit shaky. "They're siblings and their parents died. They're currently living with their aunt but she can't afford to keep them and she asked Eve to take them. Eve couldn't, but maybe we can."

That was an awful lot for all of us to take in, and though I still had a lot of questions, I also wanted them to know that we had their backs, without question. "We'll do whatever you need. Have you spoken to a lawyer?"

Noah shot me a grateful look. "Not yet. We literally only found out about this yesterday, but Eve was already in touch with the charity that's helping the family and they've set up this video call this morning with us and the charity's director. We might even be able to see the kids too."

He and Olivia shared a quick, hopeful smile that had my heart melting. This obviously meant a great deal to them, and I would do anything I could to make it easier for them. We all would. "The solicitor we've been dealing with about my brother's estate works for a firm that specializes in international family law. He might be able to connect us with someone who can help."

"Already on it," Cole announced from beside me, his phone in his hand.

"Let's wait and see how the meeting goes first," Jackson suggested, taking a calmer approach than Cole, as usual. "One thing at a time. When are they calling?"

Noah glanced down at his watch. "In about five minutes. Anyone want coffee first?"

"Tea," Holly and I requested in unison, to no one's surprise. Noah and Jackson went to take care of drinks while Holly moved over to the couch next to her daughter, wrapping her arms around Olivia as the two of them whispered to each other.

"Did you know about this?" I asked Cole quietly.

"Not all of it. I had no idea they were thinking about adopting, but do you know what this means?"

It meant an awful lot of things, so I asked him which one he meant. "What?"

"We're going to be grandparents. Really soon."

That *would* be a big change, and I had to point out one more thing. "And so are the Hanmers. I guess neither you nor Jackson wins your little bet."

Cole chuckled, his deep laugh sending a wave of affection through me. "Actually, I think we both win. Hopefully, we all do."

~Noah~

The well-stocked kitchen in our suite had a coffee maker and plenty of tea, and Jackson and I set about putting everything together in a production line without a word exchanged between us. My father-in-law hadn't said *anything* to me yet and eventually, his silence threw me so much that I had to voice the thought foremost on my mind.

"You probably think this is some kind of karma."

Jackson stopped in mid-motion, his hand hovering above the tea bags as he looked up at me in surprise. "What do you mean?"

A lump formed in my throat as I looked down at the coffee cups in front of me, concentrating on pouring a little milk into my own so I didn't have to look at him. "I know you've never approved of my lifestyle. You haven't made it an issue between us, and I appreciate that, but somewhere in the back of your mind, you must be thinking that I deserve this."

Because I was looking down, I didn't see Jackson moving towards me until he gently grabbed hold of my shoulders and turned me to face him, refusing to let me look away. "The thought never crossed my mind, Noah, but I'm guessing it's crossed yours."

The lump in my throat grew bigger, threatening to cut off my air entirely. He couldn't possibly understand all the times I wondered what I'd done to bring this struggle into our lives. Olivia stressed about whether she ate too little or too much or the wrong things, whether she exercised too much or not enough, and a million other little questions that ate away at her, and I always did my best to reassure her that nothing she did or didn't do caused our infertility. How could I add to her burden by voicing my doubts and worries to her too?

But just because I didn't speak them didn't mean they didn't haunt me. Was it, as I just suggested to Jackson, some kind of cosmic retribution? Did I hurt someone during my younger, carefree days, and this was my punishment? Was Liv suffering because of me?

When I couldn't get the words out, Jackson exhaled, seeming to read most of my thoughts in my face even if I didn't say them out loud.

"You're a good guy, Noah. Do I agree with everything you've ever done? You know I don't, but you're a caring friend and son, a hard worker, a fair boss, and most importantly to me, a great husband. You make Liv happy, I've never had a reason to doubt that, and I think you'll be a great father. But more than that, even if you weren't a good guy, even if you were the world's biggest asshole, it still wouldn't mean you brought this upon yourself. Sometimes, things just happen and there's absolutely no reason behind it."

I'd used those words myself when trying to comfort Olivia, but it didn't make them any easier to accept. Swallowing down my pain, I did my best to look him straight in the eye. "Sometimes, I think I would rather have a reason, even if it was my fault."

Jackson nodded sympathetically. "You're like your dad: you want to meet the challenge head-on, but you can't when you don't even know what you're fighting against."

Somehow, he got right to the heart of things in just a few words, so I kept going, speaking my other fear out loud. "Do you think we're crazy for jumping into this potential adoption? It feels right to me, but I'm second-guessing myself too. It kind of just fell into our laps. Is it too easy?"

Taking a step back, Jackson chuckled softly. "Three kids? I don't think there'll be anything easy about it. But I think I know what you mean: after everything being so hard, it's hard to trust that anything good could happen. You feel like there has to be a catch."

"Exactly." Once again, he hit the nail squarely on the head.

"I don't think you're crazy at all." Giving me a supportive smile, Jackson went back to making the tea for Holly and my mom. "Sometimes, you need to be cautious, but other times, when something's right, you need to take the leap. When I had the chance to prove myself to Holly, I jumped right in and proposed to her after only a few weeks. Your dad did the same. Some people would say that's crazy, but when you know what you want, there's nothing wrong with making it happen. There will be challenges for you and Liv, without a doubt, but that's what we're all here for. We'll help you when things get rough. You're not alone, Noah. You never have been."

"Thanks."

There wasn't much else I could say, at least not without becoming more emotional than I should be considering I needed to be on video in just a couple of minutes. Clearing my throat, I tried to compose myself before taking the coffee back over to the others.

"Alright, let's figure out how we'll set this up."

Holly had that covered already, and Liv and I sat on the couch with our parents on chairs just beside us. They could see the screen but wouldn't be on camera until we asked them to be.

"Are Eve and Julien joining us?" my mom asked.

Since they'd been the ones to put us in touch with the charity and had already met the people involved, they would have been able to make the introductions, but I had purposefully kept them in the dark about this meeting. "It's their wedding day. They've got other things to think about, and we can handle it without them."

Olivia took my hand as I connected us to the call, and a moment later, another room appeared in front of us, a stark space with concrete walls and hard wooden chairs. It didn't look like a home, so I guessed it must have been the charity's office. A man in a suit sat closest to the camera. Beside him was a woman, probably around our own age, with a baby on her lap. Standing next to her, a little girl and a little boy, both dark-haired with dark, wide eyes, stared curiously into the camera.

Olivia inhaled sharply next to me, her hand squeezing mine, and I knew she felt it just the same as I did: we were looking at our future.

~Holly~

It felt like we all held our breath as Noah and Olivia introduced themselves to the people on the screen. I couldn't really imagine what they must have been feeling, or what would be going through the minds of those sweet little kids. Did they have any idea what this meeting was about? Had they ever seen a video call before? They certainly seemed fascinated with the screen, peering curiously at the pictures in front of them, but did they understand that the people they saw on it were real?

Nothing in the world could have adequately prepared me for this meeting when I woke up that morning. Jackson and I had been lying in bed, reminiscing fondly about our night at Paradise and wondering if Emilie would end up coming to the wedding after all when Olivia knocked on our door, and less than twenty minutes later, we were watching our daughter take the first step towards adopting children of her own.

"I wish you'd told me," I whispered to her after their initial announcement, when Noah and Jackson went to get us all drinks and Gemma and Cole carried on their own conversation, giving us a moment to ourselves.

I didn't want to make it about me or make her feel bad in any way, but I could hardly believe that she'd been going through fertility treatment for years and never mentioned it. Maybe we couldn't have done anything to directly help, but just having someone to talk to could make a difference. Jackson had taught me that, and I thought we'd demonstrated it to our girls too.

Olivia took it the way I intended: not as an admonition, but as a worry that I'd failed her somehow. "I know that I could have. I know I can tell you anything, Mom. It just felt like telling everyone would make it more real. I thought if I could deal with it myself, it would mean it had never been that big a problem. Now that I say it out loud, it sounds stupid, but..."

"No, it doesn't," I quickly cut her off. "It sounds a lot like me when I was younger."

Most of the time, she took after her dad, but in her more stubborn moments, I could see myself in her too.

Our foreheads rested against each other as I squeezed her tight. Back when she was little, whenever she got sick, I'd wish that I could be the one to suffer instead. This felt the same, but a hundred times stronger. I hated that she'd had to go through all of the disappointments and uncertainty, but I was also incredibly proud of her. She refused to let it defeat her. They were still going to get the family they wanted, just in a slightly different way.

That pride carried over as I sat just off-screen, watching her and Noah trying to sell themselves as parents.

"Olivia and I both work for our family's hotel business," Noah said, making it sound much less impressive than it actually was. "We enjoy our work, but we're able to take time off as needed. I can work from home too. It's flexible."

"I can stay home for an extended period of time while the children get settled," Olivia added. "We know it'll be a big adjustment for them, and we want to make it as easy as we can."

Her voice had a breathy, nervous quality untypical for her. It couldn't be clearer how much she wanted this, and when I glanced over at Jackson, tears glistened in his eyes. Gemma looked just the same. Cole was dry-eyed, like me, but he gave me a short nod when our eyes met, letting me know he was just as invested in this as the rest of us were.

"And you're sure you'll be able to financially provide for the children, even if you take time off work?" the man from the charity asked.

Obviously, he had no idea exactly who he was speaking to, but Noah answered the question in a restrained, humble manner. "That won't be a problem. We own our home and we have some savings put aside. We're financially secure."

"And there's room in your home for three children?"

Olivia fielded that one. "We have a four-bedroom apartment, so the children could each have their own bedroom, or they could share if they're more comfortable that way. We would let them decide."

"The children don't speak any English," the man warned them next. "How will you communicate until they can learn?"

Noah had a ready answer for that too. "I've located a nanny who speaks their language and also has experience in teaching English. She's willing to start with us immediately."

How the hell had he pulled that off? And how much had he offered the woman?

He really did take after his dad in a lot of ways.

Since there was nothing the man could say in response to that, he moved on to the next line of questioning. "Do you have any family support?"

Noah reached down and turned the laptop so that the camera pointed at the four of us. "These are our parents: Holly and Jackson Hanmer, and Cole and Gemma Stamer."

We each waved as we were introduced and I couldn't help speaking up even though no one had asked us a question yet. "We're really one big extended family already. Gemma's been my best friend for almost forty years, two of our kids got married, the other two are best friends, and we're all very excited to get some grandchildren. I'm just about to retire, so I'll have plenty of free time if Olivia needs some help."

Jackson and I had talked about my retirement that morning too. After what he said to me in the club the night before, I understood much better why he wanted me to step back from work, and I felt more confident about doing it too. Now, I had an even better reason.

Gemma nodded enthusiastically beside me while Cole offered a more practical perspective. "Trust funds will be established in each child's name. They'll be provided with excellent schooling and the opportunity to study at the college of their choice."

He might have been jumping the gun a bit there, but the man on the screen looked impressed. "And what if you end up having children of your own?" he asked, and Noah quickly turned the screen back to himself and Olivia.

"We've always wanted a big family," Olivia said, giving Noah a sweet, tender smile. "The more, the merrier. I don't think it's very likely, but if it did happen, it wouldn't change a thing about the family we already had."

He asked a few more questions about their relationship and what they thought their parenting style would be like. When he asked about hobbies, Jackson tensed beside me, but Noah simply mentioned golfing and visiting museums.

Overall, it felt like it went well, and the man from the charity backed that up when he asked the final question: "How quickly can you come and meet the children in person?"

Noah glanced over at his dad, who gave him another of his brief, firm nods that his son seemed to be able to translate without words.

"Tomorrow," Noah answered firmly. "My sister's getting married today so we're needed here, but tomorrow, we can be on a plane first thing in the morning."

Chapter Thirteen

WEDDING PREPARATION

~Julien~

"Hey."

Eve's sultry voice being the first thing I heard in the morning always made waking up a little easier, and I had a smile on my face even before I opened my eyes and remembered what day it was.

My beautiful fiancée hovered over me, her full lips curled into a smile, enticing as always. However, she had already gotten dressed, to my disappointment.

"Are you going somewhere?"

"Noelle wants to have a quiet breakfast, just the two of us before the madness of the day kicks off," she explained. "I didn't want you to wake up and find me gone."

That kind of thoughtfulness was just one of the many reasons I loved her. "Alright, have fun. I don't think I need to be anywhere for a couple of hours yet."

The groom certainly had less preparation to do than the bride in general. It wouldn't take me more than twenty minutes to get ready, but I grabbed my phone off the bedside table just to make sure I hadn't forgotten anything.

The calendar was empty until lunch, another segregated male/female activity, but I had a text from my mom that had come in an hour earlier. My stomach sank as soon as I saw her name on the screen. What did she want to complain about now? My father again? Did she see me and Eve at the club the night before despite our best efforts to sneak out with Mr Hanmer's help? It could be several things, but I didn't imagine any of them to be good.

"What is it?" Eve asked, reading my body language just as clearly as she always did.

"My mother." Those words were enough, but I opened the text too so I could share its contents with her. "She's asking me to go to her room to talk."

Eve's lips set into a firm line. "You don't have to if you don't want to. I can stop there on my way and tell her you haven't changed your mind."

She would always stand up for me if I asked her to, but in this case, I needed to do it myself. "No, don't worry. I'll take care of it myself. Enjoy your breakfast."

We gave each other a quick kiss before Eve left and I got dressed in some casual clothes that would work until I needed to change for the wedding. Outside my mother's hotel room door, I took a deep breath to compose myself before knocking sharply.

"Bonjour," my mom greeted me as she opened the door. Her hand tapped against her thigh, a little nervous tic she'd always had, but that was the only sign she gave me that she felt any trepidation about seeing me after the way she'd stormed out of dinner the night before. Otherwise, she actually looked rather relaxed. Certainly the happiest I'd seen her since she arrived, and she even wore a dress that would be nice enough for the wedding, as if she were actually planning to come.

What had I missed?

"Come in," she invited me in French, gesturing towards the small table in her room. Although everyone else had booked suites for their stay, my mom had insisted on taking a regular double room and paying for it herself, even though the Stamers paid for everyone else. "Do you want some coffee?"

"Non, Maman. I didn't come here for coffee. You said you wanted to talk, so let's talk. If you're just going to repeat what you said last night..."

"I'm not," she interrupted, gesturing again to the table. "Sit down, Julien. Please."

Reluctantly, I lowered myself into one of the plush, soft chairs. I still had no idea where this conversation might be headed, and if I needed to leave in the middle of it, I would. She wouldn't ruin this day for me; I wouldn't allow it.

As soon as she sat down opposite me, she dove in. "I owe you an apology."

No words could have surprised me more, and I couldn't be entirely sure they weren't a trap. "Okay?"

My obvious suspicion made her smile. "I know, it's out of character, but I mean it. I'm sorry for last night, and I would really like to be there for your wedding."

Those were all the right words, but I still didn't entirely trust them. "If this is a ploy so you can come and make a scene during the ceremony..."

She cut me off again. "It's not. Mon Dieu, is that really what you think of me?"

"What else should I think? You've been acting like a spoiled child. If I had ever behaved this way growing up, you'd have grounded me for a month."

Again, she didn't argue. "I know. I see that now."

What could have inspired such a complete turnaround? Only one thing came to mind. "Did you speak with Mr and Mrs Hanmer last night?"

She nodded slowly. "I did, and they were very nice, but nothing they did or said changed my mind."

"What did, then?"

Something had to have happened. A near-death experience, maybe? Had she been visited by three ghosts like Ebenezer Scrooge? Maybe it was a Christmas miracle.

"I met someone. A man." She blushed on the last word, and my jaw nearly dropped. I couldn't remember my mother ever blushing over a man before. I couldn't remember her ever dating for that matter, either. "I told him about my situation and he told me about his. In particular, he told me about how he lost touch with his children because winning the blame battle against his ex-wife was more important to him than making sure they were happy. He hasn't seen them in years. I don't want that to be us, Julien."

Finally. I had been trying to make that point for her for ages.

"It doesn't have to be. That's what I've been trying to tell you, Maman: there is no winning or losing here. We all know that my father made a mistake. We also know that you were wrong not to let him into my life, which you seem to have forgotten. But either way, the past is the past, and I don't care who was right or wrong then. I care about now, and the future. I want my child to grow up surrounded by love from as many people as possible, and I don't want them to ever feel that any argument was more important than that."

I could have been speaking theoretically when I mentioned my child, but the baby already growing inside Eve was top of my mind, and somehow, my mother seemed to pick up on that.

"Do you mean... is Eve... are you having a baby?"

Tabarnak. I really *couldn't* keep a secret. It seemed pointless to lie about it, especially with the genuine joy that lit up my mother's face. It made her look ten years younger. "We haven't told everyone yet, but yes. We just found out."

"Oh, Julien. Congratulations." She leapt from her chair to hug me, and though I appreciated her enthusiasm, I still didn't entirely trust her new outlook.

"Julian will be the baby's grandfather. He will be in the baby's life too. Are you going to be able to accept that?"

My mom took a deep, cleansing breath as she stepped back and gave me a firm nod. "Yes. I will find a way to make peace with it, for you and for the baby."

Really? Just like that? "It must have been some date."

Her cheeks flushed again as she sat back down. "It's been a long time since I felt truly wanted by anyone. You're grown now, starting a family of your own, you don't need me anymore. But he made me see that I'm not quite dead yet."

We were veering uncomfortably close to talking about my mother's sex life, which neither of us wanted. "I'm glad that you had a good time," I said to steer us back on course.

She had one more surprise for me. "Would it be okay if he comes to the wedding? He doesn't need to join us for dinner or anything, but..."

I had no idea if there would be enough food, but if it would keep her this happy, I would cook for him myself. "I'm sure we can figure something out. I'm glad you changed your mind."

"I am too. And I'm happy that you and Eve found each other. Finding the perfect partner in life isn't guaranteed."

No, it wasn't, but I knew without a doubt that I had. And now, I felt more confident than ever that our marriage would get the start it deserved, with all of our family there to celebrate it with us.

~Noelle~

Eve swept into the restaurant where I'd booked us a table for breakfast, looking impossibly fresh and relaxed for a bride on the morning of her wedding. At *my* wedding, I'd been such a mess, worried that everything would go wrong and people wouldn't have a good time, that Eve practically erected a protective barrier around me to stop any negativity from getting through. I thought I could do the same for her with this breakfast, but it didn't look like she needed it. She had everything under control, as usual.

"The hair and makeup people Tessa hired aren't going to have anything to do when they get here," I teased her as she took a seat opposite me. "You already look amazing."

Eve rolled her eyes before giving me a teasing smile. "I thought you'd already be in your dress, just in case the world ends and you don't have time to change."

"Actually, I started to put it on but Aaron convinced me that I might spill something on it, so I should wait."

"Seriously?" Eve's lips twitched, not sure whether to believe me or not, and I shrugged in what I hoped was an enigmatic way.

"I guess you'll never know for sure."

I'd missed these little moments with her. After growing up together and four years of being college roommates, it had been a shock to my system when she spent a year abroad volunteering, and most of the next year after that travelling the world with Julien for their new charity. I couldn't be prouder of her, but at the same time, I missed my best friend. Her pregnancy news had given me hope that they might be returning to New York more permanently, but she hadn't said anything about it yet. I barely even knew the guy she was about to marry. I knew him through her, but Julien and I hadn't spent all that much time together, and I wanted to know him. Anyone important to Eve was important to me too.

I wanted to ask her about all of that, and I wanted to ask what happened with Noah the night before, since I hadn't heard anything from Olivia, but all of that fell by the wayside when the waitress finished taking our order and Eve let out an uncharacteristic sigh that immediately had my best-friend intuition buzzing.

"What's wrong?"

She winced, obviously not having meant to give anything away, but she answered my question anyway. "Julien's going to talk to his mom.

I don't really want to go nuclear on my mother-in-law on our wedding day, but if she upsets him, so help me..."

My hand shot out to take hers before she could get any more worked up. "Maybe she's realized her mistake and is apologizing. It's possible, right?"

Eve arched an eyebrow at me. "Possible? Sure. A one percent chance of anything is 'possible'."

Her sarcasm made me smile, but with her next sentence, my mouth dropped open.

"Do you want to know something weird though? She was at Paradise last night."

My hand returned to my side of the table as I leaned forward, lowering my voice to a whisper. "What? His *mom* was at the sex club?"

Eve's eyes twinkled, knowing she had my full attention. "That's not all. Your parents were there too."

She *had* to be pulling my leg. "No way. Everyone knows not to tell my dad about it. And even if he knew, they'd never go!"

Eve shrugged, trying not to smile. "I don't know what to tell you, but they were there. Your dad even talked to us. It was definitely him."

That was way too much information for me to process. "He doesn't know I went there, does he?"

"I don't think so, but I have bad news for you, Noelle: when he finds out you're pregnant, he might figure out that you and Aaron actually have sex!"

"Smartass." I picked up one of the rolls from the basket in the centre of the table and threw it at her just as the waitress appeared with our drinks. Eve and I managed to keep our laughter in until she walked away, but as soon as she had gone out of earshot, we completely lost our composure, giggling so hard that the other diners in the restaurant all sent curious glances our way.

"This is exactly how I wanted to spend my wedding day," she told me when we finally got ourselves under control. "I'm so glad you're here, Noelle."

The rest of our breakfast flew by as we gossiped and laughed together, and before I could realize how much time had passed, Tessa appeared at our table. "I heard I could find you here, Eve. Are you ready to get ready for your big day?"

"Ready as I'll ever be, I guess." Eve shot me a grin that was 99% excitement and only a tiny touch of nerves. "Are you coming with me?"

"Always."

We headed to Tessa's suite which had been turned into Wedding Central for the day. Gemma, Olivia and my mom were already there, and we all had our hair done before digging into the brunch that Tessa had delivered to the room.

"We all know why Eve's glowing today, but what's your excuse?" Olivia teased Tessa as we all sat around drinking the champagne and grape juice Tessa had arranged for us. "Is there a man we don't know about?"

"December is the best time of the year to fall in love," our mom added, and none of us in the room could disagree with that.

"Today's about Eve and Julien," Tessa tried to deflect, but we weren't having it.

"I love to hear a good love story," Eve encouraged her. "Or even just a lustful one. It's all good."

With a little more cajoling, Tessa gave in. "Alright, fine. There's a man. We actually met a long time ago, back when Liv and I went to Austria for Christmas."

Olivia's dramatic gasp made us all jump. "Is it Ken?"

"Wait, who's Ken?" I felt lost already.

"A guy that she hooked up with in Vienna," Olivia explained. "They were going to try to keep in touch…"

"… but long-distance sucks," Tessa finished for her. "So, we decided to just be friends. He actually got married a few years ago. When I found out we were coming here, I sent him a message just to see if he still lived in the area, and it turned out he and his wife recently divorced. He came to visit last night, and let's just say… the chemistry is still there."

Squeals filled the room as we pressed her for more details. The chatter got so loud that no one else seemed to hear the knock at the door besides me. When I got up to answer it, I was surprised to find Julien's mom on the other side.

"Oh, hello."

My greeting got everyone else's attention, and the happy buzz died down as everyone waited warily to see what Madame Labrecque wanted.

"Hello," she said, her eyes scanning the room quickly before landing on Eve. "I hope it's okay that I came. Julien said you arranged for stylist help for me too?"

As the mother of the groom, she'd certainly been invited, but after everything that went on the last few days, none of us had expected her to turn up. We all turned to Eve, ready to back up her response, no matter what she said. She would be well within her rights to send her away, but Eve had never been the type to hold a grudge.

"Come in," Eve invited her instead, as gracious as ever. "The stylists are just having a lunch break and so are we. As soon as they get back, you'll be first in line."

With a grateful smile, Emilie came inside, taking a seat next to my mom, and I exhaled in relief as I closed the door again. It looked like Eve wouldn't have to do any ass-kicking after all. Hopefully, the entire day would be just as perfect as she deserved.

~Eve~

Just before Tessa confiscated my phone, telling me nothing on it could be more important than enjoying each moment of my wedding day, I saw the text Julien sent me.

My mom promises to be on her best behaviour. If she reaches out to you, will you give her a chance?

I could hardly say no to the one request he made of me on that day, so when Emilie showed up at the door, I gave her the benefit of the doubt, just as he asked me to.

"Everything's set for your guest today, Madame Labrecque," Tessa told her as she got settled between my mom and Holly. "The kitchen said they always prepare a few extra meals, just in case, so it's not a problem."

"Your guest?" I repeated. "What guest?"

As everyone turned to her, Emilie's cheeks flushed. "Someone I met here. I don't know him very well yet, but I thought it would be more fun than going alone."

Someone she met 'here'? Did she mean at the club the night before? My eyes connected with Holly's over Emilie's head, and her lips curled into a knowing smile that told me she had the same thought I did. It seemed Paradise was a gift that kept on giving.

"Alright, everyone into your dresses!" Tessa announced when the last of the lunch had been eaten. "Makeup is last. We're on schedule so far so let's keep it moving."

She walked past me to go speak to the stylists who were just returning, but I reached out to touch her arm as she went by. "You're doing an amazing job, Tessa. Thank you for taking this on."

"Thank you for paying to bring me out here," she replied with a laugh, leaning closer to me with a conspiratorial wink. "I downplayed it before, but last night at Paradise? Best sex of my life!"

I choked back a laugh as she moved on. Yes, that club had definitely made the trip worthwhile.

Gemma, Holly and Emilie went into one room with their dresses while Noelle, Olivia and I went into the other bedroom. Olivia had chosen an understated dress with an off-white bodice and a deep green skirt, while Noelle, as maid of honour, wore a fern green dress that draped over one shoulder and cinched in at her waist. My mom had a green printed floral dress, and Holly had chosen a light green one with a lace top. Aside from telling them the colour I wanted, I'd left it to them to choose their own styles, and the various shades of green would look wonderful on the beach.

My own dress, I let Julien choose. He was the only person I cared about impressing that day, so once I had narrowed it down to a choice between four, he got to make the final decision. It seemed fair to me, since I chose everything about his outfit for the day, down to the corset masquerading as a waistcoat, and even the butt plug he'd promised to wear.

The winning dress was sleeveless and fitted, a light satin with a sweetheart neckline and a lace overlay that wrapped over my shoulders. Noelle zipped me up, and when I turned around, she and Olivia both squealed in that way that only seemed to happen around wedding dresses.

"It's stunning," Olivia declared.

"Julien's the luckiest man alive," Noelle added, exaggerating my virtues, as usual. "And nobody who saw you in that dress would ever guess you're pregnant. It fits you perfectly."

In her excitement, she must have forgotten that my pregnancy wasn't public knowledge yet. I'd hoped to give Olivia the news a little more gently after our conversation the day before, and as my eyes flew to her, she took a step back, swallowing hard. "You are?"

Instantly, Noelle realized her mistake. "Oh, shit. Damn it. I'm so sorry, Eve, I didn't mean to share your news."

Knowing she would beat herself up for it all day if I let her, I did my best to reassure her. Besides, my feelings weren't the ones I cared about at that moment. "It's okay, Noelle. Honestly. I'm not upset. Olivia, I'm sorry we didn't tell you, it just didn't feel like the right time..."

She cut me off, putting on a brave smile. "I understand. Congratulations, Eve. That's wonderful."

As much as I tried to return her smile, seeing her put her own pain aside to try to be happy for me brought tears to my eyes, and Noelle looked back and forth between us, utterly bewildered but trying to put the pieces together. "What's wrong?"

Olivia reached for her sister's hand. "I was going to tell you tonight, after the wedding. Mom and Dad already know. Noah and I don't seem to be able to conceive. We've been trying for a long time, and it's just not happening."

Noelle's face went so pale, I thought she might pass out. Olivia obviously saw it too, and hurried her story along.

"It's okay, though. We actually had a meeting this morning with some kids who need a family. We're going to be flying out tomorrow to meet with them in person."

"You are?" That part, I didn't know.

"Noah's not very patient sometimes," she said, her eyes crinkling as she smiled. "But yeah, hopefully, things will go well and we'll be able to adopt them. You might be an aunt by the end of the week, Noelle."

"You will be too," Noelle blurted out, and as she realized what she said, the colour began to return to her face, flushing it red instead. "I mean, not by the end of this week. But soon. I'm pregnant too. I'm sorry, I didn't know..."

Olivia threw her arms around her sister, pulling her tight. "What are you sorry for? That's amazing. Congratulations, Noelle."

By that point, we were all in tears, and I joined in the hug, unable to stay away.

"I'm happy for you both, I really am," Olivia sniffed. "I'm happy for us too. It's just... you can be happy and sad at the same time, you know?"

I did know. I felt just the same for them, and every time we helped those we could but couldn't help them all.

"What is going on here?!"

We all pulled apart to find Tessa in the doorway, her hands on her hips and her head cocked in disapproval as she surveyed our red eyes and tear-streaked faces.

"All of you to the makeup chairs, now! No more tears."

Ignoring her, the three of us shared one more hug. "It all changes from here, doesn't it?" I whispered to them.

"It does, but there are wonderful things still coming," Olivia told us. "For all of us."

"For all of us," Noelle confirmed. "I love you guys."

"Love each other later," Tessa interrupted again, pulling us physically apart that time. "Eve, you don't want your husband-to-be thinking you've got cold feet when you turn up late, do you?"

Julien would never believe that, but I let Tessa pull me away anyway. The love of my life would be waiting for me at the end of the aisle, and I had no intention of keeping him waiting.

Chapter Fourteen

TO HAVE AND TO HOLD

~**Aaron**~

My heart skipped a beat as I got my first glimpse of Noelle in her bridesmaid's dress when she walked into the hotel lobby, just before we all headed outside for the wedding. She always looked beautiful to me, even on the days we hung around in sweatpants in our apartment, her reading on the couch and me messing around on my computer. In fact, those days were some of my favourites, and though I knew we'd have a lot fewer of those quiet times once the baby arrived, I couldn't wait for the next stage of our lives too.

However, as much as I loved those moments with her, seeing her all dressed up reminded me of just how stunning she truly was. How I'd gotten lucky enough to be the one by her side still felt like a miracle sometimes, even three years after we first got together.

Those happy thoughts all flew out of my head when she came over to me with tears sitting in the corner of her eyes.

My hands immediately went to her face, cradling her jaw while trying not to mess up her makeup. "Hey. What's wrong?"

"I'm such an idiot. Why can't I just keep my mouth shut?"

It had been a long time since I'd heard her so down on herself. Often, I'd give her a stern reprimand for saying anything like that, but that didn't seem to be what she needed at that moment. She looked fragile, on the edge of breaking, and I wouldn't be the one to tip her over that edge.

"Tell me what happened."

Between shaky gulps of air, Noelle relayed the conversation she had with Eve and Olivia. "I had no idea what Olivia and Noah were going through. Julien said yesterday that he thought they might also be pregnant, but I wasn't going to say anything until she did. I didn't mean to say anything about Eve's pregnancy at all."

The tears welled up again, threatening to spill over and streak her mascara down her beautiful face. "You had no way of knowing," I pointed out gently. The news surprised me too. I'd spent a lot of time with Noah over the past three years, both in and out of the office, and I'd never had an inkling that he ever struggled with *anything*, to be quite honest. "And you were excited and trying to be supportive. Both Eve and Olivia know that. They know *you,* and they know you don't have a malicious bone in your body."

"Eve did say she wasn't upset with me," Noelle admitted, trying her best to blink the tears away.

"And Olivia isn't either," I added, in case she hadn't already figured that out. Noelle's sister adored her; I knew that for a fact. "Any sadness she's experiencing is *not* because of you."

Noelle nodded, wanting to believe me, so I threw a challenge in there for her too, knowing she could never resist one.

"She'll need your support as they go through the adoption process, and especially once they come home. You've already been doing research about programs in the city for kids and everything you need to know about raising a child in New York."

A spark of hope brightened Noelle's sweet blue eyes. "That's true. I've got all kinds of information put together that we won't need for years, but it might be useful to them sooner."

"And what you need to do right now is forget about all of it and be there for Eve. You can do that, right?"

"Yeah. I can." Her sweet smile looked much more like herself, and I threw in the words I knew would seal the deal.

"That's my girl."

The flush in her cheeks had my body heating up too, but we were both quickly pulled back into the moment as Tessa appeared. "Time to move outside, everyone. Aaron, you're needed with the groom. Noelle, you're with me."

I gave her a quick peck on the cheek so I didn't mess up her lipstick before the ceremony, but I had every intention of messing it up later that night.

Outside, it took me all of two seconds to spot the location for the wedding, and as I made my way over, my appreciation for Tessa's planning skills increased tenfold. It looked absolutely stunning. A soft white carpet had been laid out to form the aisle, bordered by flowering plants in pots, both to be sustainable and to match Eve's green colour scheme. A large canopy of gauzy material provided just enough shade from the hot December sun while still letting the light through. The ocean provided a stunning backdrop.

Beneath the canopy, Julien and Noah were already waiting. Most of the rest of the small guest list had already gathered too. I gave Corey and the Ribars a wave and Noelle's parents a smile as I walked past them to join Julien at the front. Noah was the best man, with Noelle the maid of honour, and Olivia and I were the extra bridesmaid and groomsman.

Just a few minutes later, soft music began to play from Bluetooth speakers I hadn't even noticed half-buried in the sand, and the remainder of the wedding party started to walk in.

First, the two mothers walked in together, side-by-side. Julien had told us over brunch that his mother had decided to attend after all, and she hardly looked like the same woman who'd been making such a fuss all week. Her hair had been elegantly styled, makeup freshened her face, and making the biggest change of all, she was actually smiling. Upon reaching the front, she and Gemma gave each other a kiss on each cheek before Gemma sat down on the left side of the aisle and Emilie on the right, next to a man I'd never seen before.

Olivia walked in next, and I couldn't help glancing over at Noah to see his reaction. He and his father both had the same poker face, but I'd started to learn their tells. The tensing muscles in his cheeks gave away how hard his jaw clenched, trying to keep from reacting, but his eyes were the dead giveaway. They stayed glued to his wife the whole time, full of appreciation.

Noelle came next, and even though I'd just seen her, she seemed to sparkle even more in the bright sunshine. Rays of light danced around her, reflected off her jewelry and especially off the ring on her finger that told the whole world she belonged to me. When she took her spot at the front next to Olivia, she smiled over at me, looking much more confident than she had a few minutes earlier, and my heart swelled with pride.

Last, but by no means least, the music subtly changed to the traditional wedding march as Eve appeared. Holding her father's arm, her red hair glinted in the sun. Her white dress made a perfect contrast to the greenery around her and the warm beige sand, and her dark eyes were fixed on the man at the end of the aisle. When I glanced back at Julien, he looked overwhelmed in a way I definitely recognized. I'd felt just the same when I saw Noelle on our wedding day, and had been just as certain as he looked that nothing in the world would ever be better than that moment.

~Jackson~

I always loved weddings. Full of hope and promise, the love and joy of the couple shared with all those close to them, I couldn't imagine anything better, and when the happy day belonged to a young woman who was practically a daughter to me, it meant even more. Eve might have been the last to get married, but as she took her place next to Julien at the front, her hand over his rather than the other way around, it couldn't be more obvious that the wait had been worth it. She'd found her perfect match, just as I'd been lucky enough to do.

Cole stepped into the row directly in front of me after giving his daughter away, and though I knew my friend well enough to know that he wouldn't let emotion get the better of him, I also knew he had to be feeling it. After the emotional morning with Noah and Olivia and now seeing Eve and Julien looking so radiantly happy together, I'd bet anything his feelings were running high in his own way.

I therefore reached out to put my hand on his shoulder in support, and though he didn't turn back, he did place his hand on mine for a second to acknowledge it which, coming from him, counted as a pretty big show of affection.

It really didn't seem all that long ago that he and I were the ones standing up in front of a crowd to marry the extraordinary women beside us. Vivid memories played across my mind as Eve, looking so much like her mom, pledged her love to Julien, for better or for worse. It wouldn't always be easy, I thought, glancing at Olivia on one side of the happy couple and Noah on the other, but any challenges ahead would be easier to face when faced together.

Eve smiled up at Julien beneath the canopy as she made her vows. "Pretty much any way you want to measure it, I've been lucky in life. But the luckiest break of all had to be the one when I ended up sitting next to you at a bar thousands of miles away from home for both of us. If we hadn't met then, I would have left my meeting with you the next day never knowing I sat across from the man who would complete me in every possible way. You keep me positive when I'm overwhelmed, you keep me grounded when my head's in the clouds, and you challenge me every day to think about things in different ways. This past year with you has been many different things, but one thing it's never been is boring. I love you, Julien, and I want the whole world to know it."

Gentle laughter rippled through the audience at Eve's blunt conclusion, and she slid a ring onto Julien's finger before he took his turn.

"I didn't know if I would ever get married," he began, his eyes fixed on her as if she were the only one who could hear him. "My perfect woman didn't seem to exist, but that night in Quito, I realized that she most certainly did. I just hadn't met her yet. Even then, I nearly messed it all up, pushing you away because I thought our differences were too great. What I almost missed is that our differences are only on the surface. Deep down, you are everything I will ever need, and everything I want. My heart is yours, and my body and soul too. Yours to command, and it will be my privilege to get to love you for the rest of my life."

Gemma dabbed at her eyes as Julien put Eve's ring on her.

The minister looked out over the rest of us and asked for our approval in the most succinct way possible. "Any objections?"

Every eye under the canopy moved to Emilie, intentionally or not, but she simply jutted her chin forward and kept her mouth shut, to everyone's relief.

"In that case, I now pronounce you husband and wife. You can kiss the…"

Before he even finished the sentence, Eve reached up and pulled Julien's head down towards her, making it abundantly clear who was kissing who.

Following the ceremony, there were pictures to be taken, but Holly and I were only needed for the group one. We left Olivia and Noelle with the Stamer family and joined the Ribars back inside the air-conditioned hotel. Even in the more casual clothes that Eve and Julien had suggested for the day, the cool air came as a relief from the heat of the sun.

"That was lovely," Michelle Ribar sighed, and the rest of us murmured our agreement.

"A beautiful wedding," a new voice chimed in, and we all looked over curiously as Emilie's guest joined us. "Didn't seem right for me to be in the photos since I just met the bride and groom today, so I thought I'd wait in here with all of you until Emilie's done. Name's Anthony."

I hadn't gotten a very good look at him in the club the night before, and in the light of day, he looked a lot younger than I remembered. He had to be a good ten years younger than me, I'd guess, but he certainly didn't seem to lack any confidence, and I quickly stuck my hand out to ease over any awkwardness. "Jackson Hanmer. Nice to meet you."

"Are you Julien's father?" he asked, eyeing me up and down, as if sizing up the competition.

"That would be me," Julian interjected. "How do you know Emilie?"

"We just met. I don't know her very well," Anthony admitted. "But I'm hoping to change that."

He wandered off to the bar to get a drink while Holly chuckled beside me. "He seems like the kind of man to say exactly what he thinks. I like him already."

We got a chance to chat with Anthony more over dinner. He and Emilie sat next to us, with Gemma and Cole beside them, along one side of a large horseshoe-shaped table. The Ribars were across from us, and the wedding party took up the central part of the semi-circle. Everyone looked relaxed and happy now that the main event had been concluded and there were no more worries about Madame Labrecque causing a scene.

If there would be any scene at all, it would be because Emilie and Anthony didn't seem to be able to keep their hands off each other, acting more like two teenagers than part of the older generation.

"It's a shame that you live half a world apart," Holly pointed out, not-so-subtly.

"Not for long," Anthony corrected her. "I'm heading to Whistler to work for the rest of the ski season just after New Year's."

"That's closer, but still not all that close," Holly countered. "Quebec's on the other side of the country."

"I have been thinking about retiring anyway," Emilie told us. "Maybe this is a sign that I should. With Julien travelling the world anyway, there's nothing to keep me there."

When she decided to move on, she certainly didn't waste any time. I could have said they seemed to be moving awfully fast, but as I just told Noah that morning, sometimes you needed to take a leap. Emilie had been waiting a very long time to feel a romantic spark again. Maybe it would be worth seeing where it went.

Noelle gave a sweet toast to the newlyweds, and Cole and Gemma added one of their own as the meal came to an end. When everyone who wanted to have their say had done so, Eve stood up to make a toast of her own.

"Thank you all for being here. It means the world to me and Julien that you would come all this way to celebrate with us. There will be drinks served for as long as you want to stay and visit tonight, but I know that Noah and Olivia want an early night, and honestly, I do too. Getting married is hard work!"

Indulgent laughs echoed around the room as Julien took his new wife's hand, his eyes gleaming with pride.

"However, before we go, we have a suggestion for how you all spend your evening once you're finished here."

Eve's dark eyes twinkled with mischief as two waiters walked in with trays full of cocktails that looked suspiciously similar to the ones we'd had at Paradise the night before, and set them down on the table next to her.

"You all know about the club here on the hotel grounds. I know you all know, because every single one of you has been there."

Several startled faces turned towards me as Holly stifled a giggle. "You've shocked them all, Jackson."

Apparently so, but I still had no idea what Eve had up her sleeve.

"These are some of the club's seasonal cocktails," she explained, gesturing at the drinks, which I could now see had little cards attached to the base of the cocktail glasses. "Each pair of drinks is associated with a particular type of activity. If you're feeling adventurous, you can take one of them at random, and try exploring it with your partner. A little eggnog experiment, to make a memorable night even more memorable."

Everyone glanced around the room, some more nervously than others, to see what everyone else thought.

"I'm game," Tate offered first to break the silence. Getting to his feet, he went over and picked one of the sets of drinks at random, taking them back to his seat and offering one to Crystal Ribar. While everyone watched, he opened the attached card and read it before taking a long sip of the drink. "Delicious."

Not to be outdone, Cole, Noah, and Corey got up at almost the same time, and Holly turned to me. "What do you think?"

"I think it's a bit weird they're turning their wedding reception into a sex party," I replied honestly.

Holly's giggle made me smile too. "Hardly. It's just a suggestion, a bit of fun. Nothing says we *have* to do it, but I guess it couldn't hurt to see what it says. Think of it as a fortune cookie."

She seemed to be on board, and if I didn't move soon, we wouldn't have much of a choice at all. I arrived at the drinks at the same time Aaron did, and we both avoided looking at each other while we picked our glasses. I did *not* need to know what his and Noelle's card said.

When everyone had their drinks, Eve and Julien picked up the last pair and held them up in one last toast. "To a great night," Eve said, and after taking a sip, they left the room together, taking their drinks with them, ready for their wedding night ahead.

Chapter Fifteen

PRIMAL

~**Cole**~

Leave it to Eve to find a way to spice up her wedding reception. The apple certainly didn't fall far from the tree when it came to my kids, and I couldn't be prouder of them for living the lives they wanted, unapologetically, and finding their perfect partners to share that life with.

It had certainly worked out well for me.

Aside from my pride, the more I thought about it, the more the cocktail idea appealed to me on its own merits. It never hurt to be open to new experiences, so long as it didn't involve sharing my gorgeous wife with anyone else. I drew the line there, but pretty much everything else would be fair game. The bigger question was whether or not it would actually be something we hadn't tried before.

Actually, the biggest question of all was how Jackson ended up at Paradise, but when I asked him about it when he returned to his seat with his own drinks, he refused to answer.

"You wanted to keep it a secret, so that's what it'll be."

He looked far too pleased with himself as he took a sip from his drink.

"And you're actually going to do whatever that cocktail suggests?"

"That's for me to know and you to wonder about. Forever." Jackson spread his hands to indicate the entire eternity of time, as if he were on some damned science documentary.

"Leave him alone, Cole," Gemma admonished me when I opened my mouth to say something else. She and Holly exchanged indulgent smiles before she turned to me again. "Not everything is a competition."

I supposed so. Especially since I already had everything I wanted right next to me, wearing a floral dress that highlighted every perfect curve of her body, just as beautiful to me as the night we'd met.

With that in mind, I turned my full attention to my wife. "Do you want to see what this says now, or wait until we go back to our room?" I asked her, indicating the card attached to our cocktail glasses. "Do you prefer the anticipation or the surprise?"

"Surprise me," she murmured, her green eyes twinkling in that fucking irresistible way they always did when she got turned on. "But you can peek if you want."

I definitely did want to. Knowing what it said ahead of time would give me a chance to decide how we would implement it, and I always liked to have a plan. Gemma knew that about me, and she knew how her submission in leaving all the details up to me would affect me.

She always gave me exactly what I needed.

With a sharp tug, I pulled the card off its string and broke the seal, opening it just a crack to get a look at the contents without letting any-one else see. Written in a fancy, handwritten script were three simple words.

Predator and prey.

Taking care to ensure that my expression didn't alter, giving nothing away, I tucked the card safely into my pocket and took a drink from the cocktail, my mind already racing with ideas. Though I hadn't expected that, I could definitely work with it.

Gemma shifted in her seat, her eyes studying me closely. Though she didn't out-and-out ask me what it said, she did ask for a hint. "Will I like it?"

I answered that with an arch of my eyebrow. "I'm willing to do it. Have I ever done anything you wouldn't like?"

"Never."

Her heated smile had anticipation racing through me even stronger than before, and the longer we stayed chatting with our friends, the harder it became to concentrate. Other couples began to leave, taking their cocktails with them, and soon, I couldn't take it any longer.

"It's been a long day for all of us. We're going to call it a night."

My excuse fooled absolutely no one. "Have fun," Holly said, giving Gemma a wink.

"You too," Gemma replied, though neither Jackson nor Holly had opened their card yet. I still couldn't be sure if they actually intended to do anything with it, but I also no longer cared. Much more interesting thoughts claimed my attention.

As soon as we were out of the reception room and into the empty hallway outside, I backed Gemma against the wall, boxing her in as desire and excitement raced through my body. "Are you ready to find out what the card says?"

Gemma nodded, licking her lips as she kept her eyes on me. From my pocket, I drew the card out and held it up so she could read it. Confusion flashed across her face, but only for a second before being replaced by the same anticipation I felt. "How are we doing this?"

As usual, she wanted my instruction, and I would always be happy to provide it for her. "You're going to hide somewhere in the hotel. No going outside, and not to our room either. Somewhere that anyone could go. I'll have fifteen minutes to find you. If I do, I get to fuck you wherever you are."

A shiver ran down her spine, goosebumps sprouting down her bare arms. "And if you don't find me?"

"I will."

She didn't press me for any further answer, knowing as well as I did how we both wanted this to go.

"I'll give you a two-minute head start."

Finally, I stepped back, freeing her as I pulled my phone from my pocket and set the timer for fifteen minutes. Looking up to catch her eye, I pressed the start button.

"Don't waste time, Gorgeous. I'll be coming for you, and soon, you'll be coming for me."

~Gemma~

Other people might not have been able to tell, but I knew when Cole opened the card back at the table that he liked what he saw. Subtle signs I'd learned to read a long time ago appeared: a slight tilt of his head, a pressing together of his fingers. Nothing overt, nothing that would seem out of the ordinary to anyone but the woman who had spent the last thirty years with him. And when he showed me the card, I immediately understood what caused his reaction.

In all our years together, we'd never done anything quite like this.

The idea of him *hunting* me sent a spike of adrenaline rushing through my body that made me feel much younger, and when he started the timer and told me to go, I obeyed without question, even though I had no idea where I planned to go yet.

Maybe it would be better that way. I might throw him off if I went in a random direction, with no plan. On the other hand, he'd promised to fuck me right where he found me, and if I happened to be standing in the lobby at the time, that might not go over so well with the other guests.

I would have to apply *some* logic to the situation.

The pool and the gym were out of the question; too public. The kitchen and other staff working areas were similarly off-limits. Smaller rooms sat off the reception room we'd just been in for the wedding, but some of the other guests were still in there, and I didn't want to arouse any suspicions about what we were doing. My list of available locations continued to dwindle, and the clock kept ticking down, making my head-start smaller and smaller as I tried to make a decision.

Think, Gemma. You're an architect. You know a hotel has tons of hidden public spaces.

At last, my brain kicked in over the insistent pulse of my libido, and a flash of inspiration hit me. *The wine room.* A hotel of this quality had excellent wine, and they'd have a special, temperature-controlled room to keep it in. Often, it had plenty of nooks and crannies in it, and sometimes even a separate room for the most expensive wines. With dinner still being served, it would probably be unlocked, and though the staff might access it, there wouldn't be a continuous flow of people.

It seemed worth a shot, at the very least.

Smoothing my dress, as if the agitation I felt inside had somehow manifested itself in my clothing, I did my best to look completely unbothered as I walked into the hotel's main dining room.

"Good evening, Mrs Stamer." The hostess gave me a warm smile, recognizing me from the previous evenings that we'd dined in the restaurant. "Are you meeting someone?"

"No, thank you. I just need to use the ladies' room to freshen up, if that's alright."

On a previous visit, I had noticed the toilets were down the same hall that the staff used to access the kitchen. It made sense that the wine room would also be along that same hallway.

If the hostess wondered why I didn't just go to my room, she covered it well. "Yes, of course. Let me know if there's anything you need."

Asking for her to lie about my whereabouts if Cole came in would probably be a step too far, so I simply thanked her and headed to the hallway. Besides the entrance to the kitchen, there were three doors marked 'staff only', and I peered quickly into all three. The first led to a closet with cleaning supplies, the second to another closet with extra place settings and linens. The third opened onto a small staircase leading down, which looked far more promising. Ducking inside, I made my way down the stairs, my heart beating faster with each step. If someone caught me down there, what would I say to explain my presence?

At least for the moment, the coast was clear. The staircase led directly into the wine room, as I hoped. There wasn't even a door, other than the one at the top of the stairs. Dim lighting helped to keep the temperature down, as did being underground, and although it was far from cold, I shivered anyway simply from the change in temperature and the adrenaline still coursing through my body. The room had stacks like a library, shelves of wines sorted by country and age, and I chose the aisle with the most expensive champagnes, figuring they would be the least likely to be ordered on a regular basis.

Hopefully, no one in the dining room would be splurging that night.

Hidden from view behind the shelves, I took a deep breath, trying to bring my heart rate back under control as I checked my watch for the first time since I left Cole. It had taken me five minutes to get there. That meant I still had ten minutes to wait to see whether or not he would find me. No matter how much I pretended that I didn't want him to, the fire in my body suggested otherwise.

What I really wanted to know was exactly what he would do to me when he did.

~Cole~

Although I told Gemma I'd give her two minutes before I started looking for her, I actually gave her four. During that time, I ran through the hotel layout in my head, trying to determine, based on everything I knew about her, where she might go.

She'd avoid anywhere too public, taking me at my word when I promised to fuck her exactly where I found her. Over the years, we'd had several semi-public encounters, especially at work, the thrill of potentially being caught adding to the general excitement of the situation. However, neither of us were exhibitionists, so she would choose somewhere off the beaten path.

Nowhere where our friends or children might see us. Nothing as ordinary as a supply closet. Nothing unsanitary.

That only left me with a few options, and as the timer on my phone hit four minutes, I knew exactly where to start.

Despite the blood rushing through my veins in anticipation, I kept my pace measured and unhurried as I walked out of the hotel's events area, through the lobby, and into the dining room.

The hostess greeted me with a warm smile. "Good evening, Mr Stamer. Can I get a table for you and your wife?"

She'd seen Gemma already, then. It seemed I was on the right track. "No, thank you, but could I have a serving of apple crumble with custard delivered to my room in about twenty minutes?"

Gemma's favourite dessert would make a nice treat for her while she recovered from what I intended to do to her when I found her.

"Of course," the hostess agreed, and I walked away before she could say anything else, not bothering to explain myself any further as I headed towards the hallway to the kitchen. It took a few attempts to find the right door, but as I opened the one leading to a small staircase, I caught a hint of Gemma's perfume lingering in the air, and a satisfied smile tugged at the corners of my mouth.

It had only been six minutes since she left me, so there was no need for me to rush. I took the stairs slowly, letting my shoes land heavily on each one so she would hear me coming. I had her cornered, and I wanted her to know it.

Shelves of wine filled the room, and again, I could anticipate exactly where she'd be: near the back, so that if one of the wait staff came in, there'd be less chance she'd be discovered. Probably with the pricier wine that she thought would be ordered less often. I could have gone straight there, but I didn't, drawing out the anticipation a little bit longer as my dick swelled more with each step. I loved that she'd agreed to play this game with me. I loved that I knew her so well that I could find her that easily, and I loved that she obviously wanted to be found.

I loved every fucking thing about her, and I intended to show her that, the best way I knew how.

"There you are."

As I rounded the corner of the last shelf at the back, Gemma came into view, her body pressed into the corner as she tried, and failed, to camouflage herself in the dim light. Her cheeks flushed and her eyes bright, she'd never looked more appealing.

"You must have cheated," she complained, her voice breathy in a way that betrayed her arousal instantly. "Did you follow me? How did you find me so quickly?"

"I followed the clues you've given me over the last thirty years. I know you, Gemma, and I know exactly what you need right now."

With no further foreplay, knowing she didn't need it and knowing that we might still be discovered at any moment, I grabbed her shoulders and spun her around, placed her hands on the shelf just below her head to help support her, pulled up the skirt of her dress and pulled down her panties, exposing her gorgeous pussy to me. She shivered as I unzipped my pants, and after spitting roughly into my hand and rubbing it on my stiff cock to help ease my way, I thrust into her, claiming my prize.

~Gemma~

"Oh, fuck."

I tried to keep the words to a gasp, not wanting to be overheard as my husband kept his promise about what he'd do to me when he found me. Cole groaned as his hips pressed against my ass, his cock buried fully inside me.

"This is going to be quick and dirty, Gorgeous. Are you ready?"

"Yes," I breathed. *Fuck, yes.*

Cole's hands grabbed my arms, pulling them off the shelf and behind my back. With one hand, he secured my wrists there, and his other hand grabbed my hair, threading through it at the roots, a way of expressing his control without hurting me too much. Not any more than I wanted him to, anyway.

With me completely immobilized, Cole's hips began to move, his cock pulling out of me and driving back in again as he used my arms and hair to pull my body towards him. In each thrust, I tasted his desire, his possessiveness, his victory. He was the predator, and I, his willing prey. I would always, always let him catch me if this was my reward.

With the lust that had built up during the chase and the exquisite perfection of submitting to him, it didn't take long for my orgasm to start to build. Recognizing the signs, Cole thrust harder, slamming into me just the way I liked, but right as I approached the peak of my pleasure, the basement door opened again and we both immediately froze.

Fuck. In this position, there could be no way to hide what we were doing. Footsteps skipped down the stairs, their owner whistling cheerily, unaware of exactly what they were interrupting.

Cole's hand slipped from my hair to cover my mouth instead, muffling the sound of my breathing. My heart thudded as we both stood stock still, listening to each sound intently.

The footsteps came closer, and closer.

Just when I thought we were completely and utterly screwed, the person turned into the shelf just before us. I could hear the rattling of the bottle against the shelf as he pulled it down, and a moment later, the footsteps retreated, back up the stairs, and the door closed again, cutting off the whistled song mid-note.

"That was close," Cole whispered.

"*Too* close," I amended, my heart still pounding, and my body aching for release more than ever.

"We better finish this, then." His hand tightened over my mouth, covering my nose as well and cutting off my air as he resumed his thrusting. The lack of air made my body tighten, and combined with the thrill of nearly being caught and the feel of him filling me, my orgasm soon followed. The room around me disappeared as pleasure took me, blotting out everything else.

Cole released me as soon as I came, letting me breathe again, and his hands moved to my hips, gripping them hard as he fucked me even faster. He never let himself go until I had, but my orgasm always helped to draw his out, and after just a few more thrusts, I could feel him pumping into me as he muttered my name into the cool air.

No sooner had he finished than the door opened again, and that time, Cole quickly tucked himself back into his pants while I pulled my panties back up and my dress down. We had just finished arranging our clothes when a uniformed waiter appeared at the end of our row, exclaiming in surprise as he saw us there.

"What the fu... what are you doing here?" he gasped before making out our faces in the low light. "Mr and Mrs Stamer?"

"Good evening," Cole greeted him, coolly and calmly. "We were just taking a look at the hotel's wine offering. It's impressive."

"Thank you," the waiter replied, still sounding unsure. "Is there something I can help you with?"

"No, I think we're satisfied with what we've seen." Cole shot me a smirk before taking my hand. "Shall we?"

I gave the waiter a smile as Cole pulled me from the row, hoping my flushed cheeks wouldn't be too much of a giveaway. The poor man still looked confused, but since he wasn't about to accuse one of the world's richest men of trying to steal from the wine cellar, he let us pass unimpeded. When we reached the top of the steps, I let myself breathe out.

"I'm not sure I want to do that every day."

Cole smiled over at me, the look in his eyes softer than before. "I'm glad we did it, though. Now, how about a warm bath with some apple crumble and custard? It'll be waiting for us in the room."

"How did you..." I started to ask before realizing it truly didn't matter. Cole would always take care of me in his own way, and I truly loved him for it. "Never mind. Thank you."

"You're welcome, Gorgeous." His lips pressed against my forehead before he led me back out through the restaurant and back to our room, freshly fucked and just as in love with him as I had ever been.

Chapter Sixteen

Restrained

~Noelle~

The way Eve smiled at me when Aaron picked out our drinks concerned me. Did she already know what the card said? Did she think we were in over our heads? If it involved anything like the performance we'd seen at the club, I wouldn't be able to do it. What if it suggested involving another person? My thoughts quickly spun out of control, the whole thing putting me on edge, but since even my dad was taking part, we had to at least keep up appearances.

"What does it say?" I whispered to Aaron when he sat back down.

He smirked at me, his eyes twinkling behind his glasses. "I don't know yet. It's not written in braille, we need to open it first."

His teasing did nothing to calm the butterflies in my stomach. "What if it's something that isn't safe for the baby?"

Images of whips and chains crowded into my head while Aaron chuckled.

"Then we don't do it. But on that note, I asked Julien about the drinks: they're non-alcoholic, so go ahead."

I appreciated that, especially since my mouth had gone dry, and I took a long sip of the fruity eggnog mocktail to help bring some moisture back. Everyone else around us seemed excited as Eve and Julien said goodnight, but no matter how much I tried not to think about it, my thoughts kept returning to the little card attached to our drinks and what it might say.

Maybe I was more like my dad than I'd realized before. The idea of doing anything truly kinky kind of terrified me.

Gemma and Cole left the room first, followed shortly thereafter by the Ribars, including Tate and Crystal. Julien's mom and her date disappeared next, his hand on her ass as they walked out, leaving just the Hanmer family behind, along with Aaron and Noah.

"Go on, then. Don't let us stop you," my mom teased, but her eyes softened when she looked over at Liv. "Are you sure you don't want us to go with you tomorrow?"

Olivia nodded firmly. "I'm sure. We appreciate your support so much, but we need to do this on our own. Besides, it might not work out and we don't need to disrupt these children's lives any more than absolutely necessary."

"But on that note, we should go get some rest," Noah added, kissing Liv softly on the temple. "We'll let you know as soon as we have any news."

We all wished them a good night and good luck the next day, but though Noah said they were going to sleep, I noticed that he still took his glass and the attached card with him.

That left Aaron and I alone with my parents, and I quickly began to babble before things could get awkward. "That was a fun wedding, wasn't it? Eve looked so beautiful. I mean, of course she did, she always does, but even more than usual. And I'm glad Julien's mom came around. I think she forgot that Mr Ribar was here at all. I can't wait to see the pictures from outside. I thought I was going to melt, but I bet they'll look great."

My mom cut me off with an affectionate smile. "Noelle?"

"Yes?"

"Go to bed."

My cheeks flushed as I got to my feet. "Alright. Good night."

"Good night," Aaron added, grabbing our drinks to bring them along with us, which made my cheeks even redder.

"They totally know what we're going to do," I whispered to Aaron as we walked down the hall to our room.

"Actually, I think they were trying to get rid of us so they could go to bed too," he countered. "Can you open the door? My hands are full."

I managed to get the keycard out of my purse and let us into the room, my heart still racing at the idea of what the card might say. Aaron must have known it, because he handed my drink to me as soon as the door closed behind us.

"Put yourself out of your misery. See what it says."

My fingers shook as I pulled the small card from its envelope. One single word stared back at me, bold and unyielding.

Bondage.

~Aaron~

From the way Noelle's eyes widened, I knew that whatever the card said was outside of her comfort zone. And yet, I caught a spark of interest in her expression too. She didn't hate the idea, whatever it might be. She only felt uncertain about it, and as always, I would take it upon myself to make her more comfortable.

"What does it say?"

She flipped the card around to face me, and as I caught sight of the word, my tension eased too. That wasn't so bad. I'd been afraid it would be something so extreme that we wouldn't be able to participate, which would leave Noelle feeling like she'd failed. I understood her better than she understood herself sometimes, but bondage, we could work with. We'd even experimented with it a little bit before, though certainly not anything like the BDSM rooms we'd seen at the club. And we didn't *have* to go that far. We could adapt it to our own comfort level and make it fun for us.

Yes, it could definitely work.

"I guess the first thing we need to decide is who's tying up who."

I mean it as a joke, but the startled look in Noelle's eyes suggested she might actually have some interest in reversing the expected roles.

"Eve has told me a little bit about how she restrains Julien," she admitted, her cheeks a deep red but her eyes bright. "Some of it actually sounds kind of fun."

Well, now she definitely had me curious, and I had no objections to the basic premise. I could praise her just as well for tying me up as I could for allowing herself to be tied up, and as long as we kept that element of our usual dynamic, we would still have a good time.

"What do you tell her about *our* sex life?" I couldn't help wondering. If Eve shared those kinds of details, Noelle must reciprocate in kind.

"Only what I need to," she replied, flashing me a confident smile that had blood rushing to my dick. Now that she no longer feared the card, her sweet, sassy self was returning, and I found it just as irresistible as always.

I let that answer go, eager to move onto the more pertinent questions. "What are you going to tie me up with?"

We didn't have any handcuffs or rope or anything like that, but Noelle already had an answer in mind. "Eve says she uses neckties."

She pointed to the one around my neck at that moment, and I immediately pulled it off for her. Luckily, I had brought an extra one for the trip, just in case. I always liked to be prepared, and once I located it in the closet where I'd hung all my clothes neatly, I presented that one to Noelle too.

"Now what?"

Excitement lit up her beautiful face. "Now, you can take your clothes off and lie on the bed. Please."

A dominatrix, she would never be, but I obeyed anyway, simply because she asked so sweetly. My dick had already begun to swell with anticipation, and as Noelle leaned over me to tie my wrists to the headboard, her breasts hanging over my face in her pretty bridesmaid's dress, I counted myself very lucky indeed.

"You should keep that dress on while you fuck me. You look incredible in it."

Her cheeks flushed at the compliment, the praise affecting her as it always did. It took her a few tries to get the knot to stay, but eventually, I was restrained. Sort of. If I tugged hard enough, I could probably pull myself loose, but I didn't mention that to her. I'd happily play along if it made her happy.

Grinning with anticipation, Noelle pulled her panties off and lifted the skirt of her dress as she climbed onto the bed. She didn't immediately straddle me, though. First, she bent down to flick her tongue across the head of my dick, and it instantly jumped towards her as my blood pumped through it harder.

"Mmmm, you always make me feel so good." The words came out low and rough as Noelle's tongue slid slowly down my shaft and back up again. She always gave a wonderful blowjob, but that night, thinking that I couldn't do anything to hurry her along, she seemed bolder than ever. Slowly, she flicked her tongue down my entire length before sucking lightly on my balls. My eyes rolled back of their own volition as a satisfied groan rumbled through my chest.

Fuck, maybe I should let her tie me up more often.

After teasing me a little while longer, her impatience won out. Hiking up her skirt again, she swung one leg over me to sit on me, her warm pussy pressing down directly on my hard cock.

"Beautiful," I confirmed. The sight of her on top of me combined with the feel of her had me primed and ready, and though I yearned to touch her, I kept my hands where they were, leaving Noelle in charge. She rocked against me, her hips moving just enough to give me a bit of friction, but not nearly as much as I wanted. "If you don't fuck me soon, I'm going to tell Eve she needs to give you better pointers."

"You wouldn't," Noelle asserted, but with just enough tremble in her voice that I could tell she didn't feel entirely confident of that. Just to be sure, she reached between her legs to lift my dick, positioning it just right so that she could sink down onto me, and my eyes closed again in pleasure.

"No, I won't. Not as long as you keep riding me with that perfect pussy of yours."

The flush in her cheeks spread downwards, the praise and the pleasure of the contact between us working to heat her body in a way that satisfied us both. With my hands tied, I couldn't do anything but let her use me and watch her do it, which worked just fine for me. I couldn't imagine a better view.

"You might not be the kinkiest woman here, but you are definitely the right one for me. I couldn't take my eyes off you today. I dreamed about having my dick inside you with you in that dress, and here we are. You make all my dreams come true, Noelle. Always."

She whimpered beneath the weight of my words, her body beginning to tremble as her pace increased, her hips lifting and falling ever faster, stroking my dick until I didn't think I could last another second. I would have to pull out the big guns to get her to finish before me.

"Fuck, you're beautiful. Now, come on my dick like a good girl," I stuttered, and that did it for both of us. Noelle's body shuddered above me as my dick pumped inside her, our bodies responding to each other in perfect harmony, just like everything else about our relationship.

She lay down on top of me, with me still inside her, cuddling into me until my arms began to tremble with the exertion of holding them up.

"Think you can untie me now?"

Her head popped up with that startled look in her eyes I loved so much. "Sorry."

"Don't apologize. I think that experiment was a great success all around."

She leaned down to kiss my lips softly after she pulled the ties loose. "I think maybe we should repeat it when we get home, just to be sure."

"Yes, we fucking should." With my arms free, I wrapped them around her, pulling her the rest of the way down so I could make her come again, as many times as she'd let me.

Our night had only just begun.

Chapter Seventeen

REMOTE

~Eve~

Julien chuckled as we made our way back to our hotel room, his arm around my waist. "You're pretty proud of yourself, aren't you?"

"Shouldn't I be?" The reaction to the cocktails had been everything I hoped for, and based on the enthusiasm they were greeted with, I had a feeling most of our guests were in for a very good night.

"You sowed chaos," Julien chided me.

"Sexy, fun chaos. That's an important distinction."

After all the drama of the past few days with Julien's mom, discovering our pregnancy, learning about Noelle's pregnancy and Noah and Liv's struggles, it felt almost impossible that the wedding had gone off without a hitch. Everyone seemed to have a great time. *We* had a great time. I would remember that moment on the beach forever, when Julien told everyone we cared most about just how much he loved me.

The idea for the cocktails came to me just after the ceremony, when I looked around at all the guests, all broken off into couples. Even Emilie had her new man there, whatever the relationship between them might be, and so, I thought it would be fun to give them all a bit of a challenge. Other weddings had party favours; mine had sex games. It seemed entirely appropriate, somehow.

"Nobody complained," I reminded Julien as he unlocked the door and let us in. "And I don't think you're complaining either."

"I'm not," he agreed, coming over to wrap his arms around me as soon as the door closed behind us.

His firm corset beneath his clothes served as a reminder to both of us of his commitment to me, and I knew he wore the butt plug as well. I'd asked him about it earlier, whispering to him as we stood before the officiant at the wedding about whether he could feel it, and it had given me a secret thrill to think about it every time I saw him all day.

"I am, however, curious about what our card says," he added.

It would be a surprise for me too. I hadn't rigged the game in any way, unlike Noelle and Aaron did on that Christmas in Leavenworth years earlier. Julien and I chose a pair of cocktails at random just like everyone else did, and hopefully, it would add a little extra flair to our wedding night. Julien had already taught me so much about myself over the past year, but I had a feeling we would keep on learning things about each other and about ourselves for many years to come.

He removed his suit jacket to get more comfortable as I slid my nail beneath the seal of the envelope and pulled out the little card inside. Printed on it were two words and a QR code, which I hadn't expected.

"Remote domination," I read aloud before looking up at Julien curiously. "What does that mean?"

"I'm not sure," he confessed. "I guess we could scan the code and see what happens?"

That would be the quickest way to find out, so I grabbed my phone from where I'd left it earlier that day and scanned the code. The page that loaded wasn't from the Paradise website, but an adult entertainment site instead.

Again, I read the information out loud to Julien. "Choose a performer or performers and have them act out your wildest fantasies. They'll do whatever you tell them to, within reason."

His face softened in understanding. "Ah, so you are controlling them. It's like voyeurism, but more interactive, and they can't see us."

I noticed how he said *I'd* be controlling them, not that he would. "Does that idea turn you on?"

Julien took a moment to consider it. "Yes, I think it would. I love to see you take charge, but I wouldn't want to share you with anyone. This way, I can enjoy watching you control them, but no one gets to see you but me. It's a good compromise."

I could see his point, and even though I'd never considered doing anything like it before, I was willing to give it a try. Pictures of individuals and couples filled the rest of the page, like a dating app, and I decided on a couple about our age. She had long, blonde hair and he looked like he spent an awful lot of time at the gym. Telling him in particular what to do might be kind of fun.

When I tapped on their photo, we were taken to a live feed that showed them in their bedroom, wherever they were in the world. They were already down to their underwear and sitting next to each other on the end of their bed. They must have gotten some kind of notification that we'd joined them because they both looked over towards the camera expectantly.

"It says I can press down this button to speak to them, and it will distort my voice," I explained to Julien. "Let me try."

Clearing my throat, I started with something simple.

"Kiss her neck, not too hard."

Immediately, the man leaned forward, burying his face in the crook of his partner's neck as her head dropped back, her eyes closing in pleasure, and satisfaction pooled deep inside me at seeing my order so instantly obeyed.

Yes, I could definitely have some fun with this, and even more so if I got Julien involved.

"Everything they do, we're going to do too. Agreed?"

"Oui, Madame." His eager agreement sent another rush of anticipation through me, mixing with the feeling of power the control gave me and my general lust at the thought of celebrating my wedding night with the man who completed me in every way.

That night, it would be hard not to feel like I truly had the world at my feet.

~Julien~

The day had gone better than I had dared to hope after all the drama of the past week.

"Julien, this is Anthony," my mother introduced us after the ceremony, and I shook the man's hand though I still had no idea where he'd come from or what he did to effect such a change in my mother's outlook.

"Great wedding," Anthony told me in a broad Australian accent. "You've got a beautiful bride, and it's clear she adores you."

"The feeling is very mutual, I assure you."

"Eve is wonderful," my mom added. "I liked her from the first time I met her."

That might have been true, but over the past week, she certainly hadn't been acting like it. "You have a funny way of showing it sometimes, Maman."

She didn't deny it, offering me a sheepish shrug. "My concern was never with Eve. She makes you happy, that much is clear, and I want you to be happy. Congratulations, Julien."

She kissed me on both cheeks before moving away, and Julian and his wife approached me next. "We're so glad we could be here for this," my father said, moisture dotting the corners of his eyes. He had been nothing but grateful to be included, and though we still didn't know each other well, I hoped that would continue to change.

"I am too. I'm sorry if my mother made you uncomfortable."

He shrugged in a way that unconsciously mimicked my mother's actions. "She has a right to feel how she feels, but I'm glad she was able to put it behind her for today."

That made two of us.

The rest of the day went off without a hitch, and back in the hotel room with Eve, ready to consummate our marriage properly, I couldn't wait to see exactly what she had in mind.

"Take off the corset," she commanded first as the couple on the screen continued to kiss each other, slowly and sensually, just as Eve had instructed. "Take it all off except your underwear. We're going to be just like them. You'll have to unzip me too."

Gently, I unzipped Eve's delicate, beautiful wedding dress, and as I got my first look at the white, lacy lingerie underneath, blood rushed to my cock, which in turn made my ass clench around the plug I still wore. Every time I felt it, it made me think of Eve, and since I felt it pretty much every time I moved, she had rarely left my mind for a second all day.

As I released the tight lacings of my corset, my chest expanded, adding another sensation to the mix. Its tightness during the day, though not painful, also acted as a kind of discipline, just enough to remind me that Eve held the key to my comfort, and for her alone would I allow myself to fully relax.

When I had removed everything but my underwear as she'd asked me to, Eve issued her next command, both to me and into her phone. "Have him take off his underwear and kneel on the bed, on his hands and knees."

Both the man on the screen and I obeyed. My cock hung half-stiff already between my legs as I climbed up onto the bed, my butt plug still in. Eve smiled at the sight of it as she laid the phone down on the bed beside me where we could both see it while she gave her next order.

"Climb up behind him. Stroke him with one hand, and finger his ass with the other."

Curiously, I glanced down to see if the couple would obey. They had said they would do anything 'within reason', but of course, everyone had different definitions of reasonable. However, in this case, they did exactly as Eve said. The woman grabbed a bottle of lube at the same time Eve did. Eve had to remove my plug first, and after wearing it for so long, it almost felt strange *not* to have it in. That emptiness didn't last long, though, as Eve's finger took its place, at the same time that the woman on the screen pressed her finger inside her partner. Watching it at the same time as I felt Eve's hand in me added another layer to the whole experience, and as her other hand wrapped around my cock, my body jolted, yielding to the pleasure she provided.

"Get him close," Eve's sultry voice commanded. "But don't let him come. Not yet."

As Eve's hand stroked me firmly, her finger pumping into my ass in perfect harmony, the couple on the screen mirrored our movements. The man's shoulders tensed as the same sensations I could feel went through his body, connecting us even though he had no idea I existed.

Knowing she didn't want me to come turned me on even more, my cock swelling in response to Eve's perfect touch, and when she felt me getting close, she instantly stopped, moving to the next step.

"He can undress you. Lie back and let him do all the work until he makes you come."

Eagerly, I took up the challenge. Eve's pretty bra and panties hit the floor as I undressed her, my mouth and my hands running over her exposed skin, exploring every inch. After helping her to get comfortable, I positioned myself between her legs, just as the man on Eve's phone did, and together, we both began to eat.

The other woman was beautiful, certainly, but I knew without a single doubt that I was the luckier one. Eve's taste hit my tongue as I buried my face in her pussy, making me groan in pure happiness. No matter how calm and in control she appeared, her body always told me the truth, and the wetness that greeted me was all the proof I needed that she found the situation just as titillating as I did. No matter where we went in the world or how much hardship we encountered, running my tongue along her clit always felt like home. Somehow, the most incredible woman I'd ever met had agreed to spend her life with me, and I would do everything in my power to ensure she never regretted it.

Eve's body shuddered around me as her first orgasm took her, but I didn't stop. I wouldn't until she told me to. My fingers fucked her as my tongue stroked her clit, working in tandem until she couldn't take it anymore. Her hands threaded through my hair, pressing my face more tightly into her as she came a second time.

"Flip her over," Eve gasped into the phone breathlessly. "Press her face into the mattress as you fuck her."

Grabbing her hips, I twisted her so that she ended up face-down. With her legs pressed together, I slid my hard and ready cock between them, finding her entrance and pushing inside it as Eve moaned. Every now and then, she liked it rough, and however she liked it was how I wanted to give it to her. With one hand on the side of her head, I pressed her face down just as she instructed while my hips pumped into her, her beautiful body taking each stroke of my cock until I could tell she was right on the edge.

"Ma femme," I grunted out in French, each word punctuated by another thrust. "Aujourd'hui. Toujours."

My wife. Today. Always.

Eve's body contracted again, the waves of pleasure rippling through her and into me as her pussy clenched around my cock and my own orgasm hit. The room disappeared around me as I melted into pleasure, and when it started to come back into focus, I could hear the man's panting through the phone as he hit his climax too, after his partner already had.

Four thoroughly sated people, sharing in the afterglow of their satisfaction, all because of the amazing woman I got to call mine.

Chapter Eighteen

STRANGERS

~**Holly**~

I reached over to take Jackson's hand once we were left alone in the reception room. "This has been a pretty great day, hasn't it?"

"It has." His warm smile in return warmed me right through. Well, it mostly came from him, anyway. The champagne I had earlier might have played a small part too. "I hope things go well for Livvy tomorrow."

I did too, obviously, but I also didn't want to spend the evening dwelling on it. We couldn't do anything to influence the outcome, and everyone else had gone off to spend their nights in a decidedly more carnal manner. I'd been hoping we could do the same.

"What does that card say on the drink? Now that nobody's around, we should find out."

"You really want to do this? It seems kind of silly."

Jackson tried to laugh it off, but I'd known the man long enough that I could tell the difference between a real laugh and a forced one. He couldn't fool me for a second.

"What are you afraid of?" I teased him. "That it's going to tell you that you have to share me with the local motorcycle gang?"

His eyes widened in horror. "Well, *now* that's what I'm worried about."

With a laugh, I plucked the card from his hands. "Come on, let's end the suspense. If it sounds like fun, we'll do it. If not, no harm done. We already had a wonderful night at the club last night, so you don't need to prove yourself to me, Jackson. I love you just as you are. You know that."

He did know it, deep down, but I could see him relax when I stated it out loud anyway. "Alright. What does it say?"

It took me a couple of attempts to get the envelope open, and when I finally ripped into it, I managed to rip the card too. However, it held on by enough of a thread that we could still make out what it said.

"Stranger roleplay?" Jackson read out loud, phrasing it as a question, and a wary one at that. "What does that mean?"

I could guess that his uncertainty came from the fact that it mentioned a stranger, but he didn't have to worry. Neither of us wanted to involve a third party, and that didn't have anything to do with the suggested activity anyway.

"It's where we pretend that we don't know each other. We go out somewhere separately, act like we're strangers, and end up hooking up. I think it sounds like fun. I could be the second woman you've ever slept with!"

The corners of Jackson's blue eyes crinkled as he smiled, enjoying my humour as always, but he still didn't quite get it. "So, you'd be pretending to be someone else?"

"Not necessarily. We could be ourselves, but from an alternate reality where Holly and Jackson never met in London. We could be the versions of ourselves who are alone in their fifties, but who feel an instant spark when they meet. What do you think?"

The more I thought about it, the more it appealed to me, and Jackson fed off my enthusiasm. "That could be interesting. I'm willing to try. How should we begin?"

There shouldn't be anyone else in the hotel bar we knew. Everyone else had probably gone back to their rooms for the night, so it would only be strangers there. No one would know me or Jackson, and they wouldn't know we were together. It would be our secret.

"I'll go to the bar and get a drink. You can wait five minutes or so and join me. Approach me like you'd approach any stranger at a bar that you found attractive. We'll see if you remember how."

"It's been a long time," Jackson had to agree. "But I'll see what moves I can pull out of the vault."

That was the spirit. "Give me your wedding ring. I'll put them both in my purse so we don't look like cheaters."

Jackson handed me his ring while I slipped mine off too, the beautiful one he'd given me in front of Rockefeller Center all those Christmases ago. If someone had told me then that I'd still be finding new ways to have fun with this amazing man as we got close to sixty, I probably wouldn't have been able to imagine it.

With my stomach bubbling with excitement, I gave him a quick kiss and headed to the bar. The room was actually busier than I expected, but a few stools sat empty at the bar itself, so I headed there and ordered myself a chocolate martini.

"Is this seat taken?" a gruff Australian voice asked when I had taken just a couple of sips. With a smile, I turned around, thinking that Jackson had put on an accent just for fun, but to my surprise, another man stood there. A little bit younger than me, I would guess, and much more casually dressed.

Force of habit wanted me to say that I was waiting for someone, but that would defeat the purpose of the game. We were supposed to act like we'd never met, so how could I be waiting for Jackson to arrive?

"It's all yours if you want it," I replied instead, and the man lowered himself into the seat next to me with a smile.

"That's a pretty accent. Where are you from?"

"London." My accent hadn't faded at all, even after thirty years of living in America. "What about you?"

"Melbourne. Just here for business."

"Me too." The lie slipped off my tongue easily as I caught sight of Jackson walking in the door. He saw me immediately, and his body tensed as he caught sight of the stranger giving me his full attention. Would my husband keep up the game, I wondered, or would he charge over and claim what was his?

Honestly, I wouldn't mind either way.

~Jackson~

My first instinct when I saw the man at the bar next to Holly, his body turned towards her, far too close for my liking, was to walk straight over and make it clear that she was already spoken for. It didn't shock me that she'd been approached, not when she looked the way she did that night, but the speed of it still came as a bit of a surprise.

However, as I took a breath to clear my head, I thought better of it. She could have any man she wanted, and after more than thirty years, she still chose me. If I'd ever needed a reminder of just how lucky I was, that would be it, and that night, she wanted to play the game. For her, I'd do anything, and so, I walked over as if I didn't know her at all, taking the seat on the other side of the man instead.

"Whiskey, neat," I ordered when the bartender glanced my way, and Holly leaned forward onto the bar to look at me.

"It's an international crowd in here tonight," she said as she took a sip of her martini, looking sophisticated and utterly gorgeous. "Are you here on business too?"

The man between us turned to me, not thrilled to have lost her attention. His eyes scanned me quickly, sizing me up as competition, and he must have quickly come to the conclusion that I didn't pose much of a threat because he relaxed as he leaned back, taking a sip from his own drink.

"That's right. I'm in the hotel business, here from New York. What about you two?"

"I'm British and he's Australian," Holly told me, her eyes twinkling with amusement and appreciation that I was committing to the game. "He was just about to tell me what he does for a living."

"Software sales," the man answered, addressing himself to Holly more than to me. "I just made a big sale today, so I'm celebrating tonight.

"Congratulations." Holly's blue eyes focused back on him, which I took as a challenge.

"Oh, so you two aren't together?" I asked, turning up the heat just a little bit as I made my interest clear.

"We just met. I'm Holly."

She offered her hand to me, and I held it for just a second longer than necessary, squeezing her fingers gently before letting them go. "Jackson."

"Keith," the man in the middle introduced himself as he shook her hand next. "What do you do, Holly?"

"I'm an interior designer. Hotels, mostly, so I guess Jackson and I have something in common."

She shot me a smile that Keith didn't appreciate very much. "Did you design this place?" he asked, leaning forward so he could gesture to the bar around us, but also effectively blocking her from my view.

"I wish I could say I had, but no, this isn't one of mine. It's lovely though, isn't it?"

Though she asked Keith the question, I answered it. "It's nice, but I've seen nicer. The one in the Stamer hotel in London, for example, has to be my favourite hotel bar in the world."

Of course Holly designed that one, and she smiled as she leaned forward so she could see me again. "You have good taste."

The conversation continued that way for a few more minutes, Keith doing his best to box me out and me stubbornly refusing to give in.

Eventually, he pointed into the distance. "Look, a table by the window just opened up. The view's gorgeous from there. Would you like to join me, Holly?"

It couldn't be clearer he wanted to get rid of me, and Holly's eyebrows raised as she looked in my direction, waiting to see how I would respond.

Although she had said to pretend like we'd never met, I couldn't resist the chance to push her buttons a little bit. "Actually, there's a better view from the bed in my room. Maybe you'd like to join me there?"

She nearly choked on her drink as Keith's lips pursed in disapproval. "Show some respect, mate."

"I'm just giving the lady another option."

"And the lady says yes, please," Holly giggled, downing the rest of her martini in one gulp. "Have a good night, Keith."

She slid off her stool and came over to link her arm through mine as Keith stared at us both in disbelief. "You've got to be kidding," he muttered.

I gave him a shrug. "Sometimes, you can't deny chemistry. Better luck next time."

We managed to hold it together until we got back to the hallway to our room. Holly broke first, her laughter ringing down the hall as she held onto me. "The look on his face!"

"The poor guy." Although it had been fun, I felt a bit bad for him. "I hope he doesn't try that line with anyone else."

"You never know. Maybe it'll work."

She was still chuckling as I let us into our room.

"That wasn't exactly how I envisioned it going, but it was still fun," she told me, wrapping her arms around me as soon as we were alone. "You were very sexy."

"You looked amazing," I told her honestly, bending down to kiss her neck. "I can't blame him for taking a shot, but I'm going to remind you why you made the right choice in coming back here with me."

"Mmmm, yes, please." Holly's body melted into mine as I kept kissing her. My hands found the zipper on the back of her dress easily, and when it hit the floor, I picked her up to carry her into the bedroom, placing her down gently on the bed.

From beneath half-closed eyelids, she watched as I undid the straps of her shoes, removing them one by one before pulling off her panties and bra. Honestly, that man at the bar couldn't even begin to imagine how much he was missing. I'd never seen anything more beautiful.

"I don't need any foreplay," she grinned, reaching out for me. "You've already got me hot and heavy for you, Jackson. Make me yours."

How could I resist that?

My suit took a little longer to remove, and by the time I got my underwear off, my dick was practically begging me for relief. Holly spread her legs as I climbed onto the bed, calling to me like a siren.

"I don't even want to imagine a world where we never met," I told her as I rubbed my dick against her entrance, getting it nice and wet for her. "You're the best thing that's ever happened to me, Holly. And this? This is the best fucking feeling in the world."

I thrust into her hard, all the way in, as Holly's back arched and a low, raspy moan slipped from her lips. "I...have to... agree... with that," she gasped.

"I want you thinking about it every time another man looks your way." My pace was hard and fast, reminding her with each stroke that she belonged to me, just as I completely belonged to her. "I want you thinking about it when you're on your own. I want it to come to you at completely random times, just to make you smile."

"Oh, fuck, yes."

Her legs wrapped around my back as I continued to fuck her, and when my hand slipped between us to find her clit, those legs began to tremble.

"You're the only stranger I ever want," she promised me just before her body surrendered to the pleasure overwhelming it. "Oh, God. I love you."

Those words were always the sexiest ones I could ever hear, and I came too, completing the game, at least for that night.

For as long as we were together, we would both continue to win.

Chapter Nineteen

CAPTIVE

~Olivia~

It had been a long, emotional day, but as Noah and I headed back to our hotel room, I felt pretty optimistic. We had the support of our extended family, and a real chance at starting a family of our own, much sooner than we could have imagined. A few days earlier, things felt pretty hopeless, but after reconnecting with Noah and our kink at the club, talking to our parents, making contact with the charity and celebrating Eve and Julien's marriage with all the people dearest to us, a flicker of light had started to creep back in again.

Noah's heated smile when we were alone helped to fan that flame even higher. "If you want to go straight to sleep, I understand, but I'll be honest: I'm very curious about what's on this card."

It had me curious too. Noah and I were pretty experienced when it came to kink. We'd tried an awful lot of things in the eight years we'd been together, but I would never presume to imagine we'd tried everything. And even if it was something we'd done before, it might be nice to revisit it as part of Eve's game.

"Honestly, if we get into bed right now, my brain will be going a mile a minute. I'd rather take my mind off tomorrow, at least for a little while."

"That's exactly what I was thinking." He pressed a firm kiss on my forehead before opening the small envelope attached to his drink. His only reaction was a slight raising of his eyebrows, not nearly enough to give me any indication of what it might say.

"Well?" I pressed when he didn't speak.

He turned the card around to show me the two words printed on it: *Hostage fantasy.*

"Interesting."

I let that word linger in the air between us as I thought it over. Power dynamics weren't usually our sweet spot, but we could probably find a way to adjust it to our own personal preferences.

"Hopefully the one my parents got wasn't quite so kinky." I couldn't imagine that my dad would do anything like that. I still couldn't believe he'd gone to Paradise in the first place. When Eve announced that everyone had been, he didn't deny it, but my imagination refused to summon any scenario that made it seem plausible.

Noah chuckled even as he winced. "I'd rather not be thinking about your parents right now."

"Fair." We shared a quick smile before I laid out my initial thoughts. "How about you're not the one who kidnapped me, but you work with him? You're not happy about having me around. You think I'll be trouble."

"Oh, you're always trouble, Liv. The best kind." Noah's smirk still managed to make my knees weak, no matter how many times I'd seen it. "I think we can make that work. Do you want to be tied up?"

"Sure. Lightly." We didn't usually go for bondage, but it would help to set the scene. Noah sat me down in one of the chairs in the centre of the suite's living room and used one of his spare power cords to loosely tie my hands behind my back. When he had me set up, he went into the next room to get into character and make an entrance.

No matter what we did together, he always fully committed, and I couldn't wait to see exactly how this would play out.

~Noah~

In the hotel bedroom, I took a moment to clear my head. Ever since the meeting that morning, it had been hard to think about anything other than our upcoming trip. My sister's wedding had been a helpful distraction, thankfully, and Olivia had just agreed to give me another one. If things went well the next day, we might not have many more uninterrupted nights ahead of us, so I planned to take full advantage of this one.

With the details Liv suggested for our roleplay, I filled in the blanks, concocting a backstory for myself that would have me walking in on a beautiful woman I'd never seen before, tied up in the next room. Seeing her tied up did nothing for me on its own; that had never been my kink, but the scenario as a whole could work for us, if we played it our own way.

I pulled my phone out of my pocket, pretending to be talking on it as I walked back into the room where I'd left Olivia. "Are you crazy, bringing her back here? What if they track her down? You'll lead them right to us." I paused for a second, as if my imaginary partner were speaking to me. "Whatever, just hurry up and take her off my hands."

Jabbing at the screen, I shoved the phone back into my pocket and glared down at Olivia, who didn't seem intimidated in the slightest as she curled her lips at me in a snarl. "You're so screwed. My father runs this town, and when he finds out you've taken me, he'll have your dick on a plate."

The corners of my mouth twitched at her colourful turn of phrase, but I loved how she jumped right into the game. "Are you thinking about my dick, sweetheart? We haven't even been introduced."

"Don't flatter yourself." Though she said that, her eyes dropped to the front of my pants, and my dick twitched in response. Fuck, she could always turn me on. "What are you after? Money? I can pay you. Just let me go."

"What if it's not money I want?"

"What else, then?"

That time, I let my eyes roam across her body, her blonde hair pulled back for the wedding, her pretty white and green dress looking perfect on her. Though I could see her body responding to my gaze the same way I had to hers, she tried to hide it.

"You've got to be kidding," she snorted. "I'm completely out of your league."

She wasn't wrong. Olivia Stamer was in a league all her own. "Fine. If you're not interested, we'll just wait for 'daddy' to come through with the information my partner wants."

Taking a seat on the sofa across from her, I pulled my phone out again and pretended to ignore her, though I could still see every subtle movement from the corner of my eye.

After a couple of minutes where she struggled half-heartedly against her restraints, she'd had enough. "What are you offering?"

My lips curled into a satisfied smile as I looked back up at her. "Simple. You suck my dick and I'll let you go."

"That's all?" she mocked. "I bet it wouldn't even fill my mouth."

The chuckle I let out was only half faked. "No, that's not all. I'm going to record you doing it. I'm going to put it on public display so anyone who wants to see it can watch you on your knees."

The shiver that went down Olivia's spine didn't surprise me at all. The idea of anyone watching would always turn her on.

She pretended to think it over for a moment. "Just as long as you don't send it to my father."

I couldn't resist the chance to tease her, even if it broke character. "I think we both know I'm not the one with a history of sending things to your dad."

Olivia couldn't hold her laugh in, but she quickly got back into her role, her beautiful blue eyes still twinkling. "Alright. You've got a deal."

Untying her only took seconds since I hadn't tied anything very tight to begin with. As Liv got down on her knees, I pulled my half-hard dick out and held my phone up above her, pressing the red record button for real. We had a very private, very secure server where we saved some of our own videos, for the two of us to watch together when the mood took us. This would make a nice addition to that collection.

Through the screen, I watched as Liv lifted my dick to her lips and slowly took me all the way in, never taking her eyes off me. A tight groan left my lips as my head hit the back of her throat. She'd never given me a bad blowjob, and I could already tell this would be no exception. When she gagged while taking me in a second time, I had to laugh.

"I thought you said you wouldn't feel it. Looks to me like you might choke on it, sweetheart."

A strand of saliva hung between her lips and my dick as she pulled back. "I'll bite it if you don't let me do it my way."

"My apologies. Go right ahead."

Her hand went to my balls, stroking them while she continued to fuck me with her mouth. She looked incredible and she felt even better, and before too long, I had to put a stop to it or the whole scenario would all be over much quicker than either of us wanted.

"I changed my mind." Pulling my dick out of her mouth, I took a step back. "I want to fuck you too."

"That wasn't our deal," she argued, even as excitement flared in her eyes.

"It is now. Take it or leave it."

Liv got back to her feet, crossing her arms as she pretended to think it over. "Fine. Just make it quick."

That wouldn't be a problem after how close she'd just gotten me, but I would make sure she enjoyed herself too. "Bend over the chair."

I pushed her gently down towards the chair she'd just been sitting on and lifted the back of her dress, exposing her perfect ass. Still recording,

I pulled her panties down just enough that I could slide my dick in. Already wet from her mouth, and with Liv's own wetness adding to the lubrication, I had no trouble pushing all the way in, and she moaned as her grip on the chair tightened.

"That's right, sweetheart. Let me hear you. Let them *all* hear you."

Just the suggestion of anyone else watching sent a shudder through her body while I began fucking her in earnest. One hand still held the phone, capturing every thrust of my hips against her, but the other reached around her to find her clit, and as I began to rub it, Liv dropped the act entirely. "Oh, fuck, Noah. Right there."

"Just like this?" I confirmed, pressing down with my fingers as I rotated my hips against her ass, pushing into her as deep as I could go.

"Yes. Fuck, yes!"

She came moaning out my name, and I pulled out of her to finish myself off, making sure to capture the moment on camera as I shot ropes of cum across her beautiful ass.

It took a moment for my vision to clear afterwards, and for me to remember exactly what I'd been trying to forget about in the first place.

"*Now*, I think it's time for bed," Liv said, standing up to give me a kiss before she headed into the bathroom to get ready.

We had a big day ahead of us, but I would never forget that night either.

Chapter Twenty

FAMILY

~Olivia~

Falling into bed satisfied and curled up with the man I loved helped sleep to come faster than it otherwise might have. Even so, I woke up an hour before our alarm, and as soon as I stirred, Noah lifted his head too. "Is it time?"

"No, not yet. Go back to sleep."

"Not likely," he groaned. "We might as well get ready and go. Sitting around here won't do us any good, and it's going to be a long day."

In the early dawn light, we both got dressed, packed a small bag of essential toiletries and extra clothes, just in case, and headed out to the lobby. Derek was standing at the front desk as we went over to order a taxi, and he gave us a friendly smile. "Are you two up early or just coming in?"

Any other day, it might have been the latter, but that morning, we were on a mission. "We're flying out on a trip today, but should be back tonight," Noah told him. "Can I speak to you for just a second? Liv, ask for the car, okay?"

That wouldn't be a problem, but I glanced back over at Noah and Derek curiously once the order had been placed, wondering what Noah might be up to. With him, it could honestly be anything.

The taxi arrived in just a few minutes, and it didn't take much time at all to get to Sydney's international airport on the traffic-light highway. Besides the early hour, it was also December 24th, so a lot of people would have the day off. Eve had wanted to get the wedding out of the way before her birthday and Christmas, so if all went well with our flights, we'd be back by late that evening, ready to celebrate Christmas with everyone the next day.

"Could we pick up a few Christmas gifts for the children?" I asked Noah as we drove up to the airport drop-off. "Would it be okay to give them something?"

He kissed the side of my head, his grip a little firmer than usual. "I think that would be great. We can board the plane whenever we're ready, and they'll squeeze us in for takeoff when there's an opening."

Having the Stamer private plane at our disposal definitely made things easier, and when we arrived at the toy store in the airport to find it hadn't opened yet for the day, Noah refused to let that stop him either. Before long, he had a manager on site to open it early just for us, and while I normally didn't approve of him throwing his financial weight around, in this case, I appreciated it.

"I don't know what they'll like," I fretted, feeling overwhelmed as I looked over the aisles of dolls, stuffed animals and electronics. "We don't know them at all yet."

"It's the thought that counts," Noah assured me. "Stick to something small but heartfelt. Don't go too crazy."

He said that as if there were a danger I would, and I accordingly scaled my ambitions back. In the end, I bought three stuffed Australian animals: a kangaroo, a koala and a platypus. Hopefully, when we met them in person, I could decide which animal belonged with which child. I also picked up some candy bars from the airport's convenience store, feeling fairly certain that every kid liked chocolate.

The flight would take about four and a half hours to the small Pacific island, so Noah tried to tell me to nap when we got in the air, but there was no chance of that happening. My whole body felt on edge, my stomach fluttering in a way that had nothing to do with the change of altitude.

Talking would help to pass the time, so I tried my best to make conversation. "I guess it's lucky that Eve and Julien were working in this part of the world. If they'd been in South America, we wouldn't be able to do this trip in a day."

"I think it's more than luck," Noah countered. "Some things are meant to be, like how you chose Vienna for your Christmas vacation the same year I happened to be there."

That had certainly been serendipitous, but were we reading too much into the current coincidence? I didn't want him to be too disappointed if it didn't work out, so I tried to put down a bit of a cushion beneath us. "They're not the only kids in the world who need a family, though. If this doesn't work out..."

"Don't go making your backup plans yet," he cut me off. "If it doesn't work out, we'll deal with it together, like we deal with everything. But for right now, let's go in believing it's going to work, okay?"

That was easier said than done after all the disappointments we'd been through, but I promised him I'd try.

A car was already waiting for us at the airport when we landed. Noah had hired a driver for the day to be available for us when we needed him, and he drove us through the city where we'd landed towards its outskirts. The paved streets gave way to dirt ones, the houses becoming smaller and less sturdy, sitting on stilts to protect them from flooding. By the time the driver stopped, the slatted wooden houses slanted dangerously towards each other, with laundry lines strung across the street between them. Barefoot children ran over to see the car, peering curiously through the windows at us.

Although Eve had told us about the poverty the family lived in, seeing it for ourselves was still overwhelming. "Have you ever been anywhere like this before?" I asked Noah.

His hand squeezed mine, his jaw firmly set as he looked out the windows. "No. Maybe I should have before now."

The driver got out first, nudging the children away from the door so I could get out. Seeing the bright, curious faces made me wish I'd brought more gifts with me, or at least more chocolate. Maybe we could send something for the neighbourhood after we got back. The small bag clutched in my hand didn't contain enough to go around.

Looking into each face, I tried to recognize the boy and girl we'd seen on the computer screen the previous morning, but none of them looked familiar to me.

"Mr and Mrs Stamer, hello." From the porch of one of the houses down the street, a man waved to us, the same man we'd spoken to during the meeting the previous day.

Noah put his arm around my waist, giving all the children surrounding us a friendly wave as he led me towards the people we'd come there to see.

The man's smile grew warmer as we approached the porch. "I hope your flight went well. Are you hungry?"

I hadn't eaten anything yet that day, my stomach too much in turmoil to even want to try, and the thought of taking food from the family that lived in this house sent another pang through it. "No, thank you," Noah answered for the both of us. "Did you receive the information from our lawyer?"

I didn't know the lawyer sent anything, but the man confirmed he had. "Yes, we received the criminal record checks and financial records. Everything is in order, Mr Stamer. Please, come in and meet the children."

My lungs seemed to forget what to do as Noah took my hand and we followed the man from the charity up the steps into the small house. Small gulps of air didn't do much to ease the tightness in my chest. I couldn't remember the last time I'd been so nervous.

Inside, the house was just one big room, with a few curtains hung from the ceiling to give a bit of privacy. The woman who had been on the call, the children's aunt, sat on the floor with the baby in her lap. The other two children sat beside her, looking just as unsure as I felt.

Heaven only knew what they had been told about the whole situation. They wore faded but clean clothing, and though skinny, they didn't look malnourished. Their aunt had clearly been doing her best by them, but looking around, it was pretty clear that having three extra bodies to care for would have been a burden. Their dark hair almost matched Noah's, but their dark eyes and light brown skin would make it clear at first glance that they weren't our biological children. We would have to learn the best way to navigate the inevitable questions when the time came.

Behind one of the curtains, I could see more little feet and hear whispered conversation in the local language. Those must have been the woman's own children.

"Hello," Noah greeted the woman with a nod, but I couldn't tear my eyes away from the children. Desperately wanting to set them at ease, I went and sat next to them, opening the bag to give them their gifts first, to give them something to do rather than simply sitting there awkwardly.

"These are some animals from Australia," I explained, though I knew they wouldn't understand me. "We don't live there, but we're staying there right now."

They wouldn't care about that even if they could understand me, so I quickly changed tack, pulling the kangaroo out of the bag first.

"This is a kangaroo. She jumps like this."

The soft kangaroo in my hand made exaggerated bounces along the floor, and the girl watching me almost smiled, so I handed the animal to her.

"This one is a platypus. He's got a bill like a duck, and a tail like a beaver. I think he's cute."

The little boy examined the animal in my hand seriously before reaching out to take it. When his little hand made contact with the soft hair, his eyes widened in awe.

They both seemed pleased with their presents, so I handed the koala to the woman with the baby in her arms. "This one's for her."

"Thank you," she replied in accented English before turning to the kids. "Say thank you."

They both repeated the words as if they'd been practicing them, which they probably had, but their eyes never left their new toys.

"Sit down," the man from the charity invited Noah, and he lowered himself onto the floor next to me. There was only one chair I could see in the house, but no one used it. "The children aren't used to being around men, so they are a little nervous. It's normal."

That made sense since their father had passed away before the little one was born. In fact, based on the timeline Eve had given us, I didn't think the littlest one could even be the child of their mother's husband. She was born too long after his death, but everyone seemed to ignore that fact. I supposed they figured her young life was already difficult enough without also being labelled as illegitimate.

"What are their names?" Noah asked softly. He looked just as captivated by them as I felt. We hadn't asked their names during the meeting the day before, since that meeting had been more about us as potential parents than about the kids themselves.

"You can choose new names if you like," the man offered, but Noah quickly shook his head.

"We don't want to change anything. We just want to know."

"She is Maria," their aunt said, gesturing towards the older girl with her chin. "He's Daniel, and she's Sera. They are good children. No crying."

My chest tightened again, but I tried to keep the smile on my face and not betray any signs of being upset, no matter how much my heart ached for them. "They're allowed to cry. That's okay. Could I... hold her?"

The baby in the woman's arms snuggled in so peacefully there, it didn't look like she would mind coming to me, at least for a few minutes. Her aunt handed Sera over to me without complaint, and as I hoped, after a few seconds of squirming to get comfortable again, she settled right in, her little face pressing against my chest and her tiny fingers wrapping around my thumb.

My heart felt so full I thought it might burst as I fought to keep the tears from my eyes.

Noah cleared his throat beside me, a sign that he was affected just as much as I was even if he didn't show it as much outwardly. "We have some chocolate too. To eat." He mimed eating before pulling the bars out of the bag and handing them to the children. They took them as seriously as they'd handled everything else, but when they got them open and took a bite, some smiles began to show, first to each other and then, much more shyly, towards Noah.

We sat there together for nearly an hour as the woman told us about her sister and about why she couldn't care for the children herself. Maria shuffled closer to me, curious about my blonde hair, so I passed Sera to Noah so I could give Maria my full attention. I sang her a few nursery rhymes I remembered, and though she didn't understand all the words, she seemed to like the tunes. Daniel still kept his distance, but when Sera fell asleep in Noah's arms, he went over to inspect the situation.

"I have a little sister too," Noah explained to him, keeping his voice soft and gentle. "But she's not so little anymore."

The idea of all of us being at Sera's wedding one day, just as we'd all been at Eve's, brought tears to my eyes that I couldn't stop from spilling over the edges. Maria looked up at me in concern, reaching up to wipe them off my cheeks.

Eventually, their aunt told them all to go behind the curtain to have a nap, except for Sera who stayed with us. Without the children there, we focused on specifics.

"Are you interested in taking them?" the man from the charity asked us bluntly.

I looked over at Noah, but I already knew his answer as much as I knew my own heart. "Yes, we are. How quickly can we make it happen?"

"There is some paperwork," he warned us. "They will need medical tests and passports, along with the legal adoption papers. However, your lawyer said that you can send the necessary funds to have it expedited."

Noah would have given those instructions already.

"In which case, they can probably be ready to travel with you in two to three weeks."

Although I knew how fast that was in the grand scheme of things, the thought of being separated from them for even that long felt like a lifetime. Noah clearly felt the same because he turned to me to try to soften the blow. "We need time to put things together at home anyway. You and your mom can redecorate. We'll meet the nanny, find all the best programs. And in the meantime, we can pay for extra food and clothing for the whole family here."

Everything he said made sense, so I tried not to be too upset as we handed Sera back to her aunt and returned to the car that still sat at the end of the road, waiting for us. With the return flight and drive back to the hotel in Wollongong, we should arrive back just before Christmas Eve turned into Christmas Day, with the best present we'd ever received.

We were finally going to be parents.

~Eve~

Julien's arm slipped around me as soon as I woke up the next morning. "Happy birthday, Eve. Bonne fête."

"Thank you." With a hum of contentment, I turned to face my new husband. His stubble-lined face looked as handsome as ever in the morning light. "I'm happy I get to spend it with you."

"Moi aussi." He often spoke more French first thing in the morning, as if his brain hadn't totally woken up yet in order to translate, but he quickly switched back to English after saying 'me too'. "It's the first one we spend together, the first as director of your own charity, as Mrs

Labrecque, and as a mother-to-be. With all those firsts, it's bound to be a good one."

I had to agree. That morning, absolutely anything felt possible.

We had some decaf coffee together as we got ready for the day, before meeting the rest of our guests for breakfast, all except Noah and Olivia who must have already left on their trip. Emilie's friend Anthony was still there, which suggested that he had spent the night. I'd never seen Emilie looking so relaxed and happy.

"Happy birthday, Noelle." I gave my best friend a tight hug as she and Aaron came in, not the first ones to arrive for once. "Did you sleep in? Was it that good a night?"

Her blush was all the answer I needed, even though she didn't give me any details. "We had fun. I hope you did too."

"Absolutely. I think it was a very successful experiment all around."

Looking around the table, it certainly seemed like everyone had enjoyed themselves.

"Tessa has arranged a day for us in Sydney to see some of the Christmas sights," Julien announced as breakfast wrapped up. "There's room for anyone who wants to come along, but you are under no obligation to."

After some discussion, Tate and Crystal decided to come with us, but Maribel and Corey and the elder Ribars chose to stay behind. Emilie and Anthony also elected to stay.

"We don't have a lot of time before I go home," Emilie explained to me, sounding sincerely apologetic. "We'd rather spend it alone. I hope that's okay."

"It's definitely okay," I assured her. "Although maybe the four of us can have a private dinner together sometime before you leave?"

If she was as serious about Anthony as she seemed to be, it might be a good idea for Julien and I to get to know him at least a little.

"I would like that. Thank you, Eve. And happy birthday." My new mother-in-law gave me a hug as Julien shrugged at me over her shoulder.

He found her change of heart as baffling as I did, but neither of us were about to complain.

My parents, Noelle and Aaron, and the Hanmers also decided to come along, so the ten of us loaded into the minibus that Tessa had hired for the occasion. The drive to Sydney took about an hour and a half, and the time went quickly as we all reminisced about past Christmases. Tate shared some stories about Noah in college that we'd never heard before, and Crystal told us all about the Ribar family Christmas traditions, which naturally interested Julien quite a bit. Those might have been his own traditions, had things been different between his parents.

One decision could alter our lives in ways we could never fathom at the time. People were brought together in the most random circumstances, and the best we could do was try to recognize the important people when they showed up, and do our best to keep them in our lives in a happy and healthy way.

If I had let Julien go after he tried to push me away a year earlier at the charity benefit my dad had thrown, I would have never known the perfect bliss of that Christmas Eve a year later, and I whispered a grateful 'thank you' to the universe for making me stubborn enough to hold on.

Our first stop of the day was at the pop-up Tinseltown, and as we all piled out of the bus, the hot summer air hit us with full force. "I'm not sure how much we'll be able to get into the Christmas spirit," my mom wondered, but as soon as we walked inside, all of our worries disappeared.

The place had been decked out in floor-to-ceiling Christmas with hanging garland and balls above our heads, and even an upside-down Christmas tree hanging from the ceiling further inside. A cozy fireplace and Victorian furniture gave the room a nostalgic feel that made us all quickly forget the scorching heat outside.

"What do we do here?" my dad asked.

"We can start with decorating cookies."

Noelle immediately began to giggle, recalling our gingerbread cookies that had led to her and Aaron hooking up for the first time.

Jackson gave her a curious look. "What's so funny?"

I jumped in to distract him. "Look, there are cute Christmas aprons! Jackson, this one is perfect for you."

We each decorated a cookie for our significant other, and one more for the people who weren't there with us. I made Emilie a Québec flag I thought she would appreciate.

"Not bad," Julien praised me. "And you look beautiful in that apron."

"You'd look better with nothing under yours," I teased him.

After making cookies, we took turns on a curling lane that had been set up next door, and had some pictures taken with Santa as well. My mom was definitely feeling more Christmasy by the time we finished.

"Where to next?" she asked, linking her arm through mine.

"Time to see some decorations!"

We checked out the windows at the David Jones department store, which led Holly to reminisce about the first time she saw the Fifth Avenue store windows in New York. Afterwards, we visited the Queen Victoria Building, a five-storey shopping centre that had a four-storey tree inside, stretching up towards the central dome in the middle of the building, making it easily one of the biggest ones any of us had ever seen. Since Tate and Crystal had never heard the story before, we convinced Jackson to tell us about how he proposed to Holly under the Rockefeller Center tree. Even though I'd heard the story many times before, I still loved to hear him tell it.

"How did you propose, Julien?" Crystal asked her brother when Jackson had finished.

"I don't think I've heard this story either," Holly exclaimed.

Julien's cheeks turned an adorable shade of pink. "I'm afraid it's not as romantic as Mr Hanmer's story."

I disagreed with that, and no one was about to let him off that easy. "Tell us anyway," they all begged.

Slipping my arm around his waist, I took over. "We were sitting on a beach in Thailand at night, watching a meteor shower. I joked that if one shooting star granted a wish, then a night like that must mean you could wish for anything to come true. I asked Julien what he'd wish for, and he said it would be to marry me. When I looked over at him, he had a ring in his hand."

The women all squealed in delight, making Julien's cheeks go even pinker.

We visited The Tea Room in the same shopping centre for a break, enjoying the specially themed Christmas high tea. "This will be your everyday life when you go back to England," I teased my parents.

"I think it will be spreadsheets and contractors rather than teas and parties," my mom countered. "But when you come visit, we'll pull out all the stops."

Full of tea and cake, we ventured over to Martin Place, with another enormous Christmas tree and choirs performing all our favourite Christmas songs, and wandered around the city's commercial district some more, looking at all the lights before ending up in Darling Harbour to watch the fireworks. By the time we got ourselves loaded back on the bus to return to the hotel in Wollongong, it had been a perfect Christmas Eve day.

"I take it all back," my mom declared. "It does still feel like Christmas in Australia, at least when we're all together."

We agreed to meet up in my parents' suite in the morning to exchange gifts, and when we returned to the hotel, Julien and I went back to our room to exchange our stockings in our very own Christmas tradition.

The previous year, we had a week's worth of items we'd bought each other, but that night, we had a whole year of them. Across the world as we'd travelled, I'd picked up things that reminded me of him, and he'd done the same for me. Those little mementos meant more to me than any big gift ever could, and as we fell asleep in each other's arms, I could honestly say it had been my best Christmas ever, even though the day itself was yet to come.

~Gemma~

"Merry Christmas, Gorgeous."

Cole's greeting on Christmas morning put a smile on my face before my eyes were even fully open. "Merry Christmas. What time is it?"

He sat beside me in bed, his phone in his hand. "Only seven. I'm sorry if I woke you, I was just checking if Noah had sent an update."

Noah's name woke me the rest of the way up. "Has he?"

He sent a message the day before when he and Olivia were on their way back, saying that things went well, but he didn't give any further details on exactly what that meant. He promised they'd share the full story when we were all together on Christmas morning.

"They got back safe and sound just before midnight, and they'll be here with everyone else this morning. How about some breakfast first?"

I thought he meant he would order some, but as I put on one of the hotel's bathrobes and followed him into the Christmas wonderland that made up the living room of the suite, I found everything already set up: tea, croissants, fresh fruit, and a gingerbread woman with my name on it.

"When did you do all this?" Obviously, he hadn't *just* woken up.

"You know I never give away my secrets." Cole's hands cupped my face as he pressed a kiss to my lips. "I'm not about to start now."

For all the happiness he brought to my life, I could definitely live with that.

We'd already put our presents under the tree, and not long after we got dressed, Holly and Jackson knocked on the door, bearing their own gifts which they added to the pile before taking a seat on the large sofa next to us. Besides the four-seater couch, there were three loveseats which would each seat another couple. It seemed to have been designed just for our extended family that morning, and knowing Cole, it well could have been.

"Have you heard anything from Liv and Noah?" Jackson asked me while Cole brought him a coffee and Holly some tea.

"Just that they're here. Nothing more."

"Does this mean you two have called off your ridiculous bet?" Holly asked our husbands. "What was the prize going to be, anyway?"

Cole and Jackson exchanged smiles, Jackson a wide grin and Cole his usual smirk, before Jackson answered. "The loser would have to wear a t-shirt that said 'world's best grandpa' on it, with an arrow pointing at the other one, for all their first photos with the kid."

The idea of Cole agreeing to that struck me as almost as funny as the idea of him actually wearing it. "You must have been pretty sure you were going to win."

"You got pregnant the one time I forgot a condom. I thought that had to count for something."

The teasing and laughter got cut off when another knock sounded at the door, and when Cole went to open it, all of our children were waiting there along with their significant others. Amid cries of "Merry Christmas", we ushered them all into the room as I gave them all a curious look. Olivia, Eve and Noelle were all wearing matching cardigans, all the same style but different colours - silver for Olivia, red for Eve, and blue for Noelle.

"Did you three coordinate this?"

Olivia looked over at my son with a warm smile. "Actually, Noah's responsible. He ordered them for us yesterday, along with the shirts underneath."

My curiosity piqued, I glanced over at Noah too, and he gave me a smirk very much like his dad's. "Don't worry, I got some for you and Holly too. But first, you have to see what they say."

Almost giddy with anticipation, the three younger women went to line up in a row while their husbands stood back with the older generation, each beaming with pride. They were all up to something, but I had no idea what it might be until the girls all opened their cardigans.

Each t-shirt said the same thing, in colours that matched their cardigans.

Mom-to-be.

For a moment, I could only stare at them all as they grinned back at us, enjoying every second of our confusion.

What did it mean? Were Noah and Olivia going ahead with the adoption? But why were Eve and Noelle wearing the shirts too?

My brain refused to make sense of it until Cole spoke the words out loud.

"*All* of you?"

All three nodded eagerly, and at last, it started to sink in.

"Eve, you're pregnant?" I asked.

"Noelle?" Jackson added.

"You signed the papers?" Cole asked Noah.

"When do we meet them?" Holly gasped.

In an instant, the room devolved into chaos. Hugs and tears and laughter filled up every inch of the room as we congratulated everyone and tried to get more details. Noah and Olivia should be able to bring the children home within a month. Noelle was expecting in six months, and Eve in eight.

Noah pulled out 'grandma-to-be' shirts for me and Holly, and we all got a picture together wearing our matching shirts and matching joyful smiles to go with them.

"The shirts are very sweet," I told Noah when we had a chance to speak privately later on. "I bet it means a lot to Eve and Noelle that you got them."

He shrugged, trying to play it off. "I think they felt a little guilty when they found out that Liv and I had struggled, but there's no need to. We're happy for them, and we know they're happy for us. It's all good."

My son might keep his emotions close to his chest, just like his dad did, but he had a soft side underneath it all, and I couldn't be any prouder of him.

By the next Christmas, our family would be completely different, but one thing that would never change would be the love we all shared. It would only get bigger as our family grew, and no matter where our lives took us, at Christmas time, we would always find a way to be together.

Epilogue

One year later

~Cole~

Gemma's head rested on my shoulder as our car drove through the familiar New York streets, already dark in the late afternoon of Christmas Eve. We'd intended to arrive three days earlier, but another small crisis at Wilby Park had kept us in England until the morning of the 24th. Though not ideal, as long as we made it in time to celebrate with the rest of the family, we really couldn't complain.

It wasn't the first Christmas Eve I spent crossing the Atlantic, and I suspected it wouldn't be the last either.

In the past year, Gemma and I had worked together more closely than ever before as we took on the properties belonging to her family. In March, I officially stepped down as CEO of Stamer Hotels, a role I'd held for 35 years, and passed the position to Noah who insisted that even with three young children at home, he could handle it.

I had no doubt that he could.

In some ways, running a worldwide network of hotels seemed simple in comparison to dealing with British rules and regulations as we sought to turn Gemma's centuries-old family home into something much more impactful. The first time I saw it, I told Gemma that American tourists would eat it up, and I couldn't have been more right. The house was now open year-round to visitors and to rent for weddings and special occasions, and those fees paid for the house's other purposes: as a training centre for young people from around Europe who were about to start placements with Eve's charity, and as a place for disadvantaged children from nearby cities to enjoy the pleasures of the countryside.

Eve's charity work had rubbed off on me, apparently, and on Noah too. Under his guidance, Stamer Hotels had just implemented a new program to help provide temporary accommodation and food for children awaiting adoption in over thirty countries around the world.

Though we were retired, in some ways we were busier than ever, especially when we factored in the trips to visit our grandchildren in New York. At least they were all in one place, since Eve and Julien had relocated there for the time being, though I suspected they wouldn't stay in one place forever.

"The babies should just be waking up from their naps," Gemma mused as we watched the skyscrapers of Midtown give way to the residential streets of the Upper West Side. "Are you sure about the costume?"

"I don't know why you think I'm going to terrify them."

"Because they're babies." She paused there a moment before her lips curled into a teasing smile. "And because you're slightly terrifying even at the best of times."

My arm wrapped tighter around her. "You were never terrified of me."

"I'm not so sure about that." Her green eyes sparkled as she looked up at me. "The first night I met you, I was terrified of the way you made me feel, and that I'd never feel that way with anyone else."

"Not the same thing." I kissed her hard just before the car pulled up outside Jackson and Holly's house. "Let's go celebrate Christmas."

Leaving the driver to unload our bags and bring them in, I got out of the car, adjusted my hat and grabbed the small bag of presents on the seat next to me before helping Gemma out. A large decorated tree filled the front window beneath the lights strung across the house's exterior, and a large, fresh wreath hung on the door, its pine scent feeling like home as we rang the bell.

Aaron answered, his eyes widening in surprise at the sight of me. "Mr Stamer?"

"Santa Claus," I corrected him gruffly as Gemma stepped into the house first, giving Aaron a hug. "Are the kids all here? And awake?"

"Yes, they're all in the living room. Hold on, I need to get my camera and warn the others."

He disappeared as I gave myself one last check in the entrance hall mirror. Without any padding, I made a rather slender Santa, but the coat, hat and fake beard made up for it.

"You look wonderful," Gemma assured me. "Maybe you can put it back on for me later tonight."

"If that's what you want, Gorgeous. Will you introduce me?"

Her eyes twinkling, Gemma went to the living room door, and cries of greeting rang out.

"Guess who I ran into on the way!" she announced. "Santa's here!"

I rounded the corner to find all the people who meant the most to us in the world inside the Hanmers' living room. On the couch sat Eve and Julien with their son, Henri. Next to her, Noelle held her daughter, Coral. Sitting on the floor by the tree, Noah and Olivia were playing with Jackson's holiday train set with their three children, and Jackson, Holly and Aaron stood behind the couch by the door to the dining room, all three of them with their phone cameras aimed in my direction.

"Merry Christmas!" Keeping Gemma's warning in mind, I kept my voice calm and not too loud, not wanting to scare anyone. "Are there some good little girls and boys here?"

"That's you," Olivia prompted Maria and Daniel as they stared over at me, their eyes wide with uncertainty.

"He's got presents for you," Noah added.

"You go, Daddy," Daniel said, wedging himself behind Noah while the adults hid their smiles.

Noah rolled his eyes affectionately. "I don't know if I've been good enough. But Sera will go, won't you?"

The sweet little girl toddled over to me willingly, her arms open wide for a hug. "Granda!"

She couldn't quite say 'grandpa' yet, but she'd obviously seen right through my disguise. Gemma tried not to laugh as I knelt down to get eye-level with Sera. "That's a secret, okay? Here's a little present from Santa."

She eagerly took the wrapped box I pulled from the bag, and once Maria and Daniel saw they had nothing to be afraid of, they came over too. We all posed for a picture together before I took the babies their presents. We'd only met 4-month-old Henri once before, and his eyes had darkened since the last time we saw him. They were a dark brown now, somewhere between Julien's lighter brown and Eve's dark eyes.

With all the presents handed out, I took my leave, slipping into Jackson's empty office to remove the Santa suit and rejoin the party in my regular suit instead.

"Merry Christmas, Dad." Eve had gotten to her feet while I'd been away, and Henri was already tucked safely in Gemma's arms. I took the opportunity to give her a hug, trying not to think about how it didn't seem all that long ago that Gemma held Eve in her arms that way.

"Merry Christmas, and happy birthday. What did I miss?"

She and Julien filled me in on the latest with their charity, while Noelle shared how things were going with Anchor Design. Noah and Aaron had stories about the latest happenings at Stamer Hotels, and Holly and Jackson told us all about the two weeks they'd just spent in Morocco.

"I couldn't wait to get home to all of this, though," Holly admitted, beaming around the room at the new generation. "Now, who wants a drink? No one's pregnant this year, right?"

Laughter circled the room until Olivia cleared her throat. "Actually..."

Instantly, the laughter died off, leaving Coral's gurgles as the only sound while we all waited for her to elaborate.

"We just found out a few weeks ago," Noah said, his green eyes sparkling just like his mom's as he took his wife's hand. "It seems like the treatments we did actually worked. It just took longer than we expected. She's almost three months along."

"Are you serious?" Holly squealed, her face a perfect mix of hope and disbelief.

"We're serious," Olivia confirmed. "Sera's going to be a big sister."

Instantly, everyone rose en masse to congratulate them, the kids all wanting hugs too even though they weren't entirely sure what we were all hugging about. As I embraced Noah, I remembered the look on his face at the hotel in Australia the year before when he found out they weren't having a baby. Those bitter tears had been replaced by happy ones, another one of life's ups and downs, but at least this one was going in the right direction.

"Four kids? You don't do anything by half."

"Why should I?" he asked, his eyes shining as he took a step back. "You showed me I can have it all, and I really do. I couldn't ask for a single thing more."

Jackson brought out a bottle of champagne so we could all toast to everyone's happiness, and Gemma leaned her head against my shoulder again in contentment as we sat down together beside the tree.

"This is perfect."

I couldn't disagree. No other word could adequately do justice to the way my life had been ever since I met her.

"That's new, isn't it?" I asked Jackson and Holly once everything had calmed down again, gesturing at a large framed canvas above the sofa. Holly changed the decoration regularly, but I couldn't remember seeing the brightly-coloured abstract piece before.

Holly looked over her shoulder at the piece before glancing over at Jackson, both of them trying not to smile. "It is. We got it in Australia last Christmas."

I couldn't think of when they would have gone shopping for art, but we hadn't spent every minute together. "I like it. It feels... energetic."

That sent them both into peals of laughter as I shot Gemma a confused look. "I have no idea," she said with a shrug.

Neither did I, but I supposed we all had our secrets, our in-jokes, our personal moments. In the end, each of the five families in the room started with two people who fell in love. None of us would ever fully know each other's stories, but the love we shared would continue to grow and multiply, especially at Christmas time.

It would always be my favourite time of the year.

MORE FROM THE AUTHOR

<u>**Contemporary Romance – 18+**</u>

Callahan Series
A Matter of Time
A Piece of Land
A Change of Heart
A Work of Art

Christmas in the City Series
Mistletoe Mistake
Candy Cane Challenge
Tinsel Temptation
Gingerbread Gamble
Stocking Standoff
Eggnog Experiment

Standalones
Leading Lady
A Set of Three
Charity Case
Hired Lover

<u>Contemporary Romance – New Adult/Clean</u>

It Figures duet
It Figures
Figuring It Out

<u>Historical Romance – 18+</u>

Lady in Waiting Series
Lady in Waiting
King in Training
Princess in Hiding

<u>Paranormal Romance – 18+</u>

Standalone
Out of My Depth

Cold Lake Pack Series
The Curse and the Prophecy
The Spell and the Legacy
The Dream and the Destiny

Mismatched Mates Series
Mismatched Mates
Misguided Motives
Mistaken Meanings

Serena's Story
The Alpha's Second Chance
The Returned Mate
The Vampire's Consort

Sacrifice Series
Blood Donor
Life Giver

<u>Paranormal Romance – New Adult/Clean</u>
The Alpha's Prey

KEEP IN TOUCH

Daily updates from my works-in-progress, bonus chapters and more can be found on my Ream account, Chilli & Chocolate, along with Emma Lee-Johnson:
https://reamstories.com/chilliandchocolate

You can find and follow me on Facebook at:
facebook.com/melodytyden

Join the Facebook group Melody's Romance Corner for fun games, interaction with the author and exclusive news and excerpts.

You can also sign up to my newsletter at www.melodytyden.com for all the latest news.

www.ingramcontent.com/pod-product-compliance
Lightning Source LLC
Chambersburg PA
CBHW070319190726
48291CB00014B/2312